"One of the best-written novels I have read this year! Crisp, on point, and very, very entertaining!" — Rabia Tanveer, *Readers Favorite*

"5-Stars! Gripping, extraordinary, humorous, suspenseful. Such detail that readers will likely feel the author must have personally lived through something similar himself." — ATAI Romance Novel Awards

"5-Stars all the way! I found myself highlighting so I could re-read and savor the depth of emotion evoked by this amazing story." — Lynda Filler, *Books Go Social*

"A love story that will not be easily forgotten!"— *Top Shelf Magazine*

"Outstanding! As a Marine myself, this book is a must!"— Douglas Nelson, USMC (ret)

"Readers, hang on! This author either did a tremendous amount of research or just really knows his stuff!" — Alicia Wright, BGS Review Club

# No Pit So Deep

The Cody Musket Story Book 1
Historical fiction inspired by real events

by
# James Nathaniel Miller II

LionsTail
# BOOKS

ISBN-13-9780692857304
ISBN-10-0692857303

## Technical Advisors

Robert W. Busby, US Dept. of Defense (Ret)
Lt. Col. Bart Wilbanks, 419th FW, USAF
Rebecca L. Mahan, domestic violence consultant

To Carla, the love of my life, my inspiration for Brandi, and to my brilliant and beautiful granddaughter Maggie, who inspired me to create the character Knoxi.

My appreciation extends to actress Stacey Danger and to Ann Busby whose insights were priceless.

Special thanks to Victoria Kendig, who made me believe I could write this story.

Cover by Delaney Design.com

# Before We Start

Writing No Pit So Deep, The Cody Musket Story changed my life forever.

Parts of this story are gut-wrenching, some of it is funny, but all of it is the story of us, as told through the progress of a pilgrim named Cody Musket and a courageous woman named Brandi Barnes. If you look closely, you may find yourself somewhere within these pages. —James Miller

---

THIS NOVEL CONTAINS REAL EVENTS. SOME PORTIONS
MAY BE TOO INTENSE FOR SMALL CHILDREN.

NO SEXUALLY EXPLICIT SCENES.

---

# MUZZLE FLASH

Cody gazed at the distant bridge that spanned the great chasm. He shaded his eyes. The latest intel was unthinkable. Capistrano's rogue army would swarm that bridge and cross the gorge any minute, with heavy soldier boots pounding the road and their vehicles growling like angry death angels. Cody and Brandi, along with fifty children and fourteen avengers would be overtaken, outmanned, and outgunned — nowhere to run, no place to hide.

Suddenly, he heard a whining, howling turbine engine. The Cessna 208 Caravan blew right past them a few feet overhead. His eyes followed as the aircraft banked left, descended, and disappeared into the ravine.

*"Daddy! Daddy!"* He looked to his right. Knoxi, age 6, was terrified, running toward him full speed. She jumped into his arms. *"Daddy!"*

Then Cody heard loud knocking. "Daddy?" The knocking continued. He opened his eyes.

"Daddy! It's time to get up." She knocked again. "You said to get you up at seventeen-thirty."

Cody rolled his eyes, momentarily disoriented. The room was dark and quiet. Brandi was still sleeping soundly beside him, although she had wormed her way out from under the sheet. He set his feet on the floor and reached for his robe, ambled to the door, cracked it open, and peeked into the hallway. Knoxi was one big smile.

"Thanks for the wake-up." He gathered a deep breath. "Uh, why are you grinnin' like that?" He nudged the door open but a few inches, because behind him, Brandi lay on the bed uncovered.

"Jeremy texted me!" She was glowing but trying to keep her voice quiet. "His agent finally got him signed with the Dodgers — a monster contract!" She jumped up and down and clapped her hands. "Is Mama up?"

"No. She's still asleep. She, uh . . . needed to chillax after her trip."

Knoxi giggled. "Uh, Dad, you need to trim your beard."

He ran his hands over his face. "My beard?"

"Hello-oo! You look like a nineties caveman commercial."

He paused and stared at his daughter. "You look all grown-up."

"What? Grown-up?" She tilted her head. "Daddy, I was —"

"Yeah. I know, I know, you were eighteen in November. You look just like your mom, and you're just about as sassy."

"Are you okay?" She reached her hand through the opening and felt his forehead. He was perspiring.

"I was dreamin' about Librador again." He broke a tight smile.

"That was a long time ago, Daddy. I was a little girl then."

"I'm fine," he assured. "I gotta get ready. I'm hosting the dinner downtown at seven." He eased the door shut.

It was 5:30 p.m. in Houston. The January sun had settled and shadows had darkened the windows of the Muskets' cozy master suite.

Cody dialed up the bedchamber lighting one notch, exposing the serene, curvy contour of the sleeping woman on the bed. He eased onto the mattress. Brandi lay facedown, her left knee bent as though she were climbing a hill, her long, dark hair gracefully covering her shoulders and flowing onto the pillow. He gently floated his hand across the small of her back, her lungs expanding effortlessly with each peaceful breath. Touching her calmed his stormy thoughts. He pulled the sheet over her.

She had returned that morning from a two-week trip to Paris and Rome with Knoxi, and had yielded to serious jetlag. She had retreated with him to the bedroom for an *afternoon delight,* after which they had fallen asleep. Now, he took care not to wake her.

A hand-crafted mantelpiece above their rustic Texas Star headboard displayed three of Brandi's most-treasured items — her All-American trophy earned while playing collegiate basketball at Stanford University, her Presidential Fighting Lady Award, and a bronze plaque engraved with the words, "Brandi Musket, Agape International Woman of the Year."

An oak cabinet nearby exhibited Cody's four American League MVP awards, his Rookie of the Year trophy, and other memorabilia from his iconic twelve-year baseball career. He had retired four years ago.

A modest, lighted niche on the west wall displayed a 16" x 24" photograph taken aboard the flight deck of the Carrier USS *Harry S. Truman.* It featured a fully-armed F/A-18D Marine Corps attack jet with a very young Cody "Babe" Musket and his airborne weapons officer, Harry "Seismo" Stanton, standing alongside the cockpit wearing full aerial combat gear.

These bedroom exhibits were Knoxi's idea. She had insisted, saying that her parents should be forever reminded of who they are, and of the lives they had touched.

After a steamy shower, Cody walked to the closet while drying off his dripping-wet, muscular, scarred body. Brandi awoke and caught a glimpse. "*Pssst!* I'm watching you, Babe."

He buttoned his britches and walked toward her, his gravelly voice as quiet as a whisper. "I was tryin' not to rouse you," he drawled. All the honchos are gonna miss you downtown tonight."

"I know." She turned over and stared up at him through weary eyelids. "People expect me at these events, but I'm not up for extra innings tonight." She yawned, then managed to force a smile. "I hope you enjoy yourself without me. Every Debbie in town'll try to make the tabloids by being photographed with my husband tonight, and I won't be there to rescue you this time."

Cody's eyes shone a spark as he reached down and seized one corner of her bed linen.

She slapped his hand away. "No peeking!" She giggled, her face coming to life. "I'll tell you when to peek."

"Just tryin' to cover you up again," he rasped. "You kicked off half the bedsheet. You wudda made a good Texas woman."

Brandi pulled the pink satin sheet up to her throat with both hands. "Texas woman?"

"Sure. I've told you before; Texas women kick their cover off when they sleep cuz they count coyotes instead of sheep."

"Oh, Babe, you're *so* yesterday." She flashed him a soft smirk. "Can you cover my feet again? It's getting chilly in here."

Brandi was accustomed to his roughrider bedroom tomfoolery, but she revelled in his strong eyes and lone-star grin, mindful that once upon a time Cody could find no reason to smile.

He picked up his bathrobe off the dresser and placed it over her feet. "I wanna take your Mustang tonight." He swagged toward the closet to find his shirt and tie.

"My Mustang?" She raised her head to one elbow. "It hasn't been outside the barn in a year. So, why —?"

"Cuz I'm feelin' wild and crazy tonight, that's all."

"Well," she reminded, "it's not exactly zero to one-seventy in two seconds, you know. It's an antique."

"But that car's special. It's — it's history," he said from inside the closet. "I remember it like yesterday; we had just met, we sneak into the parking garage, get in your car, and all-a-sudden —"

"I know, I know," she cut in. "That first night; a real-life car chase." Her voice softened. "I couldn't stop crying, then laughing, then crying again."

He reemerged from the closet carrying his freshly-pressed shirt and black tie. "Any woman wudda cried after what happened to you."

Brandi laid her head back on the pillow and looked straight up at the ceiling fan. "Cody, there's something else." She closed her eyes. "It's about Knoxi. It's serious."

"I'm listening." He put his arms through the sleeves.

She cleared her throat. "When she addressed the trafficking conference in Rome on Thursday, her story about Librador went viral. She described it all — her escape, the mud trick, even the orbiting light bulb. No one could believe she was only six when it happened."

"I know. I watched it on CNN. But we had agreed there was no reason to keep it secret any longer." He began buttoning his shirt. "So what's the problem?"

Brandi rolled onto her side to face him. "Well, now she's like a rock star, stalked for interviews, older guys approaching her. Thousands surrounded us at Da Vinci Airport before we departed Rome, and you should've seen the crowd waiting when we changed planes in New York at four this morning."

"I caught that on FOX. So, what did I miss?"

"Babe. She's leaving for Stanford in the fall and that terrifies me. There are vultures everywhere."

*"Ha!* I may have to rescue the vultures from her. God help 'em."

"Come on," she insisted. "Be serious! I know about those cool moves you're teaching her. She handles guys in exhibition matches, but could she handle someone in a dangerous situation?"

Cody walked to the mirror to straighten his tie. "Self-defense begins with learning to handle *yourself.* Do that first, then handle someone else. Knoxi catches on real fast."

Suddenly, Brandi giggled. Cody turned around. She was now sitting up on the side of the bed fully awake, his robe bundled-up in her arms. Her eyes twinkled and she wiggled her toes. "Can you teach me those moves?" She shook her shoulders. "Can you show me how to hit?"

*"Hit?* Uh, what happened to bein' serious?" He walked slowly toward her. The ceiling fan rotated quietly, breathing soft, cool swirls of air down upon them.

Brandi flushed like the pink rose of autumn as Cody lifted the robe from her hands and draped it over her bare shoulders. "You're shivering," he whispered, delicately pulling it around in front to cover her. "And you're exhausted."

Sudden teardrops softened Brandi's diamond-blue eyes. Balmy words rolled from her lips like sweet, soft kisses. "Babe, with all our rushing about, and all we've been through, do you sometimes feel life slipping through our fingertips?"

*"Maybe,"* his words whispery, growly, "but God smiles on me every time your heart thumps." He pressed his hand against her heart. "A lotta life here for a man who shudda been dead."

Brandi's effervescence reinvented itself, her cheeks blushing, blue eyes smiling. "Expedite your mission, Marine. Tell those chatty women you have no time for extra pics tonight cuz you have unfinished biz with Brandi. Do you copy?"

"Copy that, ma'am. And when I return, I'll show you moves that don't require any hitting."

They bumped knuckles like teammates celebrating a win. Cody kissed her passionately and departed smiling, visions from *Song of Solomon* filling his head.

\*    \*    \*

Brandi listened to his boot heels tap their way down the wooden stairway to the family room and then fade. He wasn't the same man she had met sixteen years before. Walls he had built around himself after Afghanistan had long since toppled.

Now she was 39. Despite permanent scars from brutal stab wounds on her breasts and abdomen and the fact she had gained twenty pounds during the past year, Cody still lavished her with long looks and a blushing smile, and it still made her cheeks turn red. His aviator call sign, *Babe,* was a tribute in more ways than she could count.

\*     \*     \*

Cody glanced at his watch and hastened his steps from the back door of their stately southwestern villa, past the pool, and onto the lighted pathway to the barn behind their home. The sun had set.

Two weeks had been way too long. Missing Brandi, he had become bored and depressed. Now his girls were home and he would share his jubilation with a classy lady who lived inside the barn.

Cody opened the doors, turned on the lights, and removed the cover from Brandi's blue 1980 Mustang. He opened the driver's side door and slipped into the worn leather bucket seat. He closed his eyes.

Memories flooded his senses. The aroma of her perfume the night they had met, her smile, her tears, her musical laughter. The two hours they had shared in this hot-blooded muscle car that night had changed their lives forever. The chase, the danger, her story about the birth of Knoxi, and her family legacy about the pit so deep — the Mustang had recorded it all and preserved it in vivid detail.

But much like this once-upon-a-time queen of the road, Cody had lately wondered if he too were a relic. At the age of 43, did anyone believe he was dangerous anymore?

He turned the engine over, felt her pulse once again, pulled the shift to first, and eased the old girl past the doors and out into the pristine evening air. He gazed up through the custom sunroof — night skies clear, visibility sixty million light-years!

It wasn't just about getting to the Walter Hodge Sports Awards Banquet where Cody was to be the host. It was as much about the ride itself — downtown and back in a chic roadstress from the past on a heavenly evening.

He came to the first intersection and turned left onto West Hammer Boulevard. Before he reached Loop 610, he was rudely forced into reality as approaching red and blue alternating strobes glared in his rearview mirror.

He sneaked a glance at the speedometer — cruise control holding at forty. *Nope, it's not me they're after.*

But within seconds, the unrelenting police vehicle pulled directly behind his rear bumper. Cody steered onto the shoulder lane, rolled down the window, and waited. A large police officer emerged. *What could this guy want?*

Rapid chatter crackled uninterrupted through the police radio. Something was up. The officer slowly stepped toward the Mustang holding a blinding flashlight in his left hand and resting his right palm on the handle of his holstered sidearm.

His nervous body language was accompanied by a deep, commanding voice. "Keep your hands where I can see them."

He shone the light at the Mustang's rear license plate as he approached, and then momentarily aimed the intrusive beam into the rear seat of the car. He asked for Cody's license and registration.

He was tall, robust, and bald with an advanced evening shadow and strong coffee breath. Sea Breezes Coffee Shop was nearby. Cody had spotted him there more than once but had never been introduced.

The officer examined Cody's driver's license, then glanced at the former ball player's face.

"Liquor store holdup. Blue Mustang. You aren't doubling as a thug these days are you, Cody?" He offered a rigid grin.

"Don't gimme any ideas, Officer. Things can get boring sometimes."

"*Haha!* I didn't recognize the car. Didn't have time to run the plates. I know where you're headed — that dinner downtown. My brother, Mike Cannon is receiving an award there tonight. I wanted to attend, but I gotta go on duty at seven — a heckuva thing."

"You're Mike's brother? He used to be my teammate. I'm supposed to present him with the citizenship award tonight."

"Nice digs, Cody. You look dressed to kill."

"Hope you didn't mean that literally." Cody chuckled and slipped his driver's license back into his billfold.

Officer Cannon turned toward another vehicle approaching from the opposite direction on the other side of the boulevard. The headlights illuminated the nameplate on the breast pocket of his dark blue uniform — Morris Cannon.

The officer was not wearing a vest. Cody didn't ask why. Perhaps he had stopped off at Sea Breezes while on his way to work and had then gotten the call about the liquor store robbery.

The burly policeman turned back again and pulled a notepad from his pocket. "Cody, I got a grandson who'd really appreciate an autograph. Any chance you could —" The officer never finished.

Without warning, the boom of a rifle shot at close range shocked Cody's senses. A muzzle flash blazed from the open rear window of the approaching sedan. Despite the sudden ringing in his left ear, Cody detected that other instantaneous and grisly sound he had hoped never to hear again — the sordid thud of a bullet penetrating a human body.

"*Ugggh!*" The stunned officer dropped the pad, fell forward against the door, clutched his chest and gasped, spitting blood as he slid down to the pavement.

Every nerve in Cody's body stood at attention. He expected the vehicle to speed away immediately, but the shooter wasn't finished. The red sedan pulled directly alongside the blue Mustang and the smoking gun barrel trained on the downed officer for another shot.

Cody instinctively reached between the bucket seats and grabbed the handle of Brandi's .380 Ruger pocket handgun. He disengaged the safety, then turned and fired, emptying the magazine into the back window of the other automobile. The surprised driver burned rubber and screeched away, but not before the rifle had fired its second shot.

Cody tried to exit the car, but the bulky officer slumped against the lower edge of the door, so he was forced to climb over the console and exit on the passenger side. He glanced at the fleeing sedan as he scooted around the front of the car and then knelt next to Cannon.

An ocean of blood was expanding rapidly underneath the vehicle. The first shot had left an entry wound below Cannon's left shoulder blade. The second shot had missed its target and drilled a hole through the back fender of the Mustang.

A BMW convertible appeared at the scene on the other side of the road. It was Cody's neighbor, Felix Anderson.

*"Call 911!"* Cody shouted, as he felt for his pocketknife. He intended to cut away Cannon's shirt around the wound so he could stop the bleeding, but his peripheral vision signaled red alert. The sedan was in reverse, barreling backward at an angry speed, tires smoking, returning to the scene.

Cody was out of bullets, and now killers bore down on him from a half block away. With the disabled officer bleeding to death before him, he heard familiar words inside his head — *analyze, stay within yourself, don't lose your head, finish it.*

He fumbled for Cannon's sidearm, still holstered somewhere underneath the officer's body. He located the weapon — a Glock 40 — heavy artillery compared to his small .380. He ripped the gun from its holster and screamed at Felix to take cover, but his neighbor, who had already dialed 911, opted to jerk his car into reverse, burn rubber, and squeal away from the scene.

Cody pointed the officer's sidearm at the approaching sedan and opened fire. The car slid to a halt and then reversed course again. It raced away at high speed, charged through a flashing red light, swerved out of control and slammed into a gigantic oak tree a quarter mile away.

Cody frantically resumed trying to save Morris Cannon. He shed his blood-spattered evening jacket and then yanked off his own shirt, rolled it up like a snowball, and crammed it against the wound. He glanced away momentarily. Flashing lights in the distance. *Help is on the way.*

"Hang in there, Morris. Hang on. Help is coming. Stay with me."

Morris struggled to speak. "Cody, Cody. I was at your last game — the World Series." He coughed and wheezed. "It was my brother's last game, too."

"That's right. It was when I had the Achilles injury."

"Help him, Cody — my brother, Mike. He's in a lot o' trouble." The officer's words were now barely audible.

"I don't know how to do it. Dammit, Cody. I don't know how to do this."

"How to do what?"

*"Die."*

"Come on, Morris! Don't give up!"

"They've killed me." Slow speech, his words were slurred. "I'm involved . . . bad stuff. Help Mike. He's in over his head. I can't be forgiven." He struggled to gain a breath and then held it.

"Extreme sin requires an extreme sacrifice to cover it," Cody said. "Jesus made that sacrifice. Give Him your heart. Ask Him. He'll forgive you." Cody spoke with urgency.

The officer clutched Cody's forearm, then exhaled his last.

Within minutes, the street was alive with emergency responders — flashing lights, police and fire vehicles, people running, scratchy radio transmissions.

*"Lemme see your hands!"* The first officer to disembark from a police vehicle was a rookie. Four others had arrived almost simultaneously.

Cody glanced up. Five weapons aimed at him. Both handguns he had fired lay on the ground next to the dead officer. Steam still rose into the cool night air from the hot muzzle of the blood-slippery Glock.

In the darkness, with his bloody face and hair, he was not recognized by any of the traumatized police. All they saw was a shirtless, bloody, unidentified man kneeling over a fallen officer. There were no witnesses present. Felix had left the scene. The nervous officers had no idea what had just occurred.

"I live just a mile from here. My name is —"

"Move away from him! Step away now and get on the ground!" The conversation was going only one direction. Uncertainty and panic were dressed in blue uniforms with badges and guns.

Cody rose from his kneeling position with his bloody hands in the air, intending to step over Cannon's body and lie facedown as instructed. They could sort it out later.

But his weak left Achilles, remnants of an old World Series injury, betrayed him and he toppled back to the ground. He reached out with his left arm to break his fall, but his hand touched the pavement only inches from the two weapons.

Five police officers fired their guns. Cody fell across the dead officer's chest.

\* \* \*

Thirty minutes later, Brandi heard her cell ringing. She stepped from the shower, reached for Cody's robe, then picked up her phone. It was the police. She screamed for Knoxi and told her the shocking news. Her sons, Raymond and Cody Junior were not at home.

"Help me find my clothes!" Brandi shouted, as Knoxi came rushing into the bedroom. "I can't think straight."

Knoxi helped her mother find everything and then tried unsuccessfully to call her brothers.

They frantically ran to the garage and jumped into Cody's truck. The rear tires screamed as Brandi backed out of the garage, turned, and then accelerated down the circular driveway toward the street.

Knoxi switched on the radio. A special report was in progress.

> ". . . on the west side of town. Former Houston Astros star third baseman and designated hitter Cody Musket, who played twelve seasons, has been shot. He was rushed in critical condition to Methodist Hospital with multiple gunshot wounds. Tina Anderson of station KPRC in Houston is standing by at the scene."

> "Thank you, Kareem. One question asked is why Musket was not driving his F-570 truck with the CODY-12 license plates tonight. Officers say they would have recognized his truck had he been driving it. But tonight, for some reason, he was in his wife's Mustang. The story gets even more bizarre. There is a dead police officer at the scene. Another vehicle has been found a half mile away with two armed gunmen dead inside. The motive for the shooting is unclear. Was Musket the target, or was it the officer? Back to you, Kareem."

Knoxi's face was flushed with tears. "Mama, how long will it take to get to the hospital?"

"I dunno. Depends on traffic. Just keep trying to call your brothers." Brandi's head was pounding as she tuned her ear to the broadcast again.

*"Also, standing by is Dancer Coleman, KPRC roving sports reporter, former Houston Astros shortstop, who is in downtown Houston at the —"*

Knoxi turned it off. "Mama, why don't you let me drive? I dunno how you can —"

"Knoxi, just try to call the boys."

"Why don't you call them and let me drive, Mama? I mean —"

"Baby, I wouldn't even be able to read the screen on the phone. My eyes are too blurry."

"Mama, if you can't read the screen, how can you drive?"

"Well, do you think you're any better off? Look in the mirror. Look at yourself."

Knoxi finally reached Raymond on his cell.

"Raymond! Where are you guys? You're where? The Riveras' home? Listen, Ray. Daddy's been shot! Turn on the news. They took him to Methodist. We're coming to pick you both up."

Raymond and Cody Junior had ridden their bicycles to the home of school friends while Cody, Brandi and Knoxi had slept. They scrambled to the Riveras' game room and tuned to the radio broadcast while they waited for Brandi and Knoxi to arrive.

*". . . and the Muskets' eighteen-year-old daughter just returned from Rome, where she addressed an international human trafficking conference. She confirmed rumors that she had indeed been rescued twelve years ago by a group of commandos led by her father. Rumors have also surfaced that Musket, a former Medal of Honor winner, has begun to lead a double life — that his Planned Childhood Foundation, which has established several safe houses on foreign*

*continents, is a front for financing illegal clandestine
child rescue missions in third-world countries . . ."*

"Not true! Why does the press always have to twist things?" Eleven-year-old Raymond was stressed and angry as the broadcast continued.

*"Brandi Musket, former Stanford University women's
basketball star and —"*

Raymond punched the off button. "Yadda, yadda, yadda. Fine. Let's go. I hear Dad's truck." Brandi was in the driveway honking the horn.

The boys said hurried good-byes to their friends and rushed to the truck outside. One look at his mother's face and eleven-year-old Raymond was ready to take matters into his own hands.

"Want me to drive, Mama?"

"No, Raymond. Just get in."

"But sometimes Dad lets me when —"

"Are you kidding? You're only eleven! He lets you drive?"

"Well, sure. At José and Mia's ranch sometimes."

"Too many crowded roads and you don't even have a license. I'm gonna have to fight traffic all the way. Three conventions in town and the Rockets are playing the Spurs tonight."

"But you're crying. How're you gonna drive like that?"

*"Raymond! Just get in!"* She sniffled and wiped tears from her face.

"Tell Mama to let me drive, Ray." Knoxi wiped her eyes, trying to look composed.

"You? Just 'cause you can fly an airplane doesn't make you a good driver."

*"Kids! Please! I'm driving, that's final. Get in, Raymond!"*

He yanked open the back door, jumped in, and then reached over the seat and twisted the keys from the ignition. He leaped from the truck, ran toward a redwood fence, pulled himself up, and catapulted into the adjacent yard.

"Mom! You let him take your keys?" Nine-year-old Cody Junior had already settled himself into the back seat.

Brandi caught her breath. She had watched her older son with both anger and pride as he gracefully breached the eight-foot fence and disappeared with the keys.

She shook her head. "He's exactly like his father."

Knoxi immediately got out of the truck and opened the back door.

"Scoot over, little brother."

*"What?"*

*"Cody! Move your butt!"*

His light dawned. "Wait. I get it. That's Mr. Sakimoto's house on the other side of the fence." Cody scooted to the middle.

Knoxi slid in next to him. "We can cry now, Mama. Neither of us will have to drive."

"I know." Brandi wiped her eyes again as she lifted herself over the console and collapsed into the bucket seat on the passenger side. Knoxi leaned forward and clutched her mother's shoulders.

A moment later, Raymond and forty-nine-year-old Yasumi Sakimoto, internationally celebrated Formula One racing driver, came bounding through a gate near the front of the property and sprinted toward the vehicle. Cody's truck was in capable hands as it blistered the road to the hospital.

# ANGELS TWO ZERO

## *Twenty years earlier*

Afghanistan skies had cleared overnight. Winds that had kicked up sand as high as fifteen thousand feet for nearly two days had subsided. The hills in northern Helmand Province were clearly visible from eighty nautical miles away.

US Marine Second Lieutenant Cody "Babe" Musket, age 23, glanced over his shoulder. Through the canopy of his F/A-18D Hornet he focused on an Afghan canyon far below — *rugged country.*

He was accompanied by his "wizo" (weapons systems officer), Harry "Seismo" Stanton, who flew in the back seat. His aircraft was part of Lima Flight — three Hornets that had launched from the USS *Harry S. Truman* at 0800.

Cody Musket, flying Lima Three, was in his element. Never mind that eighty miles ahead was a hotbed for Taliban activity, the most dangerous area of the war. The exhilaration of being in control of such power — sea level to twenty thousand feet in one minute — and then living for several hours in a different world was intoxicating. This had been his childhood dream.

"Hey, Babe, I heard you got drafted by the Phillies outta college." The transmission came from Keyshawn "Hawker" Harris, flying Lima Two.

"It was Houston. They drafted me in round twenty-seven."

"So how come you didn't play ball?"

"You kidding, Hawker? And miss all this?"

"You went to Texas A&M, Babe, right?"

"Snap ding! Hawker, you're just full of bogus intel."

"I been accused of being full o' worse. '*Snap ding?*' Wha duz that mean?"

"Just somethin' Jungle Dawg used to say."

"Detroit Pistons? That Jungle Dawg? You mean you know that guy?"

"Affirmative. I roomed with him at Baylor, home of the fighting Baylor Bears, and best of all, Lady Bears basketball."

"Hey, you gotta be pretty smart to go to Baylor, right, Babe?"

"That's gotta be a trick question."

"Well, I heard you graduated in three years, and if you're that smart, you should know what language the natives are speakin' down there on the ground. Arabic?"

"Negative. Some local dialect, not Arabic in this area."

"But if they spoke Arabic, you'd understand it, right?"

"I took Arabic in college, but I know poquito no mucho."

"Poquito no mucho?" Hawker questioned. "That's Spanish."

"Means 'a little, not much,'" Seismo cut in.

"So, Babe," Hawker rattled off, "how do you say 'a little, not much' in Arabic?"

"I have no idea."

Babe now had a visual of the target area. From twenty thousand feet (angels two zero), the beauty of the untamed mountainous world beneath was surreal. It was both desolate and magnificent, a bizarre blend of fantasy and reality. *Hard to believe there is a war goin' on down there.*

While attending flight school, Cody had been tagged by his mates as "Babe" after hitting three home runs in an exhibition game against the Pensacola Blue Wahoos, a minor league affiliate of the Cincinnati Reds. His previous call sign "Rambo," which he had worn because of his martial arts expertise, was dropped in favor of the new call sign after his home run prowess was revealed.

"Tighten it up, Marines, nearing target area. All eyes." Captain Roger "Snake" Stabler was in command, flying Lima One.

A team of Navy SEALS based on the *Truman* was trapped in the hills ahead. Cody, a Marine, had befriended the team and had worked out with them aboard the boat. Though Cody had taught martial arts while in college, the SEALs had schooled him on the mental aspects of real combat as opposed to merely fighting for sport.

The SEAL team had been dispatched to rescue eight survivors of a Chinook helicopter crash, but the Taliban had arrived first and had taken the crash survivors as POWs. The SEALs' presence had been discovered, and now they needed air support so that a helo could enter the zone and extract them from the area.

"Lima One to Badger 29, do you read me?" Snake was calling the Joint Tactical Air Controller (JTAC) embedded in the SEAL team below.

"Roger, Lima One, this is Badger 29. Read you loud and clear. Target is at our two-niner-zero, four clicks. Stand by for coordinates."

Snake answered back. "Roger that. We're comin' in for a closer look."

Then Snake barked out commands in rapid succession. "Babe, maintain angels two zero. Hawker, you're with me. Break left on three! Three, two, one, *break!*"

Babe, flying Lima Three, was to circle and observe from twenty thousand feet while the other two aircraft dropped to five thousand feet above the terrain.

Lima One soon had a visual on the enemy. The entire region was crawling with hostiles on the hunt and out for blood. Some of them were getting too close.

"Badger 29, this is Lima One with hostiles in sight. Hold your ears, gentlemen. We're gonna yell at 'em and see if we can scare 'em off."

Step 1 protocol for flying ground cover was to "show presence" or "yell" at the enemy — simply fly overhead at five thousand feet and hope the screaming rumble of jet engines would strike terror and send them wisely retreating. It usually worked, avoiding the use of deadly ordnance.

Forces on the ground were unable to make a visual sighting of the Hornets due to the bright morning sunlight. The thunderous roar echoed off the surrounding hills, making it difficult to determine the direction from which the gruesome sound came.

On this particular occasion, showing presence did not work. The proximity of the village, with the high probability of collateral damage, made the Taliban think that the Hornets were bluffing. Taliban forces simply took cover for a few minutes and then continued their advance — a bad decision.

Lima Flight received clearance to open fire on the enemy.

Cody was ordered to descend and follow the other two aircraft for a deadly strafing run. Twenty-millimeter canons and Maverick missiles would create a hellish death trap but would not create a problem for the village, according to Snake's calculations, as long as the aircraft descended low enough to avoid collateral damage while engaging.

One by one, each Hornet made a run upon the enemy. The first two dealt a collective lethal blow — more than a hundred men and weapons obliterated.

Lima Three was the third aircraft, and by the time Babe and Seismo flew over, smoke, fire, and bodies were all that remained on the rugged landscape.

Suddenly, an explosion in the forward section of the fuselage underneath Cody's right foot sent flames and smoke belching from a gaping hole and filling the tandem cockpit. His leg and foot were on fire. Lima Three shook violently. Rapid vibrations made Cody's teeth rattle, and he heard choking in his headset.

*"Babe, what hit us?"* Seismo screamed, choked, coughed, and spit. *"Babe! Babe! You okay?"*

The blaze quickly extinguished, but the blast had severely burned Cody's right lower leg and foot. *"Ugggh! My leg! On fire! What about you?"* Cody fought to keep from blacking out.

Seismo coughed and spit again. *"Nearly bit my friggin' tongue off! Blood in my throat. What hit us?"*

The flight status of the Hornet was deteriorating at dizzying speed — sluggish controls, pressure warnings, O-2 failure, too much high terrain, not enough altitude to eject. The crisis escalated when a peak at twelve o'clock threatened to obliterate them, sending the F/A-18D audible collision warning system into frantic mode. They were a split second from death when Cody was able to roll left, narrowly avoiding the mountain.

*"Babe! What's happening? Babe? Talk to me!"* Seismo coughed again.

*"I'm busy! Can't hold it much longer. I see flat terrain at ten o'clock. Brace!"*

Cody made a twenty-degree left turn, slowed the approach speed, jettisoned explosive ordnance, and prepared for a crash landing on a relatively flat plateau.

*"We're going in, Seismo!"*

With elevator and rudder deflection impossible, he was unable to slow airspeed below 220 knots. The only communication he could send off was a screaming, *"Mayday! Mayday!"*

Despite the excessive landing speed, it was a successful ditching. It could have been a piece of cake, but just before the aircraft came to rest after kicking up gigantic clouds of Afghan terrain, the right wing tip collided with a large rock. This violently whipped the Hornet into a three-quarter spin and sent it careening sideways off a ridge and down an embankment. It finally came to rest, partially buried in loose sand and rocks.

"Seismo! You okay back there?" Cody crawled out of the cockpit. Then he felt the excruciating pain in his leg and foot again. *"Ugggh.* I didn't feel a thing while I was landing. Funny how adrenaline works."

Cody shed his helmet and then bent down to check his burns. Portions of the boot seemed fried to his skin. His movements became agonizing as he lifted himself towards Harry, who was frozen to his ejection seat.

"Seismo! We gotta take cover! They're gonna be all over us here in a few minutes." Cody grimaced. *"Seismo?"*

Cody helped him out of the cockpit, but as soon as Harry's boots touched the ground he collapsed. The other two Hornets flew low over the downed jet. The noise was deafening as Cody saluted. Lima One rocked wings. Then both aircraft flew straight up into the blinding sunlight and began to circle overhead.

Cody heard steps behind him. He reached for his sidearm and then turned around to see five heavily-armed Taliban fighters standing within ten feet. These devils had just seen their comrades burned alive by American infidels from the sky. His throat tightened, and he shuddered. He had fifteen rounds in his Beretta, but he was no Wyatt Earp. He dropped his weapon and threw his hands into the air. *Am I gonna die, or are they still interested in prisoners?*

The SEAL team would be able to track his location, wouldn't they? Cody rolled his eyes left and right, hoping to see his comrades approaching. Would they come or were they pinned down?

Harry began to move around, moaning and trying to raise himself off the sand. Two more Taliban arrived, along with five young boys who appeared to be under the age of ten.

They placed a handgun in the palm of the smallest child and shouted something to him. He walked forward tentatively and pointed the gun at Harry's head. The boy's entire body was shaking. Two of the Taliban shouted at him again.

Cody looked into the eyes of this child and shook his head "no," pleading with him silently. The child hesitated and then, with a resolute expression, pulled the trigger.

*"No-ohhh!"* Cody's legs buckled. He fell to his knees beside Seismo.

A moment later, gunfire erupted from behind cover up on the ridge — fury with precision as bullets struck flesh and bone, knocking down five enemy warriors in front of him. The SEALs had arrived.

Cody started to reach for his weapon on the ground but he was immediately seized by the two remaining enemy combatants. They lifted him to his feet. One pressed a pistol to his head while the other held a large machete to his throat. They both screamed at him and at the hidden gunmen above, whose weapons fell silent.

Cody was a human shield. These two were trying to buy time. Additional enemy fighters would arrive any second.

Cody cleared his head. A ten-minute standoff meant certain death. He wasn't going to stand by and be used as a tool to get himself and his would-be rescuers killed. *Something needs to happen now.*

The one on his left, holding the gun, was shaking like a leaf in the wind, and a puddle formed underneath the other who held the machete. Cody smelled urine. These guys could be had.

His heart was pounding against his breastbone. He could either die fighting or wait to be slaughtered along with his comrades on the ridge.

As his friends remained hidden, Cody quickly executed a nifty duck, sweep, kick and spin move he had practiced several times with the SEAL team. He disarmed the gunman, distancing himself just a few feet from his captors. In a split second, as he was moving down and away, rifle fire rang out again — two deadly kill shots fired from the unseen location above. The heads of both nervous enemy warriors exploded.

Cody sustained a cut on the side of his neck, but it was not life-threatening. Blood, brain tissue and skull splinters now covered the right sleeve of his flight suit.

Two Navy SEALs identified themselves before appearing from behind cover. Cody knelt again beside Harry. The bullet fired by the shaky-handed boy had missed Harry's head but had struck him in the chest. He was alive for now. The child holding the weapon had taken a fatal gunshot through the face. The other four boys were unharmed but traumatized.

Hondo Phillips, communications specialist and sniper, and Elias Chavez, munitions expert and sometimes medic, slid down the embankment to the crashed aircraft.

Chavez examined Harry to determine his condition. "Doesn't look good. Head injury and a serious chest wound. He needs a hospital." He did his best to stop the bleeding by making bandages from some of the clothing taken from the dead Taliban.

Chavez bandaged Cody's neck. "We need to stitch this cut as soon as we can find cover again."

"We're hoping to evac the wounded sometime today if we can clear out some of these baggers tracking us," Hondo added.

"Nice shooting." Cody staggered back to his feet and leaned on the downed Hornet's right stabilizer which had been nearly hidden by a rockslide.

"What was it that shot you down?" Chavez asked.

"Dunno. We got no warning. A lucky shot with some handheld weapon, a manpad, a golden BB, a fluke." Cody's right calf and foot felt like a thousand wasp stings. He respired rapidly, his face contorted.

"Too low to eject?" Hondo asked.

"It was my call. Dodging the peaks, losing control. Then I saw this plateau. I don't know." Cody shook his head, "Maybe I should've —"

"Can't second-guess yourself now, Lieutenant. Too late. Need to slow down that breathing. Can't have you passing out on us."

Cody exhaled slowly. "I was sitting up there at angels two zero on top of the world a few minutes ago."

"Not so glorious as you thought, huh, Babe?"

Cody didn't answer. His head was pounding, his burns were barely tolerable, and the bleeding cut on his neck stung as he perspired. Each step seemed more painful than the last while they ascended back up the embankment. He tried to bring his nerves under control.

"How far away is your hideout?" Cody would be forced to make it under his own power because Hondo and Chavez had to alternate carrying Harry — a load at 225 pounds.

"Bout a mile," Chavez said. "What're we gonna do with these kids?"

"We can't take these little zits with us," Hondo mumbled. "They'll slow us down, and we'll all buy a piece of this friggin' wasteland."

"Can't let 'em follow either," Chavez added. "They'll trail us almost to our hideout and then disappear and give away our location to the enemy."

Hondo looked around nervously. "And something else to think about…" He turned and stared at the four frightened boys.

"Something else?" Cody sat down on a rock, trying to stay conscious.

"Babe, think about it." Chavez continued Hondo's thought. "If we let them go back, the Taliban will turn these kids into killers."

"And what happens if we take them with us and get caught?" Cody wrapped a towel around his head to protect against the sun, and worked on slowing his respiration.

"They'll torture and kill us," Chavez stated with conviction. "And judging from the mindset of these butchers, they'll probably torture the kids just for going with us. They'll call 'em traitors."

"I know this is your show here on the ground," Cody said, "but I vote we find a place to hide them."

"Where are we gonna hide 'em out here?" Hondo objected. "They aren't safe with or without us. Problem is, we need to expedite."

"So what are you saying?" Cody's head was clearing.

Chavez glanced at the kids and then back. "All we're saying, Babe, is sometimes there are no good answers out here. We let 'em go, and they'll be killing Marines in a couple o' years."

"Look, does either of you guys speak the language? Is there any way we can communicate with 'em?"

Chavez shrugged. "I don't think so, Babe. They don't speak Arabic around here. We can try to leave them somewhere, but they won't stay put."

"I say we finish it now and get t'ell outta here," Hondo grumbled. "They could be on us any second. They gotta be lookin' for us."

Chavez snapped back, "Stand down, Phillips. These are innocent kids we're talkin' about."

"Stand down? We're sittin' here like — I mean it's our butts on the plate."

"You're outa line, Petty Officer! SEALs protect innocents. We don't kill 'em!" Chavez outranked him.

"*Yessssir!*" Hondo scowled, as he forced an agitated salute and turned away.

"Why don't we tie 'em up? Leave them in a secure place?" Cody took a deep breath. "When the extraction helo arrives in a few hours, we can go back and pick 'em up and take them with us, turn them over to the Red Cross or something like that. Lemme try to explain it to them. What do you think?" He winced.

"It sucks either way, Babe. What if the wild animals get 'em?" Chavez stared at the four boys again who were now huddled together.

Hondo sat alone on a rock, scanning the hills with his range finder.

Chavez made the call. "Okay, Babe. Give it a shot. Like I said, sometimes there are no good solutions."

Cody tried what little Arabic he knew, but the kids did not respond to any of it. The oldest frantically pleaded and began to cry. It was useless to try to understand him.

The men found a secluded place in a ravine and tied the four children with ropes and headbands they had taken off the Taliban. They bound them hand and foot and tied them to each other, making it impossible to escape. Despite the pleading of the children, the three men left and began the trek back toward their team's hiding place with Hondo and Chavez alternating the task of carrying Seismo.

They could still hear the cries of the four boys until just before they arrived at the camp. With each step, Cody wanted to go back.

When they finally dragged into the hideout, Cody had reached his limit. He collapsed onto a large flat rock underneath a ledge. Chavez gave him a shot of morphine, then wrapped his burns and stitched the cut on his neck.

Cody looked around. They had taken refuge at the base of a cliff that extended several hundred feet upward. It was early afternoon and the sun had moved just behind the tops of the rocks, thus placing him in the shade. Positioned in the shadowy recesses along the bottom of the escarpment, he and the others hoped to make themselves invisible.

"How you doin', Lieutenant?" It was Major Simon Hendrix, commander of the mission, sitting farther back underneath the ledge. Two rounds had shattered his left shoulder and collarbone, and the resulting fall had inflicted a head injury. Morphine had slowed his speech. His face was splotched with reddish-gray mud. He wore a bloody head bandage and his dark eyes were bloodshot and puffy.

"I'll live, Sir. Looks like you took one through the shoulder? Hopefully, we can be outta here in an hour or so."

"Take another look around you, son. Reality is, this retreat is safe for now, but it's just a matter of time. Can't get a helo in here because of the rocks and the cliff behind us. We'll have to abandon this location just to find a vertical landing zone."

Even with the morphine, the major's voice was commanding, articulate, resolute.

"We also have three injured now, Babe, including Seismo," Chavez reminded. "Gonna be impossible to relocate again and avoid detection. And I can tell you for sure, Seismo won't make it if we don't get him to a hospital."

"What about the kids we left in that ravine?"

"No way, Babe. Suicide if we go back to get them without a gunship for cover. Right now, looks like we're gonna have to fight our way out of here. Shoot-n-scoot may be our only option, but the odds will be twenty-to-one."

"A Parthian shot? We gonna try it tonight?"

"Won't work, Babe," Hondo spit out. "Too hazardous without the full moon, especially carrying wounded. Bullock stepped on loose rocks in broad daylight and fell thirty feet." He pointed to the other injured SEAL, Jeffry Bullock, age 28, who was grimacing even after receiving morphine. "He's laid up over there with a broken ankle and shattered hip."

"Besides that, son, you forget that the Parthian shot required horses." Major Hendrix gutted out a smile. "And they didn't teach that at the Academy."

Due to the extended mission and additional wounded, medical supplies were running low, including pain meds. Cody's adrenaline rush now abandoned him. With morphine and the exhaustion, he fell asleep and did not awake until 0500 the next morning.

# NE'ER SAW TRUE BEAUTY 'TIL THIS NIGHT

## *Four years later*

Houston, Sunday, July 6 — Oakland right-hander Jake Grim stood in front of the pitcher's mound and glared toward home plate. His wiry hair curled upward from underneath the sides of his cap. His rugged beard, gnarly expression, and six-foot seven-inch frame afforded him an intimidating presence like that of a giant Neanderthal on steroids.

Cody Musket, rookie third baseman, stepped out of the batter's box, removed his batting helmet, and wiped perspiration from his eyes. With a full count and bases loaded with two outs, his team trailing by two runs, Cody had fouled off three nasty sinkers in a row.

It was the bottom of the ninth inning. The crowd was on its feet. It had come down to a mind game between one of the best veteran relief pitchers in baseball and a rookie hitter who had been with the big league club only ten weeks.

Astros broadcaster Bobby Dodge had the call.

> *"...Grim stretches, checks the runners. And here comes the payoff pitch again. Musket sends a soft line drive down the right field line. It's slicing...but it's a fair ball! One run across! Two runs score! And now here comes Bustamante around third! The throw to the plate is off-line! The Astros win again! The 'Stros have now won their eighth in a row as they prepare to leave town*

*for a three-game series in Philadelphia, and then three games with Pittsburgh beginning next Friday leading up to the All-Star break . . ."*

\*   \*   \*

Pittsburgh, Friday, July 11 — "Musket! Musket, wake up!" Mark Stiller, Cody's roommate, shook him by the shoulders. "Cody, wake up! You gotta come out of it!"

"Uh, what time is it, Stills?" Cody sat up and held his head in his hands.

"Man, it's almost five o'clock in the afternoon. The game's been rained out. You were losing it. When I walked in you were yelling 'mayday' again."

"Uh, did I say anything else?"

"Yeah, you said something about some kids. You're livin' in a fog, man. You should get some help. What would you do if I wasn't here? Like the other time when you got up and walked into the wall at the Marriot in Baltimore — blood all over the dang carpet, five stitches on your head."

"Hey, no sweat. I fell asleep. Just had a bad dream, that's all."

"Yeah, right. Like the time I found you lyin' in the hallway in Tampa and you didn't even know where you were? Yeah, that was a bad dream too. Man, it's been four years. Whatever happened over there, you need to get over it. But, what the hey, I mean it's your business, your life, your career."

Cody took a long breath, then walked over to the bathroom sink and splashed his face. "I heard about the game being rained out, so I took a snooze." He carried a towel back to the bed, sat on the edge and wiped his face. "Gotta find something to do with myself tonight."

"I'm leaving right now to pick up Sandy at the airport," Mark said. "We're going to her aunt's house in Harrisburg tonight." Mark put on his cap and walked toward the door. "Get some help, Musket. You don't trust me. I get that. But you gotta friggin' trust somebody."

From the eleventh floor of the Marriott, Cody could see PNC Ballpark in the distance. An early, wet darkness had befallen the city. *Still raining. Gonna be a boring night.*

This was the evening he had dreaded — his first rainout since joining the Astros. In his previous three years, in the minor leagues, he had not done rainouts well. Boredom was something he feared.

He sat in his plush hotel room looking through the *Pittsburgh Post-Gazette.* He flipped through the TV channels, stopping at local KDFG-TV in time to catch a sports report.

> *"We turn our attention to sports now, as KDFG's Peggy Kravchuk is standing by at PNC Park. Peggy, lots of rain today."*
>
> *"That's right, Cliff. And it looks like more dark clouds are on the way."*
>
> *"Well, Peggy, tell us what to expect from this red-hot Astros team."*
>
> *"Cliff, the visiting Astros have been ignited by the surprising emergence of rookie third baseman Cody Musket. At only five foot nine inches, he's leading the American League in home runs and is carrying a hefty .329 batting average. He has been up from Houston's Double-A team at Corpus Christi just since late April and..."*

He turned it off, put on a Pirates T-shirt, stepped into a pair of Wrangler jeans, and donned a Pirates baseball cap. Hopefully, wearing the Pirates gear would keep him from being recognized.

Earlier in the hotel lobby, he had been handed a VIP pass to a premiere screening of a new Superman movie. It was showing at a popular mall near the hotel. The superhero film would have to do — anything to get his mind off the boredom and bad dreams.

The rain had let up temporarily, so he took to the wet sidewalks and sloshed his way toward the mall four blocks away.

Wearing his Wranglers, Payless tennies, and the Pirates cap and shirt, he blended well while passing through the lobby of the Cinema 18 in Maxstone Memorial Matrix. It wouldn't have been this easy in Houston where he was already a celebrity, but in this mall, situated less than a mile from the Allegheny River, he was just a guy going to the movie on a Friday night without a date.

He arrived at the Cinema 18 early and decided to visit the concessions. As he stood in line, he overheard a young woman engaged in a cell phone conversation with her father. He could not see her because she stood behind a freestanding bulletin board, but he was intrigued as he listened.

> "No, Daddy, Speedy broke up with me. We went out twice, and then he asked me to move in. When I told him I wasn't going to sleep with another guy until marriage, he acted like I was violating his rights or something. Every guy I meet wants only one thing — to hit on me."

Cody strained to hear every word. His left ear had suffered hearing damage in Afghanistan, so he turned his head to get his right ear closer.

> "It's been a horrible day. First, Tanner McNair canceled for my Sunday-night show. He's leaving town right after the game Sunday 'cause he's a last-minute selection for the All-Star Game in Detroit."

Now Cody's curiosity was piqued. Tanner McNair, Pittsburgh Pirates right fielder, was his best friend from high school. *This chick must be well connected. What Sunday-night show?*

> "Then this afternoon these creepy-looking guys followed me." Silence. "Yes, I know, Daddy, but lots of editorial writers have death threats. "

Cody wanted to maneuver into position to see her, but a rail stood between him and the bulletin board. Editorials? Threats?

> "I'm going to that premiere I told you about — the new Superman movie." Silence. "I know, Daddy, but I can't let them scare me. I just need to chill."

Normally in Pittsburgh at 6:00 p.m. in July, bright daylight would be in order. But today, with foreboding skies of black clouds and drizzle, Cody saw it as a picture of what his life had become — lots of rain and thunder and very little sunshine.

Though he could not see her behind the bulletin board, something in her voice reminded him of sunlight and better days. She was going to the same movie, and she knew his best friend. *I gotta find out who she is.*

But mingling made him nervous. He was a freak. His clothing hid most of his physical scars, but what female in her right mind would want to be seen with him at a beach or similar social event? And the scars on his soul went just as deep. Who would want to endure his mental state?

Finally, she emerged. Stunning, early twenties, slender and athletic with long, dark brown hair, she reminded him of a Shakespeare quote — *"I ne'er saw true beauty 'till this night."*

The O2 rushed right out of his chest. He tried not to stare as she passed, but his captive eyes could not resist.

"Please, cowboy, leave *something* on me." The sassy filly spirited away, hastening her steps, pink flip-flops flipping and flopping underneath her heels on the worn-out carpet. Something told Cody she wasn't interested in meeting him — *not now, not ever*.

As he approached the turnstile, the skies outside rumbled again — another storm rolling across the Allegheny. He handed his free pass to the attendant, a slightly-built young man with freckles, a wad of gum in his cheek, orange hair, and wearing a micro ruby nose ring.

"Theater Five, sir, down the hall to your left. And what she really meant was, she's dying to be rode."

Cody tightened his jaw, yanked his stamped movie pass back from the attendant, and followed about fifty paces behind the captivating mystery woman. He visualized how she would look with summer sunlight shining on her face and hair.

She wore a dark brown summer blouse, the words "Coco Made Me Poor" written across the front in pink letters. With bleached cutoff jeans and a small leather purse barely large enough for her smartphone, she gracefully swayed before him like five feet, seven inches of heaven.

Was she only an apparition? Despite her display of contempt, her heavenly presence had at least temporarily calmed his storms that lurked in the night, but he would need to work up some grit just to approach her. What could he possibly say to interest her in knowing him?

Suddenly, his fantasy was shattered by a loud crash. Three men wearing ski masks had breached a nearby emergency exit from the outside. They raced into the building, brutally seized the angel of his affection, and began yanking her toward the door.

"Leave me alone! Get away! Someone call the police! Help me!" She resisted, fighting, scratching, twisting, and screaming. Her tenacity angered the abductors, so they slammed her down and dragged her across the grimy carpet toward the exit. They pulled her by the hair and from behind by the neck of her Coco shirt, which squeezed off her windpipe and ripped the blouse.

She coughed and gasped for breath while they tugged her closer and closer to the door, but still she resisted. They battered her with profane verbal abuse and extreme brutality — an apparent effort to intimidate her into submission.

Like lightning striking desert sands, the attack on this innocent woman had detonated Cody's beautiful dream into a molten rage. Adrenaline drove his legs forward like a runaway diesel. His steely forearms tightened. He was back in Afghanistan and ready to hurt somebody.

Receptors on full alert, he heard every sound and saw every movement. The rush, the horror, and the intensity — a cocktail of emotions he had tried to forget for four years.

And then he witnessed something remarkable. As though a cool breeze had swept across the young woman's face, she stopped fighting and closed her eyes. Her settled expression suggested an uncommon resolve to remain collected and to gather her thoughts.

As he charged forward, Cody never slowed, but he returned to his senses. Navy SEALs had taught him how to win — *analyze, stay within yourself, don't lose your head, finish it.*

He reasoned. They had specifically targeted her. They had it all planned out. They would have a getaway vehicle waiting in the parking lot on the other side of the exit. If they managed to get her through that door, she'd be gone forever.

"Let her go! The police are on their way!"

He had a plan — attempt to scare them off with the threat of police intervention. If that didn't work, use force. He had only seconds to decide.

Like his last mission in Afghanistan, showing presence failed to scare off the attackers. The three men ignored him. While two dragged and choked her, the third assailant attempted to place a white cloth over her nose and mouth.

Cody leaped over a rail and positioned himself in front of the door, blocking their path.

"Let go of her!"

His growling voice was now a command. "I'm not letting you get her through this door!" The words echoed in the hallway junction and resonated like that of five men.

Cody had their attention. He was a threat. If he managed to delay their getaway, they would risk the arrival of authorities. Time was not their ally. A successful abduction depended upon speed.

The individual holding the white cloth screamed a profane and loud ultimatum back at Cody — a command to either move or be cut to shreds. The shouting drew more people to the scene.

The perpetrator swung around and faced the bystanders. He waved the white cloth above his head and pointed to the battered woman on the floor.

"Let this be a lesson to anybody that friggin' goes to war with us!"

With her purse, phone and flip-flops scattered in the hallway, overpowered and held down by the other two men, she glanced up at Cody through disheveled hair that clung to her face. She tried to speak but could only gasp for air.

Cody was a coiled spring.

The assailant flung the white cloth into the air and charged toward him, brandishing a cheap but deadly AK assault knife. Cody never flinched, and the attacker suddenly hesitated. Cody then swept the legs from under the offender, separated him from his knife and slammed him facedown against the floor with extreme prejudice.

Cody turned. A second attacker, already charging forward with a knife, stopped when he saw blood and teeth lying on the floor in front of his unconscious predecessor. A grisly command from Cody put him on the carpet.

"Sit and don't move! Drop the knife and kick it away or I'll make you eat it!" The wide-eyed would-be slasher backed away, kicked the knife, and fell backwards to a sitting position.

The third man pulled his victim to her feet with a chokehold. His cold eyes snarled at Cody through the slots in his mask. He was tall and muscular, towering over her. She tried to free herself but couldn't. Struggling just to draw a breath, her urgent gasping silenced all gathering witnesses.

What remained of her Coco shirt was dangling from the front of her neck like a limp dish rag. The thin, stretchy left shoulder strap of her workout bra had been torn loose from behind and was swinging back and forth in front.

Bystanders watched in disbelief as this large man, while holding his prey by the neck with his left arm, pulled a knife from his vest and cocked his right hand back to throw the weapon. Cody was a sitting duck.

With the quickness of a cat, he sidestepped to his right to force the assailant to hit a moving target, but unexpectedly, the traumatized woman, with enough awareness, lunged slightly with all her might, threw back her right hand, and interfered just enough to misdirect the toss of the knife. It sliced a two-inch-long flesh wound one quarter inch deep into Cody's left arm, but missed his heart by twenty inches.

The big man then made a mistake. He backed up, used his victim as a human shield, held her at arm's length, and forced her into Cody's path. This allowed Cody to maneuver in between and administer a stunning right palm to the nose.

The assailant lost his grip and staggered backward, his nostrils spewing blood and his ski mask turning scarlet. Cody followed with a left elbow to the throat, an excruciating kick to the groin and a brutal takedown. The large attacker wailed in agony, and bystanders could hear the gruesome sound of ribs cracking and air rushing from his lungs as he crashed to the floor.

The instant this third man hit the carpet, several witnesses shouted, "*Look out!*"

The perpetrator sitting had retrieved his knife while Cody's back was turned. He charged, hoping to blindside Cody, who turned just in time to relieve the would-be backstabber of his weapon. He slammed him to the rug, retracted the knife blade, and then forced the handle into the mouth and down into the throat of this man to whom he had promised to feed his own knife.

Now that all three assailants were down, Cody saw red flashes. Holding the knife, hearing his defeated foe choking, a bitter taste formed in his mouth. His veins protruded and his teeth clenched. *These guys deserve to die.*

But just as suddenly as it had come, the rage passed. He pulled the knife handle away and breathed a heavy sigh of relief. He had wanted to kill the three men. What had stopped him? Never had anger overtaken him so quickly and then let go of him so soon.

He took a step backward, then collapsed into a sitting position. The nerve endings in his right foot and lower leg were on fire, but that also passed within seconds. *Thank God I didn't kill 'em all.*

Cody dragged all three perpetrators, barely conscious, into one pile. He pulled off their masks, checked them for more weapons, and then screamed into their faces a warning loud enough for everyone to hear.

"I could have killed you, but after Afghanistan I swore I'd never take another life. Nobody dies tonight, but if I ever hear that you've bothered this woman again, you will never even see me coming, and no one will ever know I was there. Do you copy?"

The witnesses stood in stunned silence and then broke into applause. Cody's eyes scanned the hallway until he spotted her. The badly bruised but gutsy woman who had narrowly escaped a violent end was now crouching in a corner near the entrance to Theater Five.

Her neck and shoulders were dappled with red streaks — brush marks left by the ends of her blood-spattered hair. Tearfully attempting to compose herself again, she would not look Cody in the eye.

Cody collected her purse, cell phone, and flip-flops from bystanders who had picked them up. He walked toward her and reached out his hand, but she moved away, lowered her head and wrapped her arms around herself.

Because a large crowd had gathered, Cody became uneasy. Curious observers were now perilously close to three dangerous men. The police were still minutes away, and only one security guard had arrived, so Cody remained with the attackers, who were injured but conscious. He would help guard them until the authorities came.

Soon, the police entered the hallway. Multiple witnesses came forward. As they described the events, it was clear that Cody had heroically prevented the abduction of Brandi Barnes, local talk show host and editorial writer.

## She's Not Too High on Men

"Sir, could I see your ID please." Detective Terrance Dupree was chief investigator at the crime scene. Cody reluctantly obliged and gave the detective his driver's license.

"Mr. Musket, I see you're from Houston. What's your business here in Pittsburgh?"

Cody breathed a sigh of relief. The detective had not discovered his celebrity status. "Well, sir, I'm a martial arts instructor, and I'm here for the weekend."

"How do you happen to know Ms. Barnes?"

"Ms. Barnes?"

"Yes, sir. The victim."

"I don't know her at all. What exactly does she do?"

"So you did not know her prior to this evening?"

"I was behind her. I happened to see what was going on and couldn't just stand by and, uh, you know. Afterward, I gave her shoes, her purse and phone to one of the female officers."

"Brandi Barnes is a writer and local sports talk show host. You're here just for the weekend you say?"

"Planning to move on by Sunday night. Uh, Detective, do you know the motive for the attack?"

"Still trying to determine that. We should know after we ID the suspects."

"Well, sir, I overheard an officer mention a possible organized crime connection. If that's the case, may I ask that you not release my last name to the press?"

"We don't know if — Stand by a moment please, Mr. Musket."

Dupree walked about thirty paces and gave Cody's ID to an officer in a dark blue uniform. The two had a brief discussion. Cody could clearly read two words from the lips of the officer in blue — *human trafficking.*

Dupree then walked briskly to Brandi, who stood with two female officers just a few feet away from Cody. The detective told her she should consider hiring a bodyguard.

"I need to get out of here. I am not feeling well. I've told you all I know." She shivered and fought back tears. They had given her a wraparound blanket to wear. One of the female officers accompanied her as she left.

While Cody waited for his ID, he had the urge to call out to Brandi as she departed, but couldn't bring himself to make a sound.

Cody asked a nearby observer about Brandi.

"She has a Sunday night sports show," the young man responded. "She also writes in the paper."

"What does she write about?"

A young woman wearing a gray University of Pittsburgh jersey emerged from the crowd and spoke up, "She's been writing exposé articles on human trafficking here in Allegheny County. They've been published in the *Gazette.*"

As she walked toward Cody, the words "This Sista Luvs Jesus" became visible on the front of her pink baseball cap. Charming, soft-spoken, early twenties, she offered Cody a pleasant smile and warm handshake, but her soft, tearful brown eyes told him she had been crying.

"I'm Sasha. I've been following Brandi's career since she played basketball at Stanford. She also played one year in the WNBA until —"

"Stanford?"

"That's right. I'm in law school here at Pitt. My older sister Latisha played with Brandi in college. If it hadn't been for Brandi, my sister wouldn't have graduated. Thank God for the rainout this evening. Without it, you wouldn't have been here, and we would've lost her tonight."

Cody looked around nervously and then gently took her arm and ushered her away from the gathering crowd.

Sasha lowered her voice. "She's been doing editorials in the *Gazette* about a trafficking ring in Pittsburgh. Children have disappeared around here in the past year — about fifty of them."

"Children?"

"Last week, she gave authorities a tip that paid big dividends. They raided a house in Peters Township. Saved seven little girls and four women and also arrested the bad guys. Now the traffickers have put a contract on her life."

"You mean she has a price on her head?"

"I know one man they won't be able to stop when he finds out about this — her father. He's a decorated US Marine like you. Those three attack dogs who assaulted Brandi might not be alive right now if Captain Barnes had been here."

"Sasha, I'd appreciate it if you wouldn't tell —"

"Their plan is to force her to give up her informants and then torture her to death. After that, her mutilated body will turn up in a public place as a warning to anyone thinking of standing in their way. It's happened before. That's why nobody has the b — Never mind, here comes Dupree. Wanna get together for coffee later?"

"Uh, no thanks. I . . . gotta meet someone. I need to ask you —"

"*Shhh.*" She placed one finger over his lips and spoke softly. "I know, Cody. I understand why you want to stay anonymous. Don't worry."

"Do I know you from somewhere?" He was certain they had never met.

Sasha closed her eyelids, kissed him affectionately on the cheek, and then stepped back with shimmering eyes.

"No, you've never met me, Cody, but I know you. My cousin was one of the eight survivors of that Chinook that went down near Helmand Province." She soft-stroked his cheek. "He wouldn't be alive today if you hadn't volunteered to…what I mean is…*thank you.*"

He thought to embrace the tearful young woman, but she turned to walk away, then stopped and smiled back at him. "And you'd better hurry if you want to catch her. She's not too high on men, but she'll like you just fine. She shouldn't be alone right now, you know. Next time, they'll have guns."

Cody saluted Sasha by tipping his cap as she departed.

Dupree returned Cody's ID and said he was free to go, but not to leave town for a couple of days. He planned to leave town after the Sunday game because, like his friend Tanner McNair, he was heading to Detroit to play in the All-Star Game.

So far, no one else had recognized him, but by now, half the population of Pittsburgh was swarming the hallway — all gawking at him.

EMS responders gave him alcohol wipes to clean blood from his arms and face. They wanted to stitch the knife wound on his left arm. "No thanks, I gotta meet someone. Could you just clean it and wrap it?"

He was frantic to depart before he was recognized, and his chances of finding Brandi diminished with every passing second. Was anyone guarding her? Did she realize the danger?

Cody trotted toward the lobby of the theater, but by the time he reached the outside door, there was no sign of her. He walked up and down the street and searched unsuccessfully. Rain began pouring down again, so he returned to the shelter of the mall, soaked.

The officers had not recognized Cody's name since he wasn't yet a national celebrity. He reasoned that if he could dodge the press, perhaps he could avoid the unwanted publicity. But Brandi *was* the press. She would eventually discover his identity — one more reason he needed to find her.

*   *   *

Brandi was 24. She had enjoyed VIP status since becoming a star athlete, and was accustomed to men throwing themselves at her. She was a popular, well-educated career woman who had no problem attracting status-seeking male suitors.

Other than her father, the men in her life had brought her only one thing — pain. Numerous disappointments had left her with serious trust issues. Ray Barnes, her father, was the only man she trusted.

Her lip was bleeding and puffy. She was battered, bruised, stinging from carpet burns on her legs and feet, but had declined a ride to the hospital from the EMS crew. She could not stop shaking from the ordeal and simply wanted to retreat to her high-rise apartment a few blocks away.

She had left the scene in a daze and wandered into a shop to purchase a jersey so she could ditch the blanket. She had stopped by a ladies' restroom and attempted to rinse the attacker's blood from her hair. Moments later, she had exited onto the street.

Even though she often walked to her apartment, Brandi had taken a cab. She was afraid to be on the street alone in the aftermath of her attack, and besides that, it was raining again.

She withered into the backseat of the cab and called her father, Ray Barnes. "Daddy, is Mama with you? You won't believe what just happened." With shaky breath, she related the events. "I'm just trying to hang on to my sanity. What? No . . . no, Daddy. Daddy, listen to me. No, I'm really okay! The men are in custody. There was this other man who showed up. I mean . . ."

She put her hand over her face. The curious driver was eavesdropping and watching in the rearview mirror. She toned it down as she told about the stranger who had defended her.

Her parents wanted to know more about her mysterious guardian. "I dunno, I had to get out of there. He was still tied up with the cops when I left. I have no idea why he helped me. I assume he's just a glory seeker like most men I've met." She scooted to the far side of the seat to escape the invasive eyes of the driver still staring at her in the mirror.

"I can't remember all the details. I breathed some of the chloroform they forced on me. I think he mentioned Afghanistan."

"If he's former military special ops," he told her, "you'd better stay clear of him 'cause I've known some of those guys to be violent."

"Oh, he was an animal, Daddy! The way he . . . I mean, Daddy, he beat the snot out of 'em!" She chuckled, then fought tears again. "He had these blue eyes, the kind that, like, go right through you, I mean . . ."

"Listen to me, baby girl, those guys don't always do well in domestic relationships, so if I were you —"

"But, Daddy, you are former military and you aren't violent at home."

"Baby girl, you need medical help. You said this guy just appeared out of thin air. Your mother and I are coming down there tonight. Go to your apartment and stay there! It'll take us a while 'cause the storm has flooded some roads. We'll call a doctor."

Just then her smartphone told her she had an incoming call. "Daddy, the police are calling. I'll ring you back."

It was Dupree. "Ms. Barnes? We've identified one of the suspects. The big guy who had you by the throat is extremely dangerous. The FBI wants him in connection with a double homicide and child abduction."

Brandi managed a shallow groan. She saw dark spots before her eyes.

"You need to get some protection," the detective continued. "These guys are part of something bigger. Your crusade has them stirred up. Lucky your date was able to handle these baggers."

"He wasn't my date," she insisted. "Who exactly is he?"

"This guy, his name's Cody. He asked what you do."

"So he didn't know who I was? He's gotta be lying."

"So you don't know him at all? You ever seen him before?"

"Never laid eyes on him."

Dupree went on, "He wasn't forthcoming about why he's in Pittsburgh. Says he's a martial arts instructor, and his ID has a Houston address. Martial arts my butt! This guy's no instructor. He's a seasoned professional who asked us to keep his last name out of the press."

"The press? Why's he worried about the press?"

"Unknown, ma'am. He has no warrants or criminal records, but why did this martial arts expert from Houston just happen to show up tonight twelve hundred miles from home at the very time and place you get assaulted? My instincts tell me he's hiding something."

"What's he not telling? I'm coming back. I'll get it out of him."

"I wouldn't do that if I were you, Ms. Barnes. He may have saved your life, but this is a dangerous man, and probably unstable."

Brandi no longer had feeling in her right hand holding the phone. She put her head between her knees in the backseat of the cab to keep from fainting. She had been a fool. Why had she just walked away? He was either trouble or an answered prayer, and she must find out which. Her stomach was like a twisted rubber band, but she was determined.

Brandi loved a mystery. Was he a devil? An angel? Why put himself in harm's way unless he expected to gain something? Was it a setup? Did that even make sense? *Think!*

Could she have found a real superhero? She managed a tight grin and then chuckled. *Hmmm, what if his last name turns out to be Kent? Cody Kent? Ridiculous!*

She asked the driver to turn around. Her cabbie could not drive fast enough to suit her. When she walked through the lobby of the Cinema 18, everyone was buzzing. She ran toward the crime scene but authorities had closed the hallway. Her superhero had vanished.

Too late. Now what? Brandi's hands were still shaking. Her palm felt cold against her forehead. Then, deep in thought, she was startled to hear a raspy male voice behind her.

"Brandi? Hi, my name's Cody."

# Devil or Angel?

B randi turned around. Her stomach, still in knots, leaped into her throat. His chiseled face was handsome in a home-on-the-range sort of way. His sculpted cheeks were partially masked by a rough-hewn beard — the obvious cover-up for scars visible through his whiskers. His nose had been broken at least once. This guy had been in some fights.

The Pirates cap he had worn earlier was now in his back pocket and his sandy blond hair wet around the sides. Did he know that his shirt had turned pink on the front? The blood spatters had faded together, partially washed off by heavy rains.

Was she face-to-face with a superhero? He was not as tall as she remembered. His fiery eyes that could have intimidated Lucifer earlier were now softer, like quiet blue waters. He offered his hand, but his shallow, forced smile told her he was not certain how she would respond. Was his shyness just an act?

*Whew!* His extended hand was attached to a massive forearm. His neck was wide and muscular, his body built to last, rough-cut from head to toe — a description that would make good print in her eyewitness report for the *Gazette*.

"I wanted to thank you," Cody told her, "for savin' my life earlier."

She could hardly believe her ears. Was it a come-on? Was his voice naturally that raspy, or just a poor attempt to imitate Batman?

"You want to thank me? Shouldn't it be the other way around?"

She extended her hand. It was cold and unsteady. Would he notice? His handshake was warm, ardent, but gentle — the same paw that had just mauled three professional tough guys. She tried to swallow her stomach back down into place but her mouth was too dry.

"Well, I wudda been a sittin' duck if you hadn't deflected that guy's arm. That was pure diehard. You got juice."

*"Juice?* You mean for a girl?"

"Uh . . . no I didn't say that. Courage knows no gender."

She tried not to laugh. The Texas accent, nearly as bad as in the movies, and one-liners about courage — where was he getting his material? Was he left behind by his Boy Scout troop?

"Why are you soaking wet?" she asked. "Did you get lost?"

"Lost? Nope. I went outside lookin' for you."

"Looking for me? Why?"

He shrugged. "Just wanted to see if you were okay."

"You're a long way from a rodeo, cowboy. I mean you obviously aren't from around here."

"Nope. What gave it away?"

Brandi fancied herself an expert at controlling a conversation, but she was on a slippery slope with this guy. She pulled out her smartphone to take notes.

"Texas. Right?" She looked up from her phone. "I think it's a good thing that God didn't make us all sound the same." She waited for a response.

He took his time. His sweet-n-soft eyes perused her face like a pair of blue searchlights looking for hidden bounty. She wondered if Lois Lane had felt the same urge to hide behind something when she discovered that Superman had X-ray vision.

"So, it's God's fault I sound this way?" he finally responded. "I like that. You're smart as a bullwhip — *for a girl.*"

Was he just messing with her? Was he trying to be funny, or just plain rude? *Does this Stony Burke ever smile?*

He was familiar but a total stranger. She should have known him but had no idea why. "Okay, let's see; 'Courage knows no gender.' Who did you hear say that?"

"It just came to me. You must have inspired me."

*Oh, how lame!* "Okay, fair enough. But why should I trust a guy from Texas who just happens to show up over a thousand miles from home right when I need a hero? Why were you here?"

"Divine appointment?" he suggested, his face like stone.

She wasn't buying it. "Okay. I get it. I'm grateful. You were wicked impressive, but I didn't ask for your help, you know."

He dropped his head and crammed his hands into the front pockets of his Wranglers. Sasha had warned him she wasn't high on men.

By now, his pupils had readjusted to the dim light. He noticed the raw skin and bruises on her throat. Her hands were still trembling. He winced at the abrasions and carpet burns on her arms, knees, and feet — the repugnant signature left behind by a gritty carpet over which she had been dragged.

As his staring eyes drifted downward, a solid knot formed in Brandi's throat. The cut-offs did not extend low enough to hide her battered legs. If only she had obtained a pair of full-length jeans when she had purchased the jersey. She put her phone away.

He raised his eyes and forced a hasty, genteel smile — an offering which seemed out of sync with his growly voice and brooding forehead.

"Well, as far as my showing up at the right time, I don't believe things like that happen by accident." His voice mellowed. "If it hadn't been raining, I wouldn't have been here tonight. I wudda been at work."

She frowned. Divine appointment? Why did he seek her out after the attack? What did he expect from her? *He works at night, but not when it rains?*

During the awkward silence, Cody glanced toward a coffee shop. "Would you wanna get coffee at the Allegheny Brew?"

"Sure," she said. "But it's on me."

As they walked, people stared. Cody covered his face with his hand, yanked his soaking wet Pirates cap from his pocket, and pulled it low over his eyebrows.

His secretive body language heightened her suspicions. "Are you here on business this weekend?"

"You might say that, but I had the night off."

"Do you play games?"

Cody raised his brow. "Play games?"

"Yes. Games. Like right now. You're just playing games with me, right?"

"*Ohhhh. Games.* Of course not, I never play games."

"So let me get this straight, you work more than a thousand miles from home at night except when it rains? Or do you just zip about looking for somebody to rescue? Someone to beat up maybe?"

"Not really," he muttered. His mechanical smile faded as he jammed his fists into his front pockets again.

She was crashing and couldn't wait to get her hands on a cup of pick-me-up. "Do you enjoy making me play twenty questions?"

"I wasn't counting." He looked straight ahead as they walked.

At the coffee shop, he ordered a double espresso, and the server gave Brandi her usual — a topped-up macchiato. They sat down.

"So can you at least tell me your last name?"

"Can you tell me why those guys were after you tonight?" he countered.

"I asked you first, Mr. Texas."

Cody drew a deep breath. "I returned from Afghanistan several years ago, and I haven't got what most people call a *real* job yet."

"A real job? How 'bout a *real name***?"

"What's your interest?" He took a sip. "Is it just so you can write a story?"

"Should there be *another* reason?"

"I was hoping . . ." He set his cup down. "Hoping we could be friends."

"So . . . look sweetie, plenty of other girls in this town would enjoy keeping company with a guy like you."

"A guy like me?" He lifted his cup before his face again and gazed at her over the top of it. "You sure 'bout that?" He took another sip.

Brandi leaned back, puzzled. "Well, to quote the famous Rodolfo LaRenzo, 'You're either a big nothing disguised as something, or a big something disguised as nothing.'"

He stared for a moment and scratched his chin. "I heard someone say you played pro basketball in the WNBA."

Brandi waved him off. "Yeah, but that was a while back." She sipped her macchiato. "What about you, Cody? Do you know any professional athletes?"

"Not any as pretty as you."

Her legs and neck were stinging and throbbing, and she was in no mood to be hit on or flattered. "So, um, Cody, do you have a girlfriend?"

"I had a blind date this week in Philly. She was a six-three hockey player from Erie."

"Erie, Pennsylvania?" Brandi took a nervous swallow from her cup.

"Yep. Didn't work out, though. We sat there at the arena coffee shop for about a half hour. We didn't talk much."

*No talking? Hmm, that's a surprise.* "So what happened?"

"Well, I cocked an eye at her, she cocked an eye at me, and we just sat there real cock-eyed for a while." He lifted his cup again.

She covered her mouth and looked away. *Oh, God, please don't let me laugh.*

"I can understand y'all wondering why I'm reluctant to tell you who I am. But there's a reason."

"I know," she said, as if a light had dawned, "you're with the Feds, or you're a front man for some politician maybe?"

Cody rolled his eyes. "Where are you comin' up with this stuff?"

"*Stuff?* Well, you do know what a politician is, right?" She crossed her legs and began kicking her foot nervously under the table.

"Oh, I'm not very political myself." He folded his arms. "In fact, to quote the famous Maxine T. Dillahogan, 'Politicians and diapers are somewhat alike — they both need to be changed often, and for the same reason.'"

Brandi covered her face with both hands and tried desperately to keep from laughing out loud, but an impulsive knee-jerk sent her flip-flop flying underneath the table. It landed on his chair between his knees. The traumatic events of the evening and the macchiato had her wired.

She wanted to disappear into her seat, but Cody never reacted. He looked away momentarily and then dropped her wayward pink leather flip-flop back onto the floor underneath her feet.

The macchiato in Brandi's stomach felt like lava. "Um, Maxine T. Dillamahoochie or whatever you said? Never heard of her. Who was she?"

The gravel in his throat rattled off again. "I just made her up." He shrugged.

Brandi leaned forward, curled both hands around her empty cup, and fought the urge to crush it with her fingers.

"Mark Twain," he rasped.

"Mark Twain?"

"It was Mark Twain — the guy who said it. About the diapers."

She crossed her arms and sat back. Her glare would have sent a papa grizzly scurrying home to mama.

Cody decided to man up. "Look. In the lobby, I overheard your phone conversation with your father. You mentioned your values."

Her mouth fell open. *Values? He was listening to my private conversation?*

Her expression reminded him of a red warning sign he had seen often while in the Marine Corps — *Danger: Explosives.* Suddenly he wished life had come with a "delete entire conversation" button like a smartphone. *Is she always like this, or do I just have this affect on women?*

Now he had nothing to lose. He folded his hands, placed them on the table, and looked into her eyes. His rugged, whispery voice was calm and direct.

"I guess I picked a bad time to tell you. I don't get out much, and I don't often meet women who share my values. I wanted to introduce myself, but I got nervous and just followed you. Then, I saw those guys grab you, and —" His mouth tightened and he shook his head.

Her eyes softened. She twirled a lock of her dark brown hair around her fingers and tilted her head to one side.

"I took a risk coming back to find you," he said. "I was afraid you would publish things that could endanger people I work with."

Her brow wrinkled, her confusion on full display. *Endanger people? What people is he talking about?*

"I knew that even if I didn't come back, you'd find out who I am anyway, so I've come to ask you to please not reveal my name to the media."

She scooted to the edge of her chair.

"My last name's Musket. I play third base for the Astros."

All life drained from her face. The deep breath she was holding instantly escaped. How could she have missed it? She had read about him — Medal of Honor and the best story in baseball this season. *Oh please, God! If I collapse right now, he'll never let me forget.*

"I'd like to keep my identity a secret," he drawled. "If organized crime is involved, it could put my teammates at risk. I took a chance, but I had to find you. I want to believe you'll keep my identity between us."

Quietly she stared down at the napkin in front of her. Her eyes became misty. "So...you're a believer? I mean you said you shared my values and..."

They waited a silent moment.

Brandi clenched her fists underneath the table. *No crying. Not now.* When she awkwardly blotted her eyes with the napkin moments later, Cody looked away.

"I still have issues," he said. "If word of what happened tonight makes *SportsCenter*, they're gonna ask me about things that — things I'm tryin' to get past."

For a few seconds, she could not look him in the eye. She was a moron. *Did I really ask Cody Musket if he knows any professional athletes?" Does he play games? Uggh!*

She expected him to leave, but there he sat. She must make amends somehow.

"I just noticed that your left arm has a fresh bandage on it. It has been bleeding again." She fidgeted and pretended to take another sip — from an empty cup.

"Yeah, so I see. The EMS guys bandaged it, but it needs stitches."

"I can take you to a clinic."

"Nah, I don't want to get recognized."

She decided to tread forward on thin ice. "Okay. So . . . would you want to come over to my place and let me bandage it better? It's the least I can do. I don't live far." She sniffled, blotted her eyes again and then snickered at herself. *Did I really invite him over?*

Despite her swollen lower lip and bruised neck, her face melted into an amiable smile which lit up her blue eyes and revealed two dimples to complement her delicate pink lips.

He reached toward her cheek. "Your face. It looks —" He hesitated, curled up his fingers, and withdrew.

She swallowed awkwardly. "It's okay, Cody. What did you start to say?" She reached across the table and took his hand. "Something about my face?" She could no longer feel the chair beneath her or the stinging carpet burns. Could he hear her pounding heart?

His gritty voice finally spat it out. "I'm sorry. I'm not good at sayin' stuff. I just don't often see a face that — What I mean is, mostly I'm just around ballplayers with faces about as soft as a steer's butt, that's all."

She wanted to laugh and wanted to cry, but which first? How could he have said that with a straight face? But the straight face seemed to be his natural one. Was it part of his act? In what way would he surprise her next?

"You got a needle and thread?"

"What?" she asked. "Needle and thread?"

"Sure. Can you stitch up my arm?"

"Your arm? Ahhh, I get it. You're kidding of course."

"I been sewed up by worse. Don't want to get infected. Can't go to a hospital."

She stared at him like a child who had just discovered the ninth wonder of the world. *Seriously?*

They walked toward the exit. Inviting a stranger to her apartment? It was a first. But was he a stranger? Why hadn't he just walked away?

"I live a few blocks from here. I'll flag a cab. Your identity is our secret." She took his arm as they walked. "So what was her name — the girl from Erie?"

"Maxine T. Dillahogan."

# Sore Feet and Blue Eyes

It was a short taxi ride to the Mayfield Tower where Brandi lived. Clouds had dissipated. From the window of the cab, they looked across the Allegheny toward a picturesque sunset of blue, red, purple and orange.

They walked through the front door of her stately third-floor apartment just as the sun finally sank. Their shoes were wet so Brandi tossed her flip-flops into the corner and Cody left his tennis shoes by the door.

He took one glance at Brandi's apartment and told her she would be a sitting duck if she didn't move out. An amateur intruder could render her security system useless.

"Would you mind if I take a quick shower?" Brandi was apologetic. "I'm not sure I got all the blood out of my hair in the ladies' room at the mall."

"Not a problem. I'll just chill for a few."

Brandi left the room, and then returned immediately holding a man-size XXL pullover shirt in her hand.

"By the way, your Pirates shirt has blood on the front. I'll throw it in the washer for you before I step into the shower. Meanwhile, you can wear this."

She tossed him the pullover. It was knee-length and light blue with the words "I Love the Son" written across the front in white letters. "I wear this around the apartment, and sleep in it sometimes."

"Okay, I'm cool with that." He disappeared into the kitchen.

"Cody?" *What's he doing?*

A moment later, he reappeared wearing her pullover and displaying a sheepish expression. He shrugged and handed her the Pirates shirt.

She walked to the washer shaking her head. *Is he that shy? Most guys would relish the opportunity to show off pectorals that bulge the top of a shirt the way his do.*

Cody seated himself on her sofa, removed his right sock and began to scratch until his foot bled. He put his sock back on when he realized he was doing himself bodily harm. He walked to the kitchen to wash blood from his fingernails and then returned to the sofa, leaned his head back, and prayed the angry itch would go away.

In a few minutes, she came back with wet hair, carrying first-aid materials to treat his knife wound. She had exchanged her jersey for a pink blouse and wore red Stanford University Athletic Department knee-length shorts.

She cleaned the wound on his arm and began to cover it with a new bandage.

"Wait," he said. "Don't you think it'll need stitches before you wrap it again?"

"Don't joke, okay?" She put her hands on her hips, hoping this was nothing more than his dry humor.

"Not joking. Can't go to a clinic tonight. Are you up for it?"

She lost the grin. *"Really?"*

She went back to her bedroom and searched for the needle, thread and other items she would need. It wouldn't do for him to think she was squeamish.

She returned and sat beside him. "I have this spray the EMS crew gave me for the pain, but I don't think it's gonna help much. *Oh God, please don't let him see my hand shaking.*

"You want me to thread the needle for you?" He held out his palm. Her face was flushed as her cold fingers handed him the needle and spool of thread.

"My father is a retired Marine," she said moments later as she pierced his arm for the first stitch. "He was awarded a Purple Heart during Desert Storm and retired four years ago with the rank of captain." Her mouth was dry, and fatigue was sneaking up on her.

"Sounds like a guy I need to meet."

She winced. "He and my mother will be here later. They live in Altoona. I told them what happened." If she could keep talking, maybe it wouldn't seem so awkward sewing a man's arm.

When she had finished, she needed to walk for a minute to settle her nerves. She shuffled around the end of the bar to her stereo receiver, tuned it to K-LOVE Radio, positioned the volume control to low, and then softened the lights in the room.

She ambled over to a window, parted the blinds, and glanced down at the street below. Something caught her attention.

"Come take a look," she said nervously. "What do you make of those four guys down there?" She stepped aside and held the blinds open for him. He walked over and looked through the opening.

"Those guys dressed in black? Standing under that streetlight?" He stared a moment longer. "Looks like they're breaking up their powwow and moving away."

She took another look. "Sorry, Cody. I'm paranoid, but they looked suspicious to me. I think you're right about this place. I'm getting nervous."

"Who could blame you?" he asked rhetorically. "I doubt they would put together another hit team tonight. Those things take planning, but you're not safe here. Maybe you should come to the hotel tonight. Our team security is tight there. Next week, you can find a safer place to live."

She crossed her arms. "The hotel? With you?"

"I didn't mean that like it sounded. I could get a room for you and your parents near where our ball club is staying."

"We just met, and you're inviting me to the hotel? Didn't you just say they wouldn't put together another hit team tonight?"

He went back to the sofa and sat down. "You can't be too safe," he said. "You just never know." He subconsciously scratched his foot again.

"I don't mean to pry, but you seem to be uncomfortable. Are you injured in some other way? I mean, you're scratching pretty hard." She walked to the kitchen and retrieved two bottles of cool water from the fridge.

"I had a mishap in Afghanistan. It itches during the summer months, 'specially when I encounter stress."

"So why don't you wear flip-flops and shorts in the heat when you aren't playing baseball? If you don't mind my asking."

"Hmmm. If my feet were as purdy as yours, I would."

She grinned. "Well, see there? You *can* compliment someone when you want to. Uh, what's wrong with your feet?" She covered her mouth. "Whoops. I'm sorry, it's none of my —"

"Bad scars from the knees down on both legs. My teammates are used to it, but I don't like to go public with it, especially around strangers."

"Both legs?" She smiled softly. "Well, it couldn't be *that* bad. I have something that might stop the itching."

Brandi displayed a small jar with a nifty blue label. "It's called Blue Tech Dermis. I know a surgeon who's using it to heal scars after plastic surgery. I used it after my shower, and the carpet burns feel a million times better."

"Yeah? I'd give 'bout anything to lose the misery."

Just then she noticed his right sock had blood on the sides. Her curiosity compelled a desire to reach down and yank it off his foot, but she fought the urge. What manner of four-year-old scars could possibly torture a man enough that he would gouge himself with his own fingernails?

"Okay," she said quietly. "So...so would you mind if I have a look? I could put some of this on the scars and try to make you more comfortable."

He lowered his eyes. "Well, sometimes the scar tissue doesn't smell very fresh after a hot day, if you catch my drift." He made a fanning motion in front of his nose.

"That's no problem. Hang on!" She bounced into the kitchen again and returned with a cool, wet towel and a small basin. She took a seat on the coffee table directly in front of him and displayed the towel. "I can take care of that easily."

"Well —" He glanced at her grandfather clock in the corner. "I — I suppose . . ."

He hesitated too long. It was easy to see he didn't share her enthusiasm. Brandi knew more than her share about men. Would he dare let her touch upon his vulnerability — wounds that caused pain of both body and soul, an area he preferred to keep hidden?

"You'll have to forgive me, Cody. I have the habit of just jumping right in when it's none of my business. When I was in college, the girls in my dorm placed a warning sign outside my door that said, *'It's best just to be yourself, but not when talking to Brandi.'* Someone even suggested I join a convent and take a vow of silence."

He was quiet, contemplative.

"Well, anyway," she sighed, "if you change your mind . . ."

"No, no." He hesitated. "I — I would like that." The sight of her cool, dripping towel had broken through his defenses. His howling puppies craved relief.

"Now you're talking." Her eager smile preceded her as she lifted his right foot and placed it on the pillow next to her. But then his drawn face told her he had second thoughts.

Brandi made eye contact and pretended she had known him always. "You said it made you uneasy around strangers, Cody. I don't want us to be strangers. I want us to be friends."

She slowly pulled the top of his sock down and watched his eyes. His reticent face began to soften, and he closed his eyelids.

She finished removing his sock and gently rolled up the leg of his jeans past his knee. The burn scars were red, uneven, twisted, and stretched. The top of his foot resembled the dark side of the moon — ridges, valleys, and craters. She proceeded to wash the blood from his self-inflicted scratches.

He opened his nervous eyes and watched hers for a reaction. She smiled as if she had uncovered his glory and not as though she had exposed a weakness.

Brandi bathed and dried his disfigured skin, then began to massage the Blue Tech into his foot and lower leg. His gray, sharpened face warmed and began to look human.

"Cody, how often do you scratch yourself 'til you bleed? I don't see you playing baseball if your feet get infected."

"They started itchin' again tonight after we left the theater."

"So the violent encounter triggered something?"

He put his hand over his forehead. "Certain things set me off, and . . . ."

Hesitation telegraphed his reluctance to proceed, so she stepped in. "Um, these burns must have been painful. Would you tell me how this happened?" Her wistful countenance was coaxing, reassuring.

Cody didn't know what to make of her. Was he now seeing the real Brandi Barnes? This one was caring, caressing, tenderly persuasive and not repulsed by his ugly wounds. Her radiant blue eyes were windows into a pure soul and a valiant heart.

Was it finally time to tell someone his story? She put him at ease, this brave woman with the soft, healing hands who jeopardized her safety to fight for children and whose father had won a Purple Heart in battle.

He leaned back on the sofa and closed his eyes again. "Four years ago, 17 May, I launched my F/A-18 Delta Hornet from the USS *Harry Truman* in the North Arabian Sea at zero-eight-hundred. My weapons officer Harry Stanton, call sign 'Seismo,' flew in the backseat. We headed to our rendezvous with a KC-10 tanker to refuel, and then flew to the hills north of Helmand Province in Afghanistan."

Cody stopped. Uncertainty paralyzed his tongue. She nudged him forward with an empathetic nod and confident smile, her hands no longer cold like when he had first met her.

He told her about the failure of the SEALs' mission due to their blown cover, and about losing the survivors of the Chinook crash to the Taliban.

His voice increased in volume. His brow became speckled with tiny droplets as he told every detail about the low-level strafing run, the bodies on the hillside, the explosion under his foot, and the harrowing high-speed pancake plunge into the sand.

"It's nearly impossible to bring a Hornet down with any handheld weapon. We never figured out what went wrong. I set a thirty-million-dollar jet down in the desert, the chance of survival less than five percent. We came to rest in one piece, but my foot and leg were cooked."

Brandi was spellbound, her hands now motionless, resting on his right foot.

"Seismo was seriously hurt. He — he had a head injury." Cody's right hand, so stable earlier, was shaking as he lifted the water bottle to his dry lips again.

Brandi didn't want to make a sound, but anticipation got the best of her. "Cody?" she asked quietly. "What happened to Seismo?"

He put his hand over his face. He could not bring himself to tell her about the children. The scars on his back began to itch as perspiration made the shirt cling to his skin.

"Cody, you don't have to tell me about your friend. It's okay." His face was ashen. He wasn't just telling his story. He was reliving it.

"Do you mind if I look at your other leg?" Brandi hoped she could bring life back to his face again. Her voice was hoarse, tender, mesmerizing. He motioned her to go ahead.

She spoke at barely above a whisper as she rolled up the other leg of his jeans. "I read that you surrendered to the Taliban. Why? Can you share that part?"

She washed and caressed the scar on his left leg. It was long, jagged, ghastly. It began at his toes and extended up the outside of his leg to above his knee. A separate scar just above the knee ran horizontally through the vertical one, thus forming a cross.

He cleared his throat. "I spent the night jammed up against a cliff with the SEAL team. At zero-seven-hundred the next morning, we spotted about fifty Taliban bearing down on us. It was just a matter of minutes before they would find us. ETA for air support was one hour — not nearly soon enough." He exhaled heavily.

"That's when I came up with a plan to walk toward the Taliban and surrender. It's a big deal for them — capturing a downed pilot. I thought it would create a diversion so the SEALs could quietly relocate to a secure place." His eyes had now refocused.

"I also hoped the enemy would take me where they had moved the Chinook survivors. That way, the SEALs could track at a distance and mount a rescue mission to save us all."

"How well did your plan work?"

He took two more swallows and set the bottle down. His gaze narrowed. "They put a bag over my head and —"

Brandi covered her mouth and caught her breath.

"I can't go on." He clenched his fists. "Harry died. Children . . . where they took me —"

"Children? What children? I don't remember reading anything about that."

"And you'll never read about something that *didn't* happen." He placed his unsteady right hand over his eyes in the attempt to hide wet streaks that made their way down the rugged landscape of his face. "I didn't know it would be this hard."

Was he tearful or just heavily perspiring? Both? She couldn't tell. With Cody's feet resting on the pillow next to her, tears filling Brandi's eyes, she could find no words. He carried heavy baggage. He was honorable. He was trouble. One part of her wanted to bid farewell to him and pretend he did not exist. The other wanted to hold him in her arms and never let him go.

"I'm sorry, Brandi. I gotta stop. You're the first person I've told since returning home." He blotted his eyes on the sleeve of the blue shirt.

She shut her eyelids. *Oh, God, what's happening to me? A night so horrible. A night so wonderful. Please don't let him be the kind of man who will ask to stay the night, but please don't let him leave.*

They were silent and motionless for a moment. Then Cody's jaw stiffened. "I've said too much. I need to get back to the hotel." He stood and put on his cap. "If you'll give me your street address, I'll send you back this shirt."

Brandi's heart fell. She had enticed him into lowering his shield — the one that had hidden his secret pain. Had she intruded too far? *Oh, God, I pray he won't resent me for it.*

She wiped her own tears with her hands. "I'm so honored that you trusted me, Cody. Please don't feel uncomfortable with me. I hope I didn't . . . Um, will I ever see you again?"

He glanced downward once more at the bruises, burns, and scrapes on her shins and ankles. Her feet were friction-burned and her soft hands trembled again. Sasha's last words filled his thoughts — *"She shouldn't be alone right now, you know. Next time, they'll have guns."*

He stepped a few paces to the window and looked down at the street with a lumbering sigh. "I've never seen evil like what I saw in that country. It can turn you into a monster. I thought I had left all that behind."

Brandi shuffled to the kitchen to get a fresh towel. She moistened it with cool water and then hastened back to him and blotted the perspiration from his brow and from behind his neck.

Cody shook his head. "I've tried to get rid of the hate, but tonight, seeing those guys degrading you, terrorizing you, it all came back. I've become just like the enemy I despise — filled with rage, anger."

Brandi gathered herself. "Before you go, I need to tell you who I am and what I saw tonight." She tenderly took his shoulders and turned him around, then looked into his eyes. "It's important."

He downed the rest of his water bottle and leaned against the wall next to the window. "Important? How's that?"

Brandi's tongue was like a dehydrated sponge. Fools rush in, and she was afraid to say another word but couldn't stop herself. She struggled down three swallows of water.

"First, come sit with me over here." She took his hand and led him to an antique chaise lounge chair.

"Okay, I'm listening," he said. "What's the big mystery?"

# FAST LANE TO THE HOTEL

They sat down on the chaise lounge.

"This chair is eighteenth century French baroque. My father's family four generations back were slaves near New Orleans during the Civil War. One night, five Union soldiers came onto the plantation for the purpose of stealing, killing and raping."

"Slaves? Your ancestors?"

"That's right." She wasn't surprised by his puzzled expression. With Brandi's light complexion and blue eyes, her ethnicity was never apparent.

"Daddy's great-great-great-grandfather helped fight off the attackers and saved the plantation owner and his wife. When the war was over, the plantation was in ruin, but the owner gave my father's ancestors this piece of furniture we're sitting on. It has been in the family ever since."

"Impressive." He paused and looked into her blue eyes. "So what's the right question for me to ask?"

"No questions. Just listen. My ancestors on my mother's side of the family had escaped to Canada before the war. They eventually settled in Pennsylvania in 1901. So that brings me to what I want to tell you. I'll probably cry. But you should hear this even if I never see you again."

She gathered a deep breath. "When my mother was just sixteen —"

Suddenly, terror seized Brandi's face. She jumped out of her skin, electrified by a loud boom outside on the street. The lights in her apartment blinked and went dark. She latched onto Cody's injured arm like a hawk clutching prey.

"Was that an explosion?" A moment later, they heard another loud pop like a canon firing in the distance. She jumped again. Cody flinched.

"What's happening? Cody, I'm scared!" Her voice quivered.

"Me too. But it sounded like a couple of transformers exploding." He looked out the window. All the streetlights were off. "Might have happened because of the storm. I see more lightning in the sky."

"Let's go to the hotel." She was frantic. "I'll take you up on your offer — uh, for security sake."

Brandi fumbled her way to a drawer on the other side of the kitchen. "I have a couple of flashlights." She pulled them out and turned them on. "Here, take one."

The two lights she was holding were shaking. Cody steadied her hands. Their eyes met briefly, and then she looked down and released her grip on one of the lights.

Brandi went into the other room to pack. When she came back, she returned his clean, dry Pirates shirt. It was awkward, but she turned her back while he changed shirts even though it was too dark for her to sneak a look.

They left the apartment with one small bag and a gigantic suitcase in addition to the large straw purse she carried.

"Whew! This thing weighs a ton. What's in here?"

"Don't even ask. Just follow me. I'll take the pointer, as you Marines say."

Cody toted both pieces of her luggage. "For the record, that's *point*. You'll take *point*. And I hope you're planning to call a cab."

"No need. We can take the third-floor crosswalk directly to the parking garage and drive my Mustang." Just then, the power came back on.

When they approached the door to the garage, he moved in front of her, slowed his steps and became quiet.

He set the bags down. "Stop. Be perfectly still."

"Something wrong?" she whispered.

"You can't be too careful." He scanned the garage, sparsely occupied with vehicles, and listened for sounds of other humans.

After a few quiet moments, he proceeded slowly. The only sounds were the squeaking of their tennis shoes on the concrete, and the rainwater dripping from a broken gutter.

"Here's my car." She pulled the keys from her handbag.

"Wow, nice ride! Looks new." He glanced at the Mustang and then nervously looked around in every direction.

When she pushed the unlock button on the remote, the beeping sound echoed through the cavernous garage.

"Quick, get inside." He opened the driver-side door and nudged her into the front seat.

"Cody, you're scaring me. What's wrong?"

"Sorry. Lotta dark places here. Maybe nothing." He scooted around to the passenger door.

Her deep metallic blue Mustang was a beauty — a showpiece on the exterior but a work car on the inside. A pink notebook sat atop a stack of folders in the passenger seat. Two half-empty mugs of stale coffee occupied the drink holders on the console.

"Just put the papers in the back. I'm working on my next editorial. I bought the car after I came back from California. It's ten years older than I am. I graduated three years ago from Stanford. Played point guard for the Stanford Cardinal women."

He moved the papers to the backseat and laid her two bags on top of them. "So after Stanford you were drafted?" He slipped into the seat.

"I played in the WNBA one season. Wanted to play longer but circumstances prevented it."

"Circumstances?"

"I'll tell you later," she said, subconsciously putting her hand over her heart.

"By the way, what's the reason you started the campaign against the traffickers? Besides the idea that somebody needed to do it?"

"Beside the fact that one of my teammates at Stanford was abducted and never heard from again? Beside the fact that kids vanish in this county every year? Beside the fact that —"

"Okay, okay, I get it. You're doing a gutsy thing, a good thing. But you need —"

"Better security? I know! You sound like my dad."

"He's right, Brandi. Got any idea what cudda happened tonight if —"

"My daddy's *always* right. I should have listened to him. I get that."

"Hey, I'm just sayin'—"

"Saying what, Mr. Texas?"

"Just sayin' that I — I really gotta meet this man who's always right."

"Oh, you will soon enough. I promise you!" She gunned the engine as she backed out of the parking spot and started down the circling ramp toward street level. "He's gonna wanna know what your intentions are toward his daughter."

"Intentions?"

"Just don't be surprised if my daddy gives you the *interrogation* of your life. That's all."

He stared out the side window and muttered, "Not a chance."

She glanced at him. "Did I say something?"

Cody was quiet for a few seconds, and then his hard brow stood at ease. It was something in the air. He drew a slow, deep breath as though the oxygen inside the Mustang were an elixir to his soul.

The corners of his lips curled upward. *"Sweet!"*

"Sweet?" she inquired, rolling her eyes back at him. "Did you almost smile, Cody Musket?" She giggled.

"I gotta ask you a really important question. How did you get those incredible — I mean how'd you get those incredible peepers. Are they real?"

Her jaw dropped and her eyebrows flashed like angry lightning. "*What! Real?*" She placed her arm over her chest to cover her modestly curvy top.

"*No, no!* Your eyes. *Blue eyes.* I mean how'd you get the blue eyes?"

Brandi totally lost it. Comic relief took her out like a Southern California wave. If the steering column had not been in the way, she would have doubled over. Cody reached out to steady the wheel.

"Sorry. What did you think I said?"

"*Never mind!*" She struggled to catch her breath. "*Peepers?* I haven't heard that word in years. Did you ask me if they're *real?*" She laughed again and wiped tears from her cheeks.

"I meant like contacts. You know. Blue contacts?"

"They *are* real, *not contacts.* Good thing I'm in a forgiving mood tonight." She giggled again and shook her shoulders. "I'll tell you about my *peepers* when we get where we're going."

He could not turn his eyes away from her. The ends of her hair were still damp from the shower. A silver ring on her right ear flashed and shimmered when she moved. Her laughing eyes, the aroma of her perfume, and the sweetness of her breath filled his head — enough to make him forget that he had once upon a time endured *interrogations* so brutal that her angelic soul could never bear the knowing.

Until tonight, Brandi had hated it when men had stared at her that way. Was she blushing? She focused straight ahead and worked hard to conceal her grin. "What are you looking at?" She waited. Would he say something truly complimentary this time?

"Do you always wear just one earring?"

Her mouth fell open. She felt her left earlobe and gasped. "I guess I forgot to put the other one on."

Then she pulled the ring from her right ear and flung it to the floor. It hit something solid and ricocheted twice, finally ending up in his lap. She laughed so hard that the blue Mustang seemed to bounce down the ramp as it galloped toward the bottom level.

"Quite a throwing arm."

She flashed her *dangerous explosives* face again and then giggled some more.

Despite the flying ring, the laughing, frowning lady, and the bouncing car, Cody had kept watch in the passenger side mirror. As they approached the exit, he sounded an alarm.

"Turn right at the street!" His growl had returned.

The road was one-way, requiring a *left turn* out of the garage. He wanted her to turn the *wrong direction.*

"What's up?"

"Look behind us. Do you own a weapon?"

In the rearview mirror, she spotted a black SUV with tinted glass. It had sped up to catch them just before they reached the exit from the garage. When Brandi turned the wrong way on the street, the black car followed.

# MEN IN BLACK

"What? A weapon? Of course I own a weapon. I'm the daughter of a Marine. Look in the glove box. She gunned the engine again.

"It's okay. Slow down."

After digging around past the owner's handbook, trip log, various maintenance receipts, coupons and ads, Cody found a mini-sized Ruger .380 handgun.

"When was the last time you fired this?"

"Umm, about six months ago."

"Ever hit anything with it?"

"I'm not bad for a girl."

Just then, the SUV driver reached out through the window and placed a rotating red light on the roof.

"What do you make of it?" Brandi's voice was nervy again.

"Could be Feds. Could be somethin' else. Turn left here." Brandi made a sharp left turn through a red light and bounced onto the road that ran directly toward the Roberto Clemente Bridge.

Cody glanced ahead and saw CoGo's Fast Lane, a well-lighted convenience store with a large Friday-night crowd.

"Pull up there!"

Brandi swerved into CoGo's parking lot. It was the first time she had ever made her tires squeal. She giggled. "Now what?"

"You think this is fun and games? Head toward the dumpster over there next to the alley — good escape route just in case we need one."

"Oh, Cody!" She laughed uncontrollably again as she sped toward the dumpster and screeched to a halt near the narrow alley.

"Brandi! Something funny? What's the matter with you?"

"Really, Cody? Escape route? *Ha-ha!* Are you serious?"

"This is not a game!" He grabbed her arm and pulled her toward the front door of CoGo's. "Why're you laughing?"

"I don't know. Makes no sense. Can't help myself."

They rushed into the store just as the SUV drove up. Brandi pulled her cell phone from her purse, only to make a nail-biting discovery. "I forgot to charge this when I got home. I had Dupree's number in my contacts, but I can't call him. Did you get his number?"

"Nope."

"Well, that's a typical male flaw."

The red light was dismounted from the roof as the black vehicle stopped near the store entrance. The driver's side door opened, and out stepped a tall individual who resembled Will Smith but with a 1960s hairstyle. He wore a dark suit and black tie, and entered the store shuffling, snapping his fingers, and quietly spinning a battered version of Stevie Wonder.

Cody lowered his voice to a near whisper. "I was gonna go to the counter and ask one of the attendants to call the police, but it's too late now, so follow me." He seized her hand and led her to the far side of the store behind the cappuccino island.

"Oh, so you're taking point now?" Then she glanced around. All eyes were staring. "The crowd thinks we're on the run, and probably assumes you beat me up." She held up her dead cell phone to conceal the scratches and bruises on her neck.

Cody glanced out the front window. "Hmmm. I don't see anybody else, but could be others inside the vehicle. Good thing it's crowded here — too many witnesses for foul play."

"Reminds me of the movie *Men in Black*," Brandi whispered.

"What?" he whispered back. "You mean Will Spence and Harrison Ford?"

"No! It was Will Smith and Tommy Lee Jones.*"*

*"Shhh — quiet!* What's with you?"

Cody and Brandi could hear the driver question the attendant at the counter. "Have you seen this woman?" He showed the clerk a picture. "Also, is there a back exit?"

Suddenly the SUV came alive. Three more individuals exited the car. One entered the front door, and the other two headed in opposite directions outside the store, obviously to circle around and cover the back. They were all dressed in black. Finally, the clerk pointed the tall driver to the cappuccino island.

"They have us," Cody said under his breath. "Don't panic. Trust me. Do exactly as I say."

Brandi nodded as Cody led her to the front corner of the room so that neither of the men in black could get behind them.

Brandi made a quiet observation, "These are the same guys who were in the street earlier."

"We know you are over there, Ms. Barnes," the driver said. "I am Special Agent Stan Bishop, FBI, and with me here is Agent Randy Graves. We're sorry we spooked you and your friend. We were afraid we were going to lose you."

*"Cody!"* Brandi whispered, shielding her mouth, "if Agent Graves had on a disguise, he'd look just like Tommy Lee Jones."

"What? Get in touch with yourself." Then Cody addressed the man who called himself Bishop. "We'd like to see your badge, Special Agent."

"Not a problem, sir, if you will take your hand off that sidearm in your right front pocket. I am holding my badge in plain sight now."

Cody focused on the badge. From twenty feet away it looked authentic enough, but he wasn't completely on board. The store was filling up with customers, and because of the drama, no one was leaving.

"Sir, I know you are a celebrity, and the police made a pledge not to reveal your identity publicly. We do not wish to violate that pledge. We are following you because we just want to make sure you are safe."

The other two men then came through the back door.

"Okay," Cody conceded. "We'll stand down."

"The police didn't figure out who you were, but I think we did," Bishop said. "Listen, I have a small favor to ask. My nine-year-old son plays fantasy football, and you are one of his favorite players. I hate to impose, but could you possibly sign an autograph for him? And by the way, how's the knee injury?"

Cody and Brandi glanced at each other, their faces reflecting their collective curiosity. Something wasn't right. Had these men actually chased them for an autograph? Did they really think Cody played football? Cody smelled a trap.

Suddenly Brandi sprang to life. "Certainly! Mr. Casper will be more than happy to sign an autograph for your son." She turned deliberately. *"Won't you, Rickey?"*

Cody's staring eyes became bigger than life.

Brandi lowered her head and spoke softly out of the corner of her mouth. "Don't panic. Trust me. Do exactly as I say."

What crazy game was she playing? Cody couldn't decide whether to draw the gun or play along.

With grace and flair, she continued, "Rickey just *loves* kids, and his knee is better now, but he still limps once in a while." She covertly pinched Cody behind his right leg — his cue to limp. "Here, just sign the cover, *Rickey.*" She handed him a magazine.

The front cover of *Sporting News,* which Brandi had just lifted from the shelf in front of her, featured a front-cover photo of Rickey Casper, five-foot-ten-inch Pittsburgh Steelers wide receiver. He had made the winning catch in the Steelers' Super Bowl victory in February. Casper had sustained a torn ACL during the play.

While wearing his football helmet, Casper looked identical to Cody, rugged beard and blue eyes included. Cody scribbled Rickey Casper's name below the picture.

Bishop introduced the others on his team to "Rickey" and Brandi, and then they all departed the store. Cody limped every other step while walking back to Brandi's Mustang.

"I'll drive, dear," she said, loudly enough for everyone to hear, "since your right knee has been flaring up a little today."

Before Brandi could drive away, autograph seekers surrounded her Mustang. The word had circulated through CoGo's — "*Rickey Casper is in the parking lot!*"

After Cody had signed everything put in front of him, Brandi backed the car up, turned, and sped away. As she turned onto the main road, she could hold back no longer, laughing so hard that Cody was forced to steady the wheel again.

"Want me to drive?"

"No! I'm fine!" she fired back. "Can't you see that? Hand me a tissue out of the box by your feet." Then she lost her composure again, playing a drumroll with her bare hands on top of the steering wheel.

He found the box and placed it on the console. "I wonder how many more crimes I'm gonna commit tonight before we get where we're going? Wonder what the penalty is for impersonating a football player?"

"Capital punishment for impersonating a Pittsburgh Steeler in this town," she chirped. Her sore ribs hurt. She tried to force herself to stop laughing. "Can you believe this? I am living a real adventure with a knight in shining armor. I didn't believe things like this happened to girls in real life. I'm sorry, Cody. I have needed to laugh like this for *so* long."

"You've seen too many old movies."

"I have a huge collection in my library at my parents' house in Altoona. I love Ingrid Bergman, Robert Redford, Clark Gable —"

Cody interrupted. "Did you really say that if Graves had on a disguise he'd look like Tommy Lee James? Well, if I had a good enough disguise, I could look like Julia Roberts."

"Come on, Cody. Don't be ridiculous. And it's *Jones.* Tommy Lee *Jones.*"

Cody was not so giddy. He checked his side mirror but saw no sign of the SUV behind them. "It's only a matter of hours before they figure out the autograph is bogus."

"Yes, but who cares? If they're Feds, they can't blame us for being too careful. And if they're impostors, at least we've thrown them off for now."

Cody frowned again. "That guy was no special agent."

"How do you know?" She sobered.

"Trust me. FBI agents don't use sloppy procedures like that."

"Never felt right to me either," she agreed. "But, how did they know the police had agreed to keep your last name out of the press?"

"Haven't figured that out yet. A mole in the police department, maybe?"

"But they don't know who you are," she reminded. "The police would have told them. They were hoping we'd tell them. So why are they interested in you? It's *me* they want. And that crazy story about wanting an autograph for his son? Come on."

"Yeah, that was a fish-n-game expedition." Cody took another look at the mirror to check the road behind them.

"Fish-n-game? Fishing for information and gaming us, right?"

"Bravo! But I gotta say, you had the better game. Yeah, you got some juice. They don't know if I'm a Fed or just a personal bodyguard, and they need to know before making their move."

She chuckled. "I said you were Rickey Casper. I think they actually believed me. *Ha-ha,* Rickey'll have something to say about that when I see him."

"Don't kid yourself," Cody cautioned her. "They didn't buy a word of it. But, you bought us time. You told 'em exactly zilch." He smothered a tense smile. "You know, you're pretty smart." He folded his arms. "For a girl."

They were quiet. Cody looked into the mirror again and then rubbed his chin in deep thought. "How come they aren't following us? They're up to something. I can smell it. Turn into this parking lot on the right."

She turned onto the lot and screeched to a halt. "Cody, I'm scared." She gazed into the rearview mirror. "I dunno what's wrong with me. One minute I can't stop laughing, then the next minute . . ." Brandi fought back tears and stiffened her death grip on the automatic shift.

He placed his hand on hers and spoke confidently. "Put it in park. Wait here. I'll be right back."

# A Bug and A Baby

C ody opened the passenger door and stepped onto the parking lot.

"Where are you going?" Brandi's voice was hoarse. She took a long look into the rearview mirror again.

"I'll be right back. Trust me."

He crawled underneath the back of the Mustang, and emerged a moment later carrying something in his hand. He trotted over to a late model sedan, reached under a rear fender, then returned to the Mustang and stood by her driver-side door.

"Just as I figured, we wuz bugged."

"We wuz? I mean we were? How did you know?"

"It was the only thing that made sense. They attached a bug at CoGo's. They wanna track our movements, find out who our contacts are. Men in black? *Ha!* Low-budget amateurs if you ask me — deadly nonetheless." He took a long look at the road — still no black SUV in sight.

"Well, if they're amateurs, we can outsmart them, right?"

"Never underestimate an opponent. Want me to drive?"

With Cody behind the wheel, the tires swished and splashed their way toward the Marriott. The were both silent. She attempted to organize the papers in her glove compartment before replacing her gun.

"I'm sorry I got you into this, Cody. I guess you've had all the excitement you want for one lifetime, huh?"

"I'm not sorry, Brandi. It's just that sometimes these adventures become . . ." He shook his head.

She dropped her hands into her lap and contemplated for a moment before breaking the silence. "Cody, I . . . I have a little girl. I was in an abusive relationship when I was at Stanford. He was a big-time football player named Billy. When I first moved to California away from my parents, I wanted freedom, adventure. I haven't always been . . ." She looked out the window. "I have no idea why I'm telling you this."

She watched his face for a reaction. Each passing streetlight ignited his fiery blue eyes, but his expression never changed.

"When Billy found out I wouldn't abort my baby, he was furious. Came in later that night in a drug-induced rage and stabbed me in the chest and stomach. I nearly died. It was the year after I had graduated. That's why I only played pro ball for one season. I have scars too, but I didn't get mine as honorably as you."

"What happened to Billy?"

"He's dead — murdered in prison."

Cody slowed down, switched on the right blinker, and turned into the Marriot parking garage. They drove past row after row of cars and up to Level 4 until they found a place next to an outside wall about forty yards from the elevator. Cody parked and turned off the engine. Everything was quiet.

"You started to say?" she asked. "Something about what adventures can turn into?"

"The morning of that last mission, Seismo and I were joking around with the other guys up there. A pilot from Nebraska named Keyshawn Harris — call sign 'Hawker' — always kidding me about going to Baylor. We had the world by the tail.

"I was sittin' up there at angels two zero in complete control of a fifty-thousand-pound supersonic video game with forty-eight thousand pounds of thrust. It was the adventure I had always wanted until —" He exhaled a long breath.

"I'm not sorry I met you, Brandi. I never thought I would have to use my aggressive skills in civilian life, but I'm glad I was there tonight. I just hope that . . ." He looked across the garage and shook it off.

She placed her hand on his knee and then pulled it back. "Cody, you know I shoot straight, so here I go again." She paused to gather herself. *No more crying!*

"I've known you for just a few hours, but if what happened tonight is what it took. I mean, like I said, I want us to be . . ."

She pulled out another tissue. "I'm sorry. I'm not usually like this. My emotions are totally stressed right now. I can't go in there looking this way. Can you hand me my small bag out of the back?"

Cody handed her the small case. She dug through it and pulled out her cosmetic kit. "I need to fix my face. Just go into the hotel. I'll meet you in the lobby."

"No way! I'm not leaving you alone." His eyes were cold blue steel, scanning the garage for signs of trouble. "I'm stayin' here. Go ahead and do what you're gonna do."

"Is that an order, Lieutenant?"

"Let's just say it's not up for discussion." He continued his visual surveillance. "What's your little girl's name?"

She brightened. "Knoxi. Her name is Knoxi." A soft, pink smile emerged. "My baby is perfect in every way, except that she has never spoken a word. She's nearly two."

"She doesn't talk at all?"

"No. Specialists can't figure out why. Three weeks after she was born, she went into respiratory failure. Rare virus, they said. She was dying. I walked the streets and wandered into a Teen Challenge mission. I was desperate, with visions of killing myself."

"I've heard of Teen Challenge. So what happened?" He resumed scanning the building.

"Well, this man, a total stranger, comes up to me and says, 'God has plans to prosper you and not harm you. Don't do what you're thinking of doing, because it's a permanent solution to a temporary crisis.' I mean how did he know?"

Cody turned. "Maybe he said that to everybody who walked in off the streets."

"Maybe so. But when I got back to the hospital, my baby girl was awake for the first time in a week. We took her home two days later."

Brandi needed another tissue. He had already pulled one for her.

"Thank you. Now I might as well start all over on my face."

Something caught Cody's attention on the other side of the garage. He turned away and then looked back at her with that cold, steely expression again.

"What's wrong?" She strained her eyes in the direction he had been looking.

"How many changes of clothes did you bring?"

"What? A couple. Why? How many am I going to need?"

He opened the glove compartment once more and pulled out her handgun.

"Now what? Whew! Just when I'm getting hold of myself. What's going on?" Her emotions were thinner than the tissue she was holding.

"See that guy over in the corner partially hidden by that pillar? He's wearing black like those other guys. This could be a trap."

"Should we start the car and try to run?"

"No. That's what they want us to do — give away our position. I don't think that guy has spotted us. It would be stupid for us to drive out of here."

"Can we call the police?" She gazed across the garage nervously.

"With what? Your phone is run down, and I left mine on the twelfth floor in my room."

"Please tell me you have a plan."

"We need to sneak into the hotel. We need disguises." Cody pulled her large suitcase into the front seat. Space was limited, so he could pry the lid only partially open.

"Cody! What are you doing?"

"This ought to be just fine." He pulled out a powder-pink Rebecca Jackson double-breasted women's raincoat with a dainty belt and skirted lower half.

"Oh, that'll look really sexy on you. Here, try the over-boots." She reached into the back floor and pulled out matching pink boots. "These fit over my shoes. You can take your tennies off and wear them. Oh, and here's a pink scarf!"

"Okay, I'll squeeze into these. Now be serious. Find something in there to put over your head, pretend to be an old woman, and follow me."

His feet made her boots bulge, and he could barely fit into the raincoat. He draped and tied the scarf over his head, which hid his beard and most of his face.

"You're ruining my raincoat! Can you even get your big feet into my boots? Oh, what I wouldn't do for another macchiato right now."

"*Ha!* That's the last thing you need. Come on. Try not to act so crazy."

She giggled. "Not act crazy? Well, what do you call what we're doing?"

He carried the large suitcase with his left hand, and the small bag under his left arm. He wanted his gun hand free.

With the Ruger hidden in his palm, Cody escorted Brandi leisurely toward the elevator door. They caught a brief glimpse of the man in the dark suit again. He had moved to a different location but was not making any effort to hide. The disguise was working.

Finally, they pressed the elevator call button. Cody had intended to remove the disguise once they were inside the elevator, but when the door opened, they were both shocked to see five members of the Astros team staring them in the face.

"Musket?" Standing in the elevator were manager Joe Moran, first baseman Pete Reynolds, reserve catcher Leo Hernandez and two coaches.

Cody's face turned as pink as the raincoat, but he took Brandi's hand and led her into the elevator as if nothing were amiss. As they descended, no one spoke a word. Brandi's snickering, however, was contagious for everyone but Cody.

When the door opened, Cody and Brandi stayed put while the other five exited into the lobby. As the door was closing, Leo Hernandez and manager Joe Moran conversed.

"Hey, Skipper, what's up with Musket?"

"He's a rookie, Nandy. Some of the veterans prolly put him up to it."

After the door closed, Cody frantically removed the scarf and raincoat. Brandi's laughing bubbles flew again, her sides aching, her face flooding with tears. "You changed out of my raincoat faster than Superman! Now I'll have to do my face again."

"Is that all you're concerned about?"

She wiped her eyes. "I should be serious, but I haven't laughed like this since — Oh, give me back my raincoat." She jerked it from him.

By the time they reached the front desk, the laughing had worn her out and she fanned her face with her hands to dry fresh tears.

They stood in line behind a man wearing a gray blazer, designer jeans, and custom Red River Valley boots. He looked familiar to Brandi. When he turned around, she recognized him — Tommy Lee Jones in the flesh.

"Hey, aren't you Cody Musket?" the venerable actor asked.

"Yes, sir. Have we met?" Cody extended his hand.

"Nice boots." He shook Cody's hand and walked away.

Brandi looked down. Cody was still wearing her pink rubber boots. "Do you even know who that was?"

"Lemme guess. Harrison Ford?"

# A KISS CAN BE A LOVELY TRICK

B randi slid her key card into the slot. Cody swung the door open. The king suite was spacious. Both rooms featured bay windows trimmed in camel draperies, with plush gray carpet, king bed, sofa, and garden tub. The entry room featured a kitchenette with fridge, mini bar and breakfast table.

Brandi had called her parents from the house phone in the lobby. Flooded roads had slowed their trip to Pittsburgh. She asked Cody if he would stay with her until her parents arrived.

"I'd rather not be alone right now," she said. "I can make decaf and finish telling you what I started when the lights went out."

"Yeah. It's been crazy tonight, and I'm curious about your story. I wouldn't be able to sleep anyway after everything that's happened."

"First things first," she said. "I *must* get out of these tennis shoes. I didn't realize how much they would hurt my feet. They're burning again."

"Roger that. Go take care of yourself. I can make the decaf, and I'll put your gun here on the bar and leave it with you tonight."

"Take it with you, Cody. My dad will have his .45."

Brandi walked into the bathroom to deposit her shoes and athletic socks. She returned with a wet towel, sat on the sofa, reached down, and attempted to bring relief to ugly carpet burns and abrasions on her lower extremities. Cody was busy with the coffeemaker.

"*Ooh!* My feet are on fire." She lost her breath. "My ribs are bruised and I'm getting stiff. It's not easy bending over like this."

She groaned and stretched but couldn't reach down past her ankles. She glanced up at Cody who simply stared back like a bronze statue.

"Yeah, your feet are really banged up. Not pretty. I mean they're pretty, but…you know what I mean."

She finally straightened up, took two deep breaths, and spouted off. "I hear that all women in Texas go barefoot."

"What? Wrong again!" He took a couple of steps toward her, still focused on her feet. She dropped the towel over them to break his gaze.

Cody smirked, "The women in Texas wear big bubba cowboy boots with huge jingling spurs and bells. It's the only way we can keep track of our females." Then he stepped closer. "Uh, could I help you do that?"

*"Too late!"* she snapped. *"I'm finished!"* She tossed him the towel. "Be sweet and ditch this rag someplace while I get the Blue Tech from my bag." She walked toward her luggage, then turned and looked back. "And for your information, that bogus crack about the boots was disgusting."

He shuffled to the bathroom and dropped the towel into the dirty laundry hamper. When he returned, he sat at the table and watched as she dug through her gear. Finally, he asked if her wounds felt better.

"I must have left the Blue Tech at the apartment. Can't find it. My ankles and feet are screaming. I couldn't reach my toes, or did you even notice?"

Cody brought a chair and placed it beside her. "Here. Have a seat."

*"What?"* Brandi bristled. "I'm not one of your Texas women or one of your subordinate military officers. What do you have in mind?"

"Please. I just wanna measure you for some boots."

"Oo-hoo, well, why didn't you just say so?" She plopped down and crossed her arms.

He knelt on the floor in front of her and reached into the left pocket of his jeans. Brandi's eyes were fixated. What was he reaching for? A tape measure maybe? Was he serious?

"Cody? What do you think you're doing?"

When he pulled his hand free, it held the blue vial she had been searching for. He reached down, gently lifted her feet off the floor, and began to massage them with the contents of the tiny bottle. "What does it *look* like I'm doing?"

She caught her breath and put her hand over her heart. "I said be sweet, but I had no idea. Where did you find my Blue Tech?"

"Picked it up at your place. It got knocked to the floor during the blackout. I saw it with the flashlight. Thought you might need it."

Her eyes twinkled. "That already feels better." She wiggled her toes. "Now if only I could get you to smile."

"Nothin' to smile about," he grumbled. "Injuries like these aren't funny."

"But I'm smiling. Look at my face, Cody Musket. I just wish —"

"I apologize for my rough hands" — he broke in — "calluses from batting practice and traces of pine tar."

She shook her head. "Don't apologize. I have nothing to compare your hands to. No other man has ever —"

"So you mean I'm the first guy you ever let rub your feet?"

"No, sweetie. I mean you're the first guy who has ever *offered*."

After he had finished, Cody walked to the coffeemaker and poured two cups. They sat down at the table. An awkward silence seized Brandi's tongue for a moment after he had served her the decaf. Could anything soften his drawn, leathery face?

"Next time I snicker-doodle through the mall," she acquiesced, "I'll remember to wear big bubba cowboy boots with jingling spurs. That should keep me out of trouble."

"Yeah. And that way I can keep track of you." He played along but his hard countenance never showed one sign of cracking.

Brandi sighed. "This has been quite the evening. What now? Will they hunt us down?" She lifted her cup.

"Well," he answered, "you're the one with the research and editorials. What do *you* think?"

"I don't really . . ." She paused. "I Don't really want to talk about that. I want to finish telling you about my roots and how it relates to what happened tonight. It might change the way you feel about yourself."

Cody nodded and lifted the cup to his mouth.

Now her pulse raced. She had rarely spoken of this to another man and her distrust of the opposite sex was a habit that did not die easily. *Why should he care about my story? He must have hundreds of women wanting him. I'm going to make a fool of myself.*

Brandi spoke slowly with feeling. "My mother's name was Whitney Bonner. When she was sixteen, she was assaulted and raped by a man wearing a ski mask. She knew only that he was white and had blue eyes. After that, she was pregnant. Her parents were dead and she had been living in a shelter."

Cody never moved a muscle.

Brandi gripped her cup with both hands. "An uncle in West Virginia had offered to pay for an abortion if my mother would come live with him, but he was a convicted molester. She scraped together the bus fare to West Virginia, but while waiting to board the bus at Pittsburgh, she became so despondent she decided to end it all with a bottle of pills."

Brandi closed her eyes and her lip began to quiver. Cody reached across the table. She opened her eyelids when she felt his fingers touch hers. Could this be the man for whom she had saved her tears?

"Go on," his voice quiet and scratchy. "I'm listening. Cry all you want to." He never let go of her hand. His expression never changed.

Brandi attempted a smile. "Right then, while holding the pills in her hand, my mother remembered something from her childhood. When she was just four, she had heard a Holocaust survivor speak at a church. Something the woman had said that day flashed through her mind again — *'There is no pit so deep that He is not deeper still.'*"

Cody reached up to brush her tears with his fingertips.

"Excuse me for a second." She got up, went back to her suitcase, and pulled out a box of tissue. "I never leave home without these." When she sat back down, her hands shook again. "I'm sorry, Cody. Tonight has been more than I can —"

"So what did your mother do after she remembered the quote from Corrie ten Boom?"

"Corrie who?"

"Corrie ten Boom, the woman your mom heard. She's the one who said it — 'There is no pit so deep that He is not deeper still.'"

"You know that quote? Um, what was her name again?"

"Corrie ten Boom, from Holland. She was from a Christian family who hid Jews in their watchmaking shop. Her whole family was arrested. She was in her fifties when she was sent to Ravensbrück and was scheduled to be gassed, but eventually the Nazis released Corrie cuz somebody screwed up — made a clerical error. Later, she was honored by Israel as one *'Righteous Among the Nations.'*"

"Cody, you sound like you're reading from a history book." She blotted her puffy eyes. "You surprise me more every minute. I can't believe you know about all that."

"I read her biography — *The Hiding Place.*"

The room was quiet. Brandi was hoarse. "You know, Cody, if it hadn't been for that woman, Corrie ten Boom, I might not even be here."

"How's that?"

"After my mother remembered Corrie and the pit so deep, she had second thoughts about killing herself. She hadn't prayed in years, but right there on that bench, crying in the bus depot, my mother prayed that if God were really there, would He please send someone to lift her from that deep pit she was in."

Cody never even blinked waiting for the conclusion. Brandi reached for his hand but pulled her hand back.

"Immediately, my mother heard a man's voice, 'Are you okay, miss?' She turned around. Standing there was the most handsome nineteen-year-old man she had ever laid eyes on wearing the uniform of a US Marine. Private Raymond Jackson Barnes loved her the minute he first saw her and took her home to his parents. He married the sixteen-year-old pregnant girl and became the only father I have ever known and the best father a girl could ever have."

The air in the room was heavy. Brandi blotted her eyes again and looked for his reaction, but Cody was pensive, inscrutable. "So . . . so my biological father was . . ."

She stopped and waited. Would he say something? Anything at all?

He finished his cup. "What an honorable family you have. What an honorable way to be born."

Brandi caught her breath, put her hand over her lips, then spoke barely above a whisper, "I suppose you can see I'm an emotional wreck tonight."

His face softened. *"Nah!* I hadn't noticed."

She chuckled. "Cody, I have never had a night like this — *not ever.* You need to hear one more thing. It's important. You said you felt like a monster tonight at the theater?"

He was fixed upon her face, curiosity wrinkling the brow above his seasoned eyes.

She spoke slowly. "My life was over tonight when those men were on top of me in that hallway." Her voice wavered again. "I knew that my parents and Knoxi would miss me. My baby girl . . ." She covered her eyes for a moment. "But just then, I remembered my mother calling out to God in that bus station twenty-four years ago when I was still in her womb, so I closed my eyes and screamed a silent prayer. 'God, please send an angel, anyone, someone to save me.'

"The next moment, I heard that cement-grinder voice of yours. I looked up, and there you stood." She paused and looked deeply into his eyes. "Cody, the light in your face —"

He stated down at the table. "Maybe you saw what you wanted to see."

"What I saw and what *they* saw was *not* a monster." She lifted his chin. "Listen to me, Mr. Texas. I tell you *they* were the monsters, and they were terrified. I could feel the wind go right out of 'em. They feared you, *not* because you were like them, but because you *weren't.*"

One tear ran down to the tip of his nose. She gently brushed it with her finger. A smile broadened across his lips for the first time, and suddenly the turbulent, spinning world around them faded from view. For one perfect moment, their universe, all that mattered, made perfect sense within the confines of a forty-eight-inch circular breakfast table.

Finally, he stood to his feet. She looked up and searched his face for a clue to his intentions. His eyes were bright, smiling, playful. After a few seconds, he came around to her side of the table, gently picked her up, cradled her in his arms, and kissed her.

"*Whew!* Where did that come from? Would that be standard procedure in Texas? How'd you know I wouldn't slap you?"

"I took the chance. Figured you were too stiff to fight back."

"Hmmm. A kiss can be a lovely trick, designed by nature to stop speech when words become superfluous. Guess who said that."

"Rodolfo Lorenzo?"

"Nope!" she declared. "It was Ingrid Bergman."

"Careful. I might do it again."

"Well, since I am your captive and too stiff to resist, I suppose I have no choice." She closed her eyes, waiting for a second kiss.

"Do you like baseball?"

She wrinkled her nose, eyes wide. "What? Do I like baseball?"

"It's not a trick question, Brandi."

She giggled and kicked her feet playfully. "Of course I like baseball."

"Good answer. So come to the game tomorrow. I can get you and your parents seats behind the Astros dugout."

"Do you know what I'm thinking?" Brandi asked, displaying the same grace with which she had charmed the men in black at CoGo's.

"This ought to be good. Nobody knows what a woman's thinking."

She reached up with both hands and grabbed the scrubby beard on the sides of his face. "I was thinking that I went to the Superman movie and walked out with a new friend — a real man of steel."

"Hmm." He reasoned. "Good friends do kiss sometimes, right?"

She licked her lips, threw her arms around his neck, pulled herself toward him, and closed her eyes. At that moment, a loud bell startled them. They looked toward the kitchen counter where she had finally plugged in her phone.

She paddled the air with her feet again. "Cody, put me down. I need to get that. My parents must be downstairs."

He set her down. She scrambled to the phone. "Hi, Daddy! Come on up." She ended the call and tossed her phone onto the bed.

"You probably want some time alone with your parents after what's happened," Cody suggested. "Mind if I wait 'til morning to meet 'em? It's been a long day."

After he had left her, Brandi did a free fall backward onto the bed and gazed straight up at the ceiling fan — turning, turning, and turning. Was she dreaming? Three hours ago, there were no good men left in the world.

But could anyone know his thoughts? He was emotional and unpredictable — cold and stoic at one moment, tender and compassionate the next. She had read that some plants take a thousand years to bloom. Others take less than a day. Can love bloom in three hours?

His smell lingered. His lips still pressed against hers. Is it true that falling in love simply means having your heart break in a good way? The Astros would leave town in two days. She would miss him. Would she have been better off had they never met?

She opened her laptop, determined to learn everything she could about Cody Musket.

# WHO IS CODY MUSKET?

Ray and Whitney Barnes arrived a few moments after Cody had left the room. "Hey, who's the security guy outside the door?" Ray spouted. "He asked for our IDs before he'd let us in."

"The Astros team arranged it. Cody insists on keeping me safe." Brandi's calm smile took Ray and Whitney by surprise — not what they had expected after their only daughter had been treated so brutally.

Whitney jumped right in. "So where is he, this Musket guy? *Musket* sounds like a violent name to me. Some sort of gun, isn't it?" She loved to pretend ignorance and lace it with sarcasm, especially around Ray. It never fooled anyone, but everyone went along.

"Oh, Mama, that's ridiculous. He stayed here with me 'til Daddy called. I asked him to stay. Didn't want to be alone. He's returning in the morning."

Ray put his stout arms around his daughter. His eyes were red and glassy. "If I had only been there at the mall. The first thing I'm gonna do is shake this guy's hand."

"I think he wants to shake your hand too. You know, Daddy, he —"

"Second thing I'm gonna do is find out what his intentions are."

Whitney with raised eyebrows, "You gonna interrogate him, Papa?" She was holding Knoxi, Brandi's twenty-month-old daughter.

"*Interrogate?* Well, I just want to find out —"

"Find out what, Daddy?"

"Oh, baby, don't let your father upset you. He's just protective. You know how these military guys are." Whitney gave her husband a token peck on the cheek. "The two of 'em will work it out between them."

Brandi took her toddler into the other room to put her in the bed and then returned. "I am so thankful Knoxi wasn't here for the last couple of days, especially tonight."

"I warned you about the serious nature of death threats," Ray asserted. "That's why I wanted you to come stay with us."

"So what's this guy like when he isn't beatin' up people?" Whitney crossed her arms. "Musket? Is that his real name? Seems like he could have come up with a gun name more modern, like Colt or Clock."

"*Clock? Ha-ha!* Mama, it's *Glock* with a *G*. Beside that, baseball players don't have stage names."

Ray snickered. "I've never figured how your mother's brain is wired."

Whitney knew how to push Ray's buttons. She loved to play the fool when it came to subjects she considered part of a man's world — guns and military protocol high on her list. She had learned to be the heroic comic after he had returned from the Gulf with his Purple Heart, depressed and aimless. He had needed the laughter.

Her act had grown old over the years, but they still played the game, and it sometimes amazed Ray how creative she could be with her ignorance.

Brandi shrugged it off. She was too hyped. "Do you wanna see who Cody Musket is? Take a look."

She sat at the breakfast table, opened her laptop, and showed them videos of Cody entertaining children before ballgames. He gave away Cody Musket T-shirts to kids in parking lots and handed out Cody Musket model baseball gloves at children's shelters. He performed corny magic acts — the kind that only small kids would appreciate.

"Daddy, Cody told me about being held by Taliban warriors — something about children involved. He was not able to finish the story because he lost his composure."

After a moment to consider, Ray spoke pointedly. "The Taliban abducts hundreds of children. Turns 'em into killers and even sex slaves." He sat down on the end of the sofa.

Brandi moved over and sat on the edge of the bed facing him. "He said something about children at the prison where they took him, but there are no reports of such a thing."

"Baby girl, there are a lot of things in war that never get reported."

"I wonder if that's why he does so much for kids. He wouldn't elaborate 'cause it was too painful for him."

"You know something, baby girl? He may *never* want to discuss it."

"I just met him, but I think — I mean is it possible to love someone after just a few hours? What am I going to do when he leaves town in two days? I know I'm rushing things, but you know how I am."

"How does he feel about you after just a few hours?"

"He didn't say much, but he kissed me."

Whitney leaned back against the kitchenette bar. "Yeah, baby, guys are good at that sort of thing — lots o' kissin' and not much talking."

"Well, he complimented me at the mall."

Mom and Dad waited.

"No man ever told me my face was softer than a steer's butt before." She giggled. Ray gasped.

"That's right. And he also said I was smarter than a bullwhip."

Whitney stood up straight and placed hands on hips. "We came down here expecting you to be a basket case, and all you can talk about is a man who said your face looked like a steer's butt and compared you to a bullwhip?" She glanced at Ray.

"Oh, Mama!" She jumped up, shuffled her feet over to the sofa, and plopped down next to her father. "That's not exactly the way it was."

"Get serious!" Whitney said. "Look, sweetie, if there are things he can't talk about, that means he has issues."

"I know, Mama. But he seems like a normal guy overall. I mean he never refuses to sign autographs for kids. Like tonight, I even got him to sign Rickey Casper's autograph for a bunch of people at CoGo's."

"You did what?" Ray flattened his large palm against his forehead.

"No. I mean it's okay." She put her hand on her father's knee. "He signed Rickey's picture on the cover of *Sporting News* and — Wait, let me back up. See, we got chased by these men in black who had this big black car, and —"

Her parents' eyes were as large as the saucers on the coffee bar, so Brandi retreated back to the bed again, sat on the edge, and offered a different approach.

"And he's so resourceful," she stepped it up. "He thought someone was spying on us in the Marriott parking garage, so he dressed up in some of my clothes and got my gun out of the glove compartment and —"

"Baby, *pleeese* tell us he's not the guy we heard about who was wearin' the red boots in the lobby."

"No, no. Of course not, Mama."

Ray leaned back on the couch and buried his face in the *Pittsburgh Post-Gazette.*

"Um, actually . . . they were *pink*." Brandi winced.

Ray slapped his knee and raised a smile, which did not escape Whitney's eye. "Pink boots!" She frowned. "I thought you'd be all over this. You act like this is funny. This is your daughter!"

"Oh, Mama. I mean it wasn't like that."

Brandi finally settled down and explained everything.

"Did you get a plate number for the SUV?"

"No, Daddy, there was no plate on the front, and we never saw the back of the vehicle. I couldn't reach Detective Dupree. I'll try again in the morning." She got up, walked back to the table, and stared at Cody's picture on her screen. "I believe Cody cares for me. I just don't know how much."

To which, Ray responded, "Well, I knew a lot of Marines who'd say anything to get a woman to —"

Brandi interrupted. "But you weren't one of them, Daddy. Isn't that true?" She retreated to the bed and sat on the edge again.

"Of course. I wasn't like that. I loved your mother too much."

"Well, there you go." She flung her arms up, fell backward, and laid her head in the center of the mattress, her legs dangling off the side.

Whitney sat next to her. "I've heard of ballplayers who have a girlfriend in every city."

"Oh, Mama." Brandi sat back up, sending sharp pain through her ribs.

Whitney wasn't finished. "Hopefully, he isn't just lookin' for a quick conquest, and then you never see him again." She folded her arms. "I can see you are in pain, baby. And look at those red places on your legs. Your feet look like they got caught in a..." She couldn't locate the words.

"Cody let me doctor his feet with Blue Tech." A tender smile softened Brandi's tone. "He has bad scars and didn't want to let me see them at first. He was so humble about it."

"Ahhh, I see," Ray said. "And you just sweet-talked him into it, right?"

Whitney cut in. "Yep! Your daughter could always talk a wall-mouse right into a trap."

"He pretends he isn't smart. It's an act. I believe he left my pink boots on just to hear me laugh. We saw Tommy Lee Jones in the lobby." She shrugged. "He recognized Cody, but Cody pretended not to know who he was. You'd think the two of them planned the whole thing."

"According to the *Gazette*, Tommy Lee Jones is here to address a film executive group," Ray said. "He's from Texas too, you know."

Brandi was silent, pensive for a moment, staring down at her feet. "He warned them."

"What? Who?"

"Cody," she said. "He ordered them to leave me alone."

"You mean he gave them a chance to withdraw?"

"Daddy, he was terrifying. I mean magnificent. I mean, his hands and feet moved so fast those guys stood right in front of him and never knew which way to look. I thought that happened only in the movies."

A tide of guarded euphoria rolled over her — calm, surreal — as if there were no men in black to worry about or hit men lurking in her future.

## PINK CHOCOLATE AND BRUISES

Saturday morning at 9:00 a.m. Brandi answered her phone. Cody was on his way.

"I awoke with a whiplash to go with the cuts and bruises," she told him. "I have to warn you, I'm sore all over."

"Roger that. I figured. You still want me to come up there?"

"Sure, but you sound tired."

"Just need some battery acid and I'm good to go."

"Daddy brewed some already."

"I heard you mention Tanner McNair last night."

"That's right. He was supposed to interview on my show tomorrow night but he's leaving for Detroit after the game."

"Yeah. I called him and gave him a hard time about that. He's my best friend in baseball. We cooked up a way to get him back on your show."

"You know him?"

"He and Julia want to take us to lunch today. They'll meet us downstairs. Your mom and dad are invited."

"What about security?"

"Got it covered."

Brandi lowered her voice. "I tried to call Dupree this morning but still couldn't reach him. I left voicemail again."

"I've thought about those guys in the SUV," Cody said. "They were about two biscuits shy of a picnic. I mean things don't add up."

"I know," she said, with a heavy breath into the phone. "Do you think they've figured us out by now? Cody, how much danger are we in?"

"We've arranged a constant security detail, and, for your safety you should…I mean, we should — never mind. I'll tell you later. This is gonna be a great day. I'll be there in a couple minutes."

Moments later, Brandi heard a knock and opened the door. Cody walked in wearing an Astros pullover game shirt with elbow-length sleeves, khaki cargos, and orange-and-blue tennis shoes.

Brandi had on a white pullover top with the words "I Love Pink Chocolate" written across the front. Gray cutoff jeans, white tennis shoes, and white knee socks covered most of her bruises. Her left elbow and right forearm carried lacerations.

"Here, take this, compliments of the Astros." He handed her a bag with Astros jerseys and hats for Brandi, her parents and Knoxi. "I had to guess at your daughter's size, but it should fit."

"Mama and Daddy will be pleased, even though my dad's a big-time Pirates fan."

"That's a nasty neck bruise. Are you gonna wear those tennis shoes? Don't you think —"

"I treated my feet again this morning with the Blue Tech. These tall socks should hide all the ugly places. Don't want to draw attention. By the way, last night, you must have thought I was — I mean, I hope you don't think that…"

Just then, her parents walked into the room.

"Oh, Cody. These are my parents, Ray and Whitney Barnes." Whitney was holding the toddler. "And this is Knoxi," Brandi said, "my miracle daughter."

Ray extended his hand. He was in his middle forties, taller than Cody at six foot two, with large hands, the physique of a basketball player, and a firm grip. His skills as a communicator were evident immediately, but his soft and friendly tone caught Cody off guard. He sported a bushy, well-trimmed mustache in contrast to the rough-cut look that Cody exhibited. His sleepless eyes were bloodshot.

Whitney was Brandi's height with shoulder-length hair that had a distinguishing streak of gray on the right side. She wore ebony designer-frame glasses and matching circular earrings, which complemented soft hazel eyes. Her amazing resemblance to the late Whitney Houston immediately captured Cody's attention, though she was a slightly more robust version.

Whitney gave Cody a proper introduction to Knoxi.

"You're gorgeous," Cody said to the child. "Uh-oh, baby girl, what do you have behind your ear?" He reached out and pretended to pull a quarter from behind her right ear. He did the same thing with her left ear. He gave both quarters to her and suggested that her grandmother could advise her on what to do with them.

The toddler's delight did not go unnoticed by anyone, especially Brandi.

The smiling girl felt behind her ears, hoping to find additional shiny coins. She had a round face, blue eyes, and dark brown hair with a pink ribbon on one side. Two dimples made her a spitting image of Brandi. Her pink "Grampa's Little Princess" pantsuit made it plain whose girl she was.

After Ray had mentioned that Knoxi was shy when meeting new people, she surprised everyone by reaching out for Cody.

That prompted Whitney. "You better hold this child, Mr. Ballplayer. She hasn't taken her eyes off you since you pulled those quarters out of her head."

Cody was hesitant, but he sat down on the sofa with her on his lap. She trained her wide blue eyes on his face and kept reaching for his nose.

Whitney folded her arms. "Well, that looks like a friendship in the making."

"Sir, ma'am, it's an honor to meet y'all."

"The honor is ours, Cody. You can call us Ray and Whitney. Say, what time is the game tonight?" Ray sat down in the recliner next to the sofa.

"Game time 6:10. After lunch, I'd like to steal Brandi away for an hour or so if that is acceptable to everyone. We got a little catching up to do"

Brandi giggled.

She and Whitney vanished into the other room to get dressed for their date with the McNairs. Brandi had attempted to take Knoxi with her, but the child was alarmed when her mother tried to snatch her away from Cody. Cody assured both women that he would be okay holding Knoxi until they returned. It was obvious the women had retreated so Ray and Cody could get acquainted.

"Thank you for getting involved last night at the theater. We would be having a very bad day if you hadn't come along." Ray's eyes fogged for a few seconds.

"I see the bruises and carpet burns." Cody grimaced. "Last night I wanted to kill 'em."

"I hear you, son. The important thing is that you didn't kill anybody. I'm fighting anger issues today as well. I keep thinking what might've happened if I had been there." Ray's voice never wavered, even as he reached up and wiped a tear from a corner of his eye.

Cody pretended not to notice. Instead, he attempted to place Knoxi's head on his shoulder, but she was more interested in staring at his face.

"Sir, your daughter...what I mean is that Brandi..." He ran out of words.

"What you mean to say is that she is a very handsome woman. I don't blame you if you're attracted to her."

A sheepish grin betrayed Cody's poker face. *Handsome* wasn't the word he had in mind.

"Of course, it's clear that she's recovering from —" Ray cleared his throat. "Well, let's just say she's a bit fragile now, if you catch my meaning."

Cody shrugged. "Truth is I hate to think what would have happened to her last night if those storms hadn't moved in. Didn't know what to do with myself, so I went to that movie."

Ray nodded. "Brandi told you how I met Whitney, but you don't know the whole story. See, I fell asleep in the depot and missed my bus home. I panicked because the next bus didn't leave for eight more hours. What was I going to do with myself in a Pittsburgh bus depot with nothing in my pocket but eight bucks and a ticket I couldn't use until zero-five-hundred the next morning? Ten minutes later, I looked up and there she was — sitting, crying, praying. I'll never forget the moment I saw her."

"So meeting Whitney was an accident?"

"Oh, not any more than you meeting Brandi last night."

Cody's face relaxed. "You mean...?"

"Yep. Missed the bus and found my future. Sometimes life is what happens to us when we think we should be somewhere else."

"Hmmm. Roger that."

"Daddy, Cody, how does this look on me?" Brandi was standing in the doorway, modeling the Astros jersey and hat.

"With you in it, that jersey couldn't look any better unless it had the Pirates logo on the front," Ray offered. Then he looked back at Cody. "I'm a lifelong Pittsburgh fan, Cody. No offense."

"None taken, sir."

Neither Ray nor Cody asked why she was wearing a blouse underneath. They knew the answer. The collar of the blouse, which extended upward through the neck of the jersey, partially covered the bruises on her throat.

Brandi disappeared again.

"You're very good at putting on a show for kids," Ray said. "And you have certainly taken to my granddaughter. Do you have any brothers or sisters?"

"No, sir, I'm an only child. My parents died in a plane crash in the Bahamas during my senior year in high school. I have always suspected sabotage, but I have no way to prove it."

"Sabotage? What did your parents do?"

"My father was a DEA agent. He directed the raid on Juanita Capistrano in Brazil in 2002. Do you remember that case?"

"Your father was the agent who brought her down? I remember reading about the operation. The hard part was putting together the coalition with local authorities since DEA is limited in foreign countries."

"He was in charge," Cody replied. "You know, sir, Capistrano was into human trafficking as well as narcotics."

"Well, you have been handed quite a legacy by your father. I guess you figured out my daughter is making things hot around here for human traffickers."

"Absolutely. And what I started to say earlier is that she's a fighter. The bad guys are afraid of her."

"So why didn't you say that when you started to say it earlier?"

"Didn't want you to think that was my only interest in her."

"Straight enough. I like that. Would it be assuming too much to ask if we will see you again after this weekend?"

"The answer would be *yes*, sir."

"And would that be 'yes, it is assuming too much' or 'yes, we might be seeing you again?'"

Cody chuckled. "I hope that you will see me again. By the way, I told Brandi that her place at the Mayfield Tower isn't safe due to poor security."

"I've been trying to tell her that," he ranted. "I don't believe those three guys acted independently. Whoever sent them will send someone else, and that's what petrifies Whitney and me."

"Sir, I want to ask Brandi to go to Detroit with me. She's not safe in this town. She should leave for a few days, at least. The Astros are arranging a security team."

"Have you asked her yet?"

"Uh, no, sir. I...I haven't mentioned it to her yet."

"So after Detroit, what then?"

Cody was silent. It was a question he had not expected. Knoxi finally rested her head on his shoulder, but his facial muscles tightened when Ray looked him in the eye.

"I've seen you play baseball on TV, Cody, but I don't know you. Brandi tells me you beat the crap out of those three guys last night." He dropped his eyes for a moment. His face twitched. "There are some things I'd like to say to you, and I hope you don't mind my being direct."

Cody leaned back. Knoxi was now asleep. "Direct is exactly what I would expect, sir."

Ray stood, walked to the window, hands in pockets, head down. "I believe you care for my daughter, but I can read your face, son. It says you carry a lot of pain."

Cody looked straight ahead and nodded. The silence was awkward but short-lived. The sweet sound of innocence — steady breathing of the sleeping toddler on Cody's shoulder — filled the void.

"Brandi has been wounded too," Ray added. "She still carries . . ."

Cody waited a moment. "I can see that, Captain."

Ray turned. "Yes, I suppose you can. For what it's worth, you used restraint last night that I might not have had. That's a sign that you're a strong man. My girls — I just don't want..." He stopped and squared his shoulders.

"Understood, sir. If she decides to go with me, I will guard her safety *and her honor* with my life."

A question arose in Cody's mind: did Ray love his daughter so much because she was amazing, or was she amazing because Ray loved her so much?

The women hustled back into the room. Whitney recognized that expression on Ray's face. "Sorry. Did we interrupt?"

Ray switched gears. "Well, looks like our baby girl is fast asleep." He took a deep breath. "She feels comfortable with you, Cody. Did you know that kids sense anxiety? If they detect that you are tense, they often won't fall asleep."

"I didn't know that. I feel pretty calm today, maybe more than usual."

Ray looked toward Brandi who had just reentered the room. "Maybe you are at ease because of the company you're keeping today, Cody."

Cody's eyes met Brandi's. "I see your point, Captain."

Whitney could not hide her tense smile when Brandi scooted to Cody's side and held his sleeve as they all departed for their lunch date with the McNairs. Knoxi had waked up. Cody delicately carried her with his other arm.

# Captain Sly

T he restaurant was one of several within the hotel complex. With one wall entirely of glass, it was a perfectly bright and airy place for lunch on a partly sunny Saturday afternoon.

When they arrived, Julia McNair was waiting inside the door. Knoxi was clinging to Cody, which caught Julia by surprise.

"Well, Cody! Who is this holding on to you?" She placed one hand on the toddler's back as she embraced Cody and kissed him on the cheek. Knoxi burrowed her face into Cody's shoulder.

"You have certainly done well for yourself, Cody Musket. Who are all these lovely people you are surrounded by?" Julia's soft brown eyes and smile were like light and music.

After they were all introduced, Julia grinned at Cody again. "Looks like she's very attached." She chuckled as she patted the snuggling toddler on the head.

"Where's ol' Cap'n Sly?" Cody asked.

"He's down in the entry signing autographs for a Boy Scout troop."

"Captain Sly?" Brandi wrinkled her nose.

"Oh. That's the new nickname he gave my husband when he shaved his head and started wearing his big earring," Julia informed.

"Yeah, I told him that with the wicked mustache and earring, all he needs now is the proper headdress and an eye patch to look like a real pirate," Cody said. "And he's earned the nickname other ways."

"How so?" Brandi asked him.

"You'll find out."

"Now, Cody, you boys need to be civil. We're in public you know." Julia loved to scold them both — part of the fun, and it encouraged the two men to be increasingly outrageous together.

The hostess led them to their reserved table. Tanner soon swaggered into the room and caused a stir — all eyes on him. Several parents with their children came to the table for autographs.

Tanner McNair, whose great-great-grandfather had starred in the Negro leagues in the 1930s, had established himself as an elite National League outfielder. He was six feet, 195 pounds, lean and fast, with a chiseled, bodybuilder physique. He wore a one-inch earring on his left ear, but not when playing baseball. His game-face scowl seemed to reinvent itself into a broad grin when the autograph seekers arrived.

Brandi was fascinated. Tanner was in his element. For some people, charm came naturally, but some charmers could turn it up several notches when they wanted to. Tanner — Cap'n Sly — clearly was in that category.

The McNairs had left their three-year-old son Jeremy with some friends. After a few minutes, Cody had the floor.

"Okay, listen up everybody. Tanner and I have cooked up a plan for tomorrow night — a way to get him back on Brandi's show."

"Yeah," Tanner interrupted. "I apologize for having to cancel on you, Brandi. We had planned to take the 7:00 p.m. flight to Detroit tomorrow, but instead of flying to Detroit, we could do the show first, then drive up there — all of us.

"Cody and I could *both* participate on your program, and since Cody's goin' to the All-Star Game too, we could all ride up in our Escalade together — the four of us and the two kids. It's just a four-hour drive. Right, Cody?" Sly's grin was the size of a Hostess Twinkie.

Cody glared at Tanner, then turned to Brandi as if he had known all along. "Well, I thought . . . I mean *we* thought —" He paused. "Uh, of course. I think it's a good idea for you to come along for — for security reasons."

"So you're inviting me to Detroit with you?" Brandi slapped Cody on the shoulder. "When were you going to tell me?"

"Well, I guess —"

"I'd love to go with you — security reasons, of course." She lifted an olive to her mouth and closed her lips around it, attempting to hide her sudden jubilation.

Julia pinched her husband underneath the table, but not before she had secretly buried her left elbow into his ribs.

After dinner, the women excused themselves and headed to the ladies' powder room together, leaving Knoxi with the men."

Most guys cannot swagger while sitting down. Cap'n Sly was the exception. Though his latest scheme had caught Cody by surprise, his friend's aggressive mischief had done Cody a favor. Brandi had been reluctant to come to the hotel with him until the blackout had scared the wits out of her. How much more unwilling might she have been to go to Detroit with a man? Now he didn't have to worry about being rejected.

"So, Cody, who were those brave individuals who attacked Brandi?" Sly's grin flashed like neon. The gloat had not left his face, and he was obviously feeling it.

"Dunno yet. The big guy who made those bruises on her neck is a dangerous professional, but the other two were a couple o' punks. They botched the whole thing, especially the scud mouth swinging a rag around and braggin' about making Brandi an example."

"I didn't hear that part." Ray dropped his fist on the table. It frightened Knoxi.

"So those characters were amateurs?" Sly narrowed his eyes.

"All three of 'em should've held knives to Brandi's throat and threatened to kill her if I didn't let 'em pass. I wudda had no choice but to step aside. Instead, they attacked me one by one — the dumbest thing they could've done. Even the big guy freaked when his two associates behaved like dud scuds."

"It was meant for you to be there, son." Ray's eyes could have fried an egg. "They weren't expecting someone to stand in their way — especially a *tuffass* Marine with an at-large disposition."

Tanner thought to lighten things up. "So, did you remind 'em not to send boys to do a man's job next time?"

Ray stepped in before Cody could respond. "That's what we're concerned about — *next time.*"

"We're trying to keep the press out of it," Cody said.

"Well, I come prepared." Tanner wore his game face again.

"So you're carrying?" Cody looked for a bulge in Tanner's coat. He had already detected the one under Ray's left shoulder.

"Nobody messes with my best buddy or his girlfriend."

Captain Sly was psyched. The idea of something secretive and potentially dangerous elevated him to red alert. "We have to be ready for anything."

Then something at the entrance caught Tanner's attention. His eyes became beady and snakelike. "Look at that guy coming through the door. He's into organized crime. I'd bet my batting title on it."

Ray and Cody took a look and then stared at each other in disbelief.

The man in question came into the restaurant followed by at least fifteen autograph hounds. He sat down at a table on the other side of the room.

Ray cracked the first smile. "That's Cody's friend. Didn't you know that?"

Tanner was completely in the dark. "That guy has to be with the underworld. I know I've seen him somewhere."

The man with the familiar face waved when Cody glanced over at him.

Cody leaned toward Sly. *"Lonesome Dove? Men in Black?"* He snickered. "Tommy Lee Jones. He's here for a screen writer's forum."

Tanner's eyes flared.

Cody leaned in further and spoke under his breath. "Just so both you gentlemen know, a security detail is assigned to Brandi and me. They're in this room right now."

Ray put his hands on the table. "I already spotted them."

Tanner scanned the room. "I don't see nobody." Then he folded his arms across his chest. "All I can say is, get ready to be hounded. Soon as those autograph vultures finish with Mr. Movie Star, they'll probably spot me."

But soon, the crowd around the actor broke up and left.

*   *   *

The ladies entered the powder room. The anteroom at the entrance was about ten by ten, with white tile trimmed in pink and two small burgundy leather sofas on either side with end tables and matching lamps. Decorating the walls were pictures of notable female Pennsylvania celebrities, including a Brandi Barnes autographed photo.

"You've fallen hard for him," Julia concluded, her eyes wild and engaging.

"What gave it away?"

"You mean other than your face lighting up the whole table when you found out you were going to Detroit with him?"

"Was I that obvious?" Brandi giggled.

Whitney was amused. The younger women were bonding like sisters.

Julia was Brandi's age and had been a runner-up in the Miss Black USA Pageant during her sophomore year at the University of Maryland. Her facial skin was tight and smooth, and her long ponytail swayed across her lower back as she walked. Her pink Summer Blossom pantsuit was a perfect fit for a well-trimmed body that visited the gym three times per week. She hosted Tanner's charity events, made personal appearances throughout the state, and was the mother of a three-year-old son.

"Cody has never invited a woman to a game. You're the first," Julia said.

"Not sure how serious Cody is about the relationship because we just met."

"Girl, are you kidding me? Have you not noticed the way his face catches fire when he looks at you? Tanner and I've known Cody a long time, and I'm tellin' you that man has stars in his eyes. Tanner told Cody last night that if he didn't invite you to Detroit, he would kick his backside blessed parts."

"No kidding?" Brandi chuckled. "Never heard it put that way."

"Listen, those two have been like brothers since Little League. The longer they hung out, the more mischievous they became. And listen to me, girl, don't even ask them about their self-defense training they did together 'cause they'll want to start demonstrating it."

"Oh, how funny!"

"Even with fame and distractions, Tanny's getting things together. He's a good father. We're active in our church, and even though he never went to college, he knows about handling money. He even holds finance planning classes for teammates who're interested."

"Is the Captain Sly routine just an act?"

"No. Not an act. But he does play dumb once in a while. He and Cody learned that from each other. When they hang out — I mean I pretend to ignore them, but they're really good together. They can't stand for the other one to get the upper hand on anything. Always competing. You know how guys are — all that testosterone."

Whitney headed back to the table while the two younger women stayed to talk.

"I noticed the bruises. Are you okay, Brandi?" They sat down on a sofa in the anteroom.

Brandi filled her in on the events at the theater the night before. "I was so emotional afterward — laughing one minute, crying the next."

"If you ever need to talk, here's my cell number." Julia scribbled the number on a notepad and handed it to her.

"Today, I'm feeling the emotional effects," Brandi said. "This morning in the shower I must have scrubbed for an hour the places where they manhandled me. I haven't told my parents or Cody. Don't want them to know how I feel."

"Cody knows. You can bet on that," Julia said, "But you need to talk to someone and..."

Brandi looked away, so Julia changed the subject. "So how much has Cody told you?"

"Afghanistan?" Brandi asked. "Not much. Do you know anything about some children?"

"He has told us very little. Tanny has become very protective of Cody. He loves him like a brother, but Cody won't share his experience with anyone."

As they walked back toward the table, Julia said something unsettling. "In the off-season, Cody makes trips to visit a woman in Springfield, Indiana named Myra Waites."

"A woman?"

"We've no idea who she is but we know she has a son. We found out by mistake."

Brandi got quiet. *An old flame? Could the son be Cody's?*

"Since Afghanistan," Julia confided, "Cody has become distant and secretive."

After lunch, Ray and Whitney returned to the suite with Knoxi. The McNairs gave Cody and Brandi a ride to the baseball park. Brandi still had not received a response from Detective Dupree.

# CENTER FIELD

P NC Ballpark is located in the downtown area of Pittsburgh on the bank of the Allegheny. The quaint setting of the park nestled between the tall buildings and the river make it one of the most picturesque stadiums in America.

Cody and Brandi arrived more than four hours before game time. "You wanna take a walk with me down on the field?" Cody took her hand.

"So this is where you work? At night mostly?"

"Yep, except when it's raining or when we have a day game."

Brandi had been there before, but not on the playing surface with her own celebrity guide.

"Cool! That screen looks amazing from here. And that bridge!" She had never been this close to the giant Jumbotron screen and scoreboard which sat above the left field bleachers. The view of the Roberto Clemente Bridge beyond center field was awesome when seen from third base.

Cody looked toward the bullpen in the deepest part of the outfield. "Wanna go out to center field?"

"Why center field?"

"Cause it's a long way from people," he said. "We can talk out there."

They began the long, leisurely walk.

"So, um, do you have a lot of girlfriends — beside Maxine, that is?" Would he dare mention Myra?

"Not really. I, uh — Why? Why do you ask?"

A good barb seemed appropriate. "Well, not meaning to be vexatious, but Julia said you're quite the ladies' man, always inviting women to your road games."

"But I've never invited one of 'em to center field."

Brandi hoped that his broad grin was because he was with her and not just because he felt at home on a baseball diamond. For Cody's hardline face, smiles came at a premium.

A few lingering clouds passed overhead and sunlight was peeking through intermittently. The heavy rains from the previous day had ceased twenty hours earlier. Field-level temperature had fallen into the middle seventies — cool for July — and it would surely shape up to be a perfect night for baseball.

As they passed by second base, she took his arm with both of hers and pulled herself closer. Someone whistled from behind them. Without looking, Cody responded, "That's enough out of you, Joey."

The whistler was José Bustamante, Houston's Dominican right fielder and the leading hitter on the club. Lately, the two had become friends. Cody had helped José improve his English, which José appreciated, and Cody loved showing off his Spanish, which José happily tolerated.

The couple walked on toward the bullpen, which was located just to the left of straightaway center field. In the pen, relief pitchers warmed up their arms prior to entering the game. A screen fence separated the bullpen from the field of play.

The sun peeked between two clouds momentarily. During the storms the night before, Cody had visualized Brandi's hair basking in sunlight. His vision had now come to life, and she was even more radiant than he had imagined. Her nearness, her tenderness, the wonder. Could the man he used to be live again? Feel again?

Should he break his silence? Tell her things that were hidden away in deep places? If so, how much should he reveal?

"I was pronounced terminal when they got me to the Army hospital at Kandahar," Cody said. "My left knee was as large as a Coyanosa watermelon and smelled worse than a dried-up water hole in the cattle country. The only chance I had was for the surgeon to amputate. Even with an amputation they didn't think I had a chance to survive."

"So what happened?" She looked down at his left foot and imagined it not being there. "Cody? Can you tell me what happened?"

"A Canadian anesthesiologist, Sergeant Nikki Corbett, asked me point-blank if I was a Christian. I resented it. I already believed in God but I didn't think I could be forgiven for what I had done. I didn't have anything left to live for. I was losing my leg, I couldn't fly anymore, I had no one to return home to, and I was responsible for . . ." He never finished.

Brandi knew not to push, although patience was not her favorite virtue.

"Nikki said that even though I believed my life was over, God might have a better plan for me than flying and being a Marine. I couldn't imagine not flying. Then she told me that if I was willing to give up my own plans in favor of God's plan, He would give me a new life."

She waited, looking straight ahead, then turned to him. "Cody, don't stop. What happened?"

"The hate I felt — I mean the hate in my head was killin' me faster than the infection. Just before I lost consciousness, I . . ." His voice trailed off.

She waited. "So . . . so how are you doing on the hate?"

"It's not that simple."

They had come to the edge of the playing field. He left her and entered the bullpen through the gate, brought back two folding chairs, and set them on the dirt track next to the screen fence. They sat down facing each other.

"I asked God for forgiveness, begged Him to take away the hate. I was definitely trending the wrong way. I told Him I would exchange the life I had made for myself for whatever life He had for me instead." He paused and waited.

"Well? What happened next?"

"When I finally woke up three days later, Nikki was sitting there. I looked down and saw five dark blue toes on my left foot, which was still attached. The infection had left before the doctor had even cut me open. Everyone at Kandahar said it was a miracle. The surgeon, Captain Jefferson, even became a believer later on."

"So, how was your left leg injured?" She waited, spoke softly, "Cody, can you trust me with that?"

"No one should hear *that* story," he said, "cuz once you've heard it, you'll never be able to unhear it."

"Something terrible happened, I get that, but if God did a miracle —"

"Yeah, but something doesn't make sense. I wanna be free from it all — the hate, the violence in my head. That's what I asked God for, but I'm still not past any of it. Like I said, it just doesn't add up." He shook his head.

"*Duh!* Maybe God isn't finished yet. Did you ever think of that?"

Cody squinted and stared off into left field. "But it's been *four* years."

"Knoxi's recovery was a miracle." Brandi changed the subject. "And I've been different ever since the incident at the mission. That day, God invaded the impossible. Since then I've found courage to do things I would never have done before."

"Like take on the traffickers?"

"Yes, but I still have issues too," she confessed. "I can't trust people — especially men — since the stabbing. I came back here to reconnect with my parents and the values they had taught me, but loneliness is an itch I still can't scratch."

Cody leaned forward. "I can trust God, but I don't trust myself." He took his cap off and set it on the ground. "I can't forgive myself."

"Forgive yourself? Forgive yourself for what?"

"I wanna ask you something." He ignored her question. "Last night at the theater, you closed your eyes and quit fighting in the middle of the attack and said a prayer. After that, I showed up, right?"

"That's right. My father has created a list of what he calls his Five Greatest Principles of Leadership. One of them is, 'In the heat of battle when you are losing ground, be still and know that He is God, and He will speak to you.'"

"So which number is that?"

"Number seven."

"Number *seven?* I thought there were just five."

"Well." She shrugged. "It started off with five, but over the years..."

"Hmmm. Well, what if you hadn't been still and prayed? Would I have still shown up?"

"That's a question for the ages. All I can say is, it was right for me to pray, and it was right for you to be there."

Cody rubbed his chin and stared down at her knee socks and tennis shoes. "Still can't bend over?"

"I'm still stiff but I plan to live." Brandi noticed he was looking at her shoes, so she quipped, "How 'bout those big bubba boots your Texas women wear? Are they comfortable?"

"Of course they're comfortable," he bragged. "They're padded with Bowie feathers."

"I don't even *want* to know what that means."

"Bowie feathers?" He raised his brow. "That's the fuzz from Texas peaches."

"Well, why not name it *Houston* feathers? Or *Musket* feathers, or —"

"Cuz Jim Bowie invented the only knife that'll harvest the fuzz without destroyin' the peach." True to form, his flintlock expression never twitched.

"I said I *didn't* want to know." She couldn't afford to give in. Laughing would hurt too much.

"No need to suffer today," he said. "You should give these up."

"What?" She stiffened. "Give what up?"

He reached down toward her ankles and opened his callused hand. Without thinking, she lifted her left foot and slipped it into his waiting palm.

He loosened the shoestrings and delicately eased the tennis shoe off her swollen foot. After a moment, the other shoe followed.

"How did you know?" she whispered.

He set her shoes beside his chair. "Wear just the socks 'till you can get some flip-flops at the team store on the mezzanine behind first base. You'll feel better."

Brandi's eyelids fell shut as the cooling afternoon air penetrated through her cotton socks. Her voice became feather-soft. "I was horrible to you last night — cruel and selfish."

Cody shrugged her off. "Nah, you weren't. Of course, you might've been a little mean and ornery. Waspish and petulant, maybe."

She tried to smile, but her chin softened and tremored. "They *meant* to bruise me, shame me, make me a public example." She placed her hand over her lips.

"It's okay," his words like a quiet breath. "Nobody can hear us."

"Afterward, I wanted to scrub every place they touched me. If you hadn't been there — I mean that's what they do. It's a warning to anyone else that . . . anyone else that . . ."

"Anyone else that stands up to 'em?"

She wrung her hands and looked away. "I was so angry. Shamed in public. I didn't need your understanding or your pity. I just had to show how tough I was, but all I did was take out my humiliation on you."

"So how do you feel now?"

"Violated. I can't help it, Cody. I didn't want you or my parents to know. I feel so exposed, helpless, ugly. I can't get it out of my mind. I hate that."

He nodded.

"Yesterday, I could never have dreamed of sitting here now with Cody Musket next to the bullpen in the middle of this huge stadium, but after last night, I wonder how much future any of us has."

"Are you scared?"

"I'd be lying if I said no. I've drawn you into my trouble. You have enough of your own. I'm a target. Maybe you should stay as far away from me as you can get."

"Right now, that wouldn't be very far." He reached for her fingers.

Her pulse raced like a little girl lost in the dark who had just found the porch light. "Cody, I regret that when I met you I was so pitiful, angry, irrational, and . . ."

Just then, the sunshine broke through again.

"May I do something?" He reached up and removed her baseball cap. "Last night, during the storm, when I first saw you, I tried to imagine how your hair would look with sunlight shining through it, just like it is now." He stroked her hair.

"Before we had even met?"

"Up 'til last night," he said, "I didn't believe anything on this planet was bolder or more beautiful than the Tyler Rose of Texas that grows down in my hometown of Big Rock."

Brandi couldn't help herself. She grinned and then laughed. "Awww shucks, John Wayne, are you trying to be romantic? Like in the movies? I shouldn't have spilled my guts about loving old melodramatic films so much."

Cody's expression faded from his lips, prompting Brandi's smile to desert her face.

"Oh, Cody, I'm so sorry." She touched his arm. "You were serious? You actually thought about the sun in my hair? The roses?" She stared. "And I just insulted you and walked away."

Cody hung his head but could not hide a guarded grin. Despite her stiffness, Brandi bent low, looked up into his face, and beamed. "Earth to Cody? So does that mean you're a serious romantic?"

He raised his eyes. "You mean like Barry Grant?"

"It's *Cary* Grant, and I knew that underneath that rough exterior was more than just a tough ballplayer who liked to wear pink boots."

"Don't be ridiculous." He motioned with his hands like an umpire ruling a runner safe.

She poked him on the left shoulder. "Do you even know what *waspish* means?" She pulled a pair of mirror sunglasses from her purse.

"Don't be so petulant. Of course I know what it means." He leaned back in the chair. "Just don't ask me to define it."

"You really think you're funny?"

"I'm a quick study." He reached down and picked up his cap.

"What's that supposed to mean?"

"It means I've already learned to read your face."

She smirked, leaned back against the screen, and crossed her arms. "Oh, you think so? Well, what does this face tell you?" She pulled her sunshades down to the end of her nose and glared at him over the top of the frames.

He pulled his cap down over his eyes, slouched back, and arrogantly folded his arms. "It tells me that underneath that frown and those shades you're laughing your head off right now."

She erupted, mirror sunglasses flying through the air. Her sweet laughter was music he had missed for a lifetime. He caught her shades before they reached the ground.

They were quiet for a few seconds.

"Cody, what are we doing? I know why you're trying to be funny."

A modest air current had coaxed a wisp of hair into Brandi's face. Cody reached over and brushed it away.

"A merry heart does wonders like a medicine," he said.

She couldn't hide her surprise. "Do you know where that quote is from?"

"Uh, I heard it somewhere. Ingrid Bergman?"

"Of course not. It's from the Bible."

"Yeah, I know," he proudly announced. "Proverbs 17:22."

"You're certainly the most *un-boring* man I have ever met."

"Un-boring? Is that all you can say?"

"No. But that'll do for now."

They listened for a few moments as players from both teams stretched and interacted on the infield. The sun retreated behind a low, restless cloud, so Brandi slipped her shades back inside her purse.

A blackbird landed on the fence twenty feet away, then crackled as it swooped down to snatch up a leftover peanut off one of the bleachers. The fluttering of its wings grew softer and softer while it soared skyward. Cody watched the bird until it disappeared, and then dropped his eyes again and shut them. The chatter on the infield died away and all was quiet.

"It was to *their* shame."

"What?"

"It was to *their* shame," Cody said, "*not yours*. The guy with the huge biceps had you in a chokehold. Your phone and your shoes were scattered among strangers. Your blouse looked like dogs had fought over it. I mean, your hair was everywhere, and your arms and stomach were cut, scraped . . . streaked with mud from that carpet. Your lip . . . it was bloody, swollen, and . . ." His eyes tightly shut. "I remember all of it."

Brandi withered into the chair and covered herself with her arms. "Cody, there are just no words."

He opened his eyes. "I know," he whispered. "I know."

She gazed into his well-tested face. For a moment, her heart seemed to stop beating. Were his sad eyes trying to tell her that he loved her? Were they saying he had already borne enough pain for them both? No more shame. She shut her eyes and dropped her hands to her lap. Easy tears escaped from her closed eyelids and rolled down across her cheeks.

Cody leaned in. "You were *not* the ugly one. He was ready to throw down on me with that knife. You could hardly breathe, but you managed to reach back and deflect his arm. Right then, you were the most beautiful woman I've ever seen — the bravest person in that hallway."

She held out her hand and searched for his knee like the blind reaching for a friend.

"You were *not* a victim," he said. "You remembered your roots and the source of your strength."

"But I was so scared. I couldn't stop trembling afterward. I wanted to crawl into a hole. I wouldn't even look at you."

"I know, but you had a job to do. You didn't stay in your hole. You came back to interrogate me. Your hands were still shaking when we were in the coffee shop."

She finally opened her teary eyes and looked downward. A beetle moved along the seam where the grass met the dirt track. Her white socks, now dusty on the sides, were toe-to- toe with those silly orange-and-blue tennis shoes Cody was wearing. She brushed back tears with her hand.

Cody's whispery words walked right through the front door of her willing heart, "You think courage means you never cry? never get scared?" He waited a moment for her to raise her eyes. "You're armed and dangerous, Brandi Barnes. That's what brought me back to find you last night."

She leaned backward against the screen. Her former boyfriend, the stabbing, and now the attack in the theater — in the aftermath of all, she had been in someone else's skin. She had convinced herself the violence had happened to that *other* person.

Now, sitting with Cody, she finally gave herself permission to own it. The abuse, the scars — yes, they were hers.

Cody placed the cap back on her head. Brandi pulled it low over her face. He waited, said nothing, but prayed the anguish would be purged from her soul. She finally nudged the cap above her eyes. "I'm sorry, Cody." She opened her purse and fumbled for some tissue.

"Don't be." He offered a clean handkerchief from his pocket.

"You're just like my father." She raised the cloth and blotted her face. "He always knows the right thing to say and . . . **a**nd *not* to say." Her voice now steady, a faint smile breaking through.

He looked toward the infield. "They're gonna start early batting practice. We better vacate. It's gonna start rainin' baseballs around here." He returned the chairs. This time, Brandi followed him into the pen.

After he had set the seats down, he did an about-face and saw her standing there. Brandi turned her cap around with the bill in the back, and then wrapped her arms around his neck.

She moved her lips close. "Do you know when I finally stopped trembling last night?"

"No, but I have the feeling you're gonna tell me."

"It was when you picked me up in your arms and kissed me."

"I don't often have *that* effect on women."

"You certainly have that effect on me." She removed his cap and held it in her hand.

"But we're in the bullpen. Are you trembling again?" He looked around, pretending to be nervous.

"Ohhhh, yesss. Definitely." She kissed him passionately and then gazed into his face. Her pupils moved side to side, searching for the hidden message in his deep eyes that were now sad again and troubled.

At that moment, a child's voice rang out from the bleachers next to the bullpen railing. "Hey, guys, you gotta see this! Come quick!"

She took his arm and pulled him back through the gate onto the field. Cody picked up her shoes, tied the strings together and looped them around his neck.

"I know now which one you are," she declared as they walked toward the infield.

"I give up. What're you talking about?" His granite face was back.

"You're a big something disguised as nothing." She held his arm with both hands as they walked. "Aren't you going to tell me I need to do my face again?"

He stared straight ahead. "Nothin' wrong with *that* face." He was broody, the smile he had worn earlier now gone.

"Cody, what's wrong? Should I not have kissed you?"

He bit his lower lip. "I got problems with relationships too."

"Oh, right. I bet you have hundreds of women throwing themselves at you."

"I dunno know how to answer that. I don't make myself available."

"So you're not available?" Her feet were suddenly heavy, dragging. "Cody, is there someone else in your life? Be serious, okay? I just need to know."

"You've seen my legs. Can you imagine anyone wanting to go to the beach with me?"

Her eyes lit up. She pulled herself close, flashed a grin, and donned her sunshades. "Well," she strutted, "there are no beaches around here."

# NIGHT TRAPS

T he weather remained perfect for the Saturday night game. The crowd of twenty-nine thousand Pirate fans was rewarded. Astros pitcher, Mark Stiller, Cody's roommate, gave up a first-inning double to leadoff hitter, Nick Colter followed by a two-out, two-run home run by Tanner McNair, and it was all downhill from there for Houston.

In the fifth inning, Cody doubled off the bullpen screen in center field, inches above where Brandi had sat that afternoon. If the ball had struck just one foot higher, it would have given him his twenty-second home run of the season.

Sandy Stiller, the wife of Cody's roomie, sat in front of Brandi. She turned and introduced herself. "How long have you known Cody?"

"Not long. So your hubby is Cody's roommate?"

"Yes. Cody's a loner, kinda' hard to get to know. You must really be special. This is the first time I've known him to invite a woman to a game."

Felicia Coleman, the wife of Houston shortstop Gerald "Dancer" Coleman, overheard. "Yeah, girl, I notice he glances at you every time he comes back to the dugout."

Brandi grinned. Knoxi climbed into her lap to get a better look whenever Cody came to the batter's box with a bat in his hand.

It was a blowout. The Pirates beat the Astros 9-3.

\*   \*   \*

After the game, Tanner and Julia took Cody, Brandi, and her family to Penn Wood River Grill, overlooking the Allegheny. Tanner rented a private room. It was a cool evening, and they opened the large sliding doors, which allowed breezes off the river to fill the room with a sweet, natural ambience.

Spirited after-dinner conversation gave Sly the opportunity he had anticipated all afternoon. "Hey, Brandi, Did Cody tell you about the first time he pitched in high school?"

"Oh, God help us," Julia said. "We should go for a walk on the deck."

"Oh, no, no, no," Brandi replied. "I gotta hear this."

"Well, it was the seventh inning and the hitter comin' up was Kenneth Davis — biggest home run hitter in the district. Our coach put Cody in to pitch."

Brandi turned to Cody. "I didn't know you pitched too."

"Well, I...in high school, I —"

Tanner stood and raised his volume. "So here was Cody, this skinny little kid, facing the best player in the league."

"*I* was the skinny kid?" Cody snorted. "You were so thin you had to run around in the shower just to get wet!"

Brandi and Julia snickered, but Sly ignored the interruption.

"So our coach tells Cody to 'deck him,' b'cuz this kid had already hit two home runs and he was gettin' too comfortable at the plate."

"Oh, I can't wait to hear how the story comes out this time." Julia tried her best to sound bored.

"Now just hear me out. Cody gets mixed up, and he's so nervous he hits the batter in the on-deck circle."

"You're kidding!"

"Of course he's kidding," Cody said. "Do you know how far the on-deck circle is from the plate?"

Sly played it right on cue. "That's what I'm talkin' about — see, the visiting coach comes out and claims that since his player on deck was hit by d' pitch, he should be awarded first base! But our coach comes out and says that if the other guy goes to first base he should be ruled out for battin' out o' turn. There was this big rhubarb, and everybody involved got kicked out o' da game, including our hero here." He pointed to Cody, then sat back down, crossed his arms and flashed his Hostess Twinkie smile again.

Cody wasn't laughing. "How many think that story was true?"

Julia and Brandi raised their hands.

"Well, listen to this." Cody bounced up. "After Cap'n Sly quarterbacked us to the district championship in football, he told reporters that his *two* greatest assets were his legs, his arm, and his brains."

Brandi and Julia erupted. Brandi knocked her water glass over, and that escalated the hilarity.

"Good thing he did a postgame interview, cuz otherwise the fans wudda never known that he looked for his open receivers, we played sixty minutes, and that our guys were a team."

Julia and Brandi laughed so hard they fed off each other's energy. The stories were not *that* funny, but the laughter was. Soon, it was contagious.

As the group left through the crowded front portion of the restaurant, the two women still could not gain control of themselves, hanging on to each other like tipsy sisters. This prompted Sly to address the Saturday night crowd.

He quoted a verse from the King James Bible. "These are not drunk as ye suppose."

The crowd applauded, and Tanner spent the next ten minutes signing autographs — the perfect way to end the night for a smiling hometown hero.

*     *     *

After arriving back at the hotel, Brandi and Cody decided to wind down with a cup of decaf in the lobby, after which they took the elevator to the twelfth floor and then walked slowly down the hall toward her room.

Brandi took Cody's arm. "Where is our security team?"

"Invisible. They have all the entrances to this floor covered."

"I didn't see anybody," she said.

"That's the idea. You probably didn't see the people watching us at the stadium either."

"Nope. Didn't notice. And the restaurant too?"

"Covered."

"You should know that you are the first man I have ever let see me cry."

"*Ha!* I find that hard to believe."

"I know. I cry easily, but not in front of men. *Not ever.*"

"I guess that makes me special."

"No. That's not what makes you special." She nestled closer. They were quiet as they approached her room.

"Cody, you said something this afternoon about your scars. If I had scars like yours, I wouldn't be ashamed for anyone to see them."

"But you haven't seen…I mean it goes deeper than that."

"And the cross-shaped scar? How deep does that go?"

"You don't give up," he concluded. "I don't want people to know what happened. What I saw. What I felt. What I still feel. Some things you just don't talk about."

"You don't look upon yourself as a hero, Cody. I get that." They stopped in front of her door.

"Do you think I would've surrendered to the Taliban if I had known what they would do to me? I wasn't *that* brave. And there are things you don't know about me — stuff you wouldn't like."

She placed her arms around his neck. "I want to know."

"Once a journalist, always a journalist. I guess it's your nature to wanna know the story even if you aren't gonna write it. I don't resent it. It's who you are."

"You think that's why I'm asking? It's my nature? Cody, the only place I want to write your story is on my heart. Can you not see that? Can't you trust me?"

"Like I told you, it's myself I don't trust."

"Cody, this afternoon in center field, you knew I was hurting. I was foolish to think I could hide it from you."

He looked away.

Brandi gripped his shoulders. "Cody, look at me. You made me feel pretty, clean, brave, loved. That's what a hero does. When you pulled off my shoes because you cared about my pain, I wanted to believe with all my heart that you're the man who'll always be there to catch me if I fall. You want to know why I called you *un-boring* earlier?"

He gazed into her face and said nothing.

"You stand ten feet tall and destroy three armed killers with your bare fists, but a few hours later, you kneel at my feet and sooth my burning skin with hands as soft as velvet mittens. You're too shy to change your shirt in front of me, but you sweep me up and kiss me without warning. You mention 'armed and dangerous' and 'Tyler Roses' in the same breath. You hardly smile, but you are the funniest guy I've ever known."

He was silent, introspective.

"You've suffered more than I have, Cody," her eyes glistening, "but you're too honorable to point that out, and you never told me to *just get over it.*"

"I'm not the guy you think —"

She put her fingers over his lips. "I have known you barely twenty-four hours, man of steel, but I make up my mind quickly. I'm either all in, or I'm all out. With you, I'm all in. I want to know why that scares you so much."

Cody's eyes were warm, wild, troubled.

"I'm not asking for a wedding ring tonight." She softly stroked his cheek. "I just want to know what's going on in this mind of yours." She tapped on his head with her fingertips. "Please let me in."

"I get that you don't waste time," he said.

"Cody, I know you care for me. Can you deny it? Time is something we may not have."

"I could fall so hard for you," he confessed. "Last night, when I first saw you, I thought I could — But now, I don't know if…"

"Do I make you nervous? Afraid you're going to throw a wild pitch and hit the guy on deck?" She searched his eyes. "You said you could read my face, Cody, but I can't read yours. Please tell me what you're thinking."

The bullpen kiss had stayed with him all through the game. All he could think about was kissing her again. But now she wanted answers he couldn't give.

He shrugged away from her and leaned back against the wall. "You wouldn't understand."

"Try me."

He eased his hands into the front pockets of his cargos and then took a long, deep breath.

"We practiced night traps on the *Harry Truman.* Landing on a carrier at night is something you never get used to. My knees were always shaking."

Brandi folded her arms and leaned back against the opposite wall. *Where is he going with this?*

"One night we returned after a mission — eight aircraft. A thunderstorm had engulfed the boat with forty-knot gusting winds, lightning, driving rain. The deck was pitchin' up and down and rolling side to side." He paused, wiped perspiration from his brow.

"The ocean reflected the lights from the carrier, so I couldn't tell where the boat ended and the water began. I couldn't tell the sky from the sea 'cause lightning flashes reflected in the waves. I got disoriented and saw myself crashing into the back of the boat. I wanted to panic."

Brandi imagined herself in the cockpit but then returned to her senses, confused. *Maybe I shouldn't ask him what he's thinking again. Where's this leading?*

"Then I reminded myself to look for my LSOs — landing signal officers — experienced aviators dressed in these funky iridescent outfits, holding lighted batons. They shine the batons toward a thirty-foot-long area on the approach end of the runway where the four arresting wires are located. You have to catch one of the wires with the tail hook to stop the aircraft.

"Flying at 130 knots at night with flashes of light and the boat bouncin' around and having to hit an area that small — scariest thing you can imagine. The first seven before me missed, and then I missed. We flew back around and tried again. In all, I made three approaches before I caught one of the wires."

"Terrifying, Cody. But your point is?"

"Disorientation, vertigo — it's what life is like for me every day since Afghanistan. I can't find the deck. Dunno where the boat ends and the water begins. I see myself crashing. It's only a matter of time."

He shook his head. "Baseball is the one solid thing in my world, and I can't do that forever."

"Cody, I'm trying to understand. I want to understand."

He pulled his hands from his pockets and crossed his arms. "I can't carry anyone with me. I'm afraid they'll be destroyed, just like Seismo."

Brandi's stomach churned. *Oh, God, I'm in over my head. This is out of my league.*

"Cody, if you watch the lightning and focus on what can go wrong, then you'll never really be alive. You need to just keep your eye on the —"

"I didn't need any advice. I just needed you to listen."

Her heartbeat advanced. Giving advice *was* her nature. Why couldn't he see that?

"Look. I just wanna get beyond all the nightmares, get away from my past. I just —"

"How's that working out for you?" she interrupted. "Flying solo? If you're afraid to let anyone get close, you've created your own prison for yourself."

"This isn't getting anywhere." He jammed his fists back into his front pockets.

Her eyes fell. "No…I didn't mean to — I mean, I know you've been in a *real* prison, Cody. I shouldn't have said — Please don't walk away. Cody, come back."

"I'll tell you after we get to Detroit," he muttered as he walked away.

"Tell me what?"

"How I got the other scar." His sad eyes looked back before he vanished into the elevator.

She wrung her hands. *Why do I always say the wrong thing?*

When she opened the door to the room, Ray was waiting. "You don't look too happy, baby girl. Is there anything —"

"Detroit. He said he would tell me more in Detroit. After that, I'll let you know if anything is wrong. Don't really want to talk right now, Daddy."

# SHOWDOWN WITH CAPTAIN SLY

On Sunday morning, Ray and Whitney left early driving home to Altoona. Brandi and Knoxi slept in. Brandi had been exuberant about Cody's invitation to accompany him to Detroit, but their hallway conversation about night traps the evening before had stunned her. She awoke under a cloud.

He was afraid to attach himself to anyone. She got that. But if he wanted to fly alone, why did he still desire to take her with him to the All-Star Game? He wasn't making sense.

Cody could be articulate, but he was moody and unpredictable. What would he be like in Detroit? The face on Roberto Clemente's statue outside PNC Park was easier to read than Cody's.

A security team accompanied her with Knoxi to the stadium before the 1:00 p.m. game. She had not talked to Cody all day. What was he thinking? Fragile emotions began to grate. How safe were they during these games? Could just a handful of security professionals protect them? She was snowballed by fear.

From her box seat in Section 11, she scanned the crowd. She and Knoxi were surrounded by a multitude of strangers, and suddenly it was the two of them against the world. She battled the urge to retreat into the concessions area where merchants sold popular baseball park specialties such as Cuban Pretzel Dogs, beer, and team gear. Should she hide in the ladies' room?

Soon, Mia Bustamante, the wife of the Astros right fielder, introduced herself. Others did the same. Felicia Coleman finally made her way to her seat in front of Brandi. Sitting with new friends, Brandi settled in and braced herself.

Knoxi was shy, but Mia was able to make friends with her and tried to teach her to clap her hands and shout, "Yaaaaay!" whenever the Astros did something exciting. The toddler smiled but made no sound.

At the end of nine innings, the score was tied 6 runs apiece. Extra innings were in order. In the top of the fourteenth inning, with the score still tied, a disruption made its way like a whirlwind through the crowd in Section 11. People in the front row stood, staring back at Brandi. Fans in the sections to her left and right pointed. Suddenly, she was the center of attention, and no one was interested in baseball anymore.

She leaned forward. "Felicia, what's going on?"

"I dunno, but I'm gonna find out." She pulled out her cell phone, punched the quick dial and raised it to her ear.

Mia Bustamante motioned Brandi to lean toward her. She spoke in broken English. "Did you and your boyfriend…did something happen Friday at picture show when we no play baseball?"

Brandi's facial skin was burning. Her head was pounding.

"Just act like nothing happen." Mia was smiling.

Felicia put her phone back into her purse. "Brandi, you got attacked? Girl, are you okay?"

"Oh." Brandi sighed and placed her hands on her temples. "I guess the news is out. We wanted to keep it quiet as long as possible."

Mia and Felicia moved close. "What happened? Something about an attempted abduction at a theater?" Felicia asked. "I just now heard."

Brandi took a deep breath. "It made the Pittsburgh news yesterday — back page. Must have just now hit the national media. Hopefully, they haven't figured out that Cody was involved. I'm okay. It's just that —"

"Oh, you no look okay, Ms. Brandi."

"Yeah, girl, we need to get you outta here right now. Are you in more danger? Something about editorials you wrote? We should get you to a quiet place. I just now noticed the bruises."

"Crowds like this make me nervous ever since — I should go somewhere and get away from all these people."

"Well, honey, wherever you go, I'm goin' with you. You shouldn't be alone right now."

"Si, Señorita Brandi. Me too! I can carry Knoxi."

The three women made their way to the exit from Section 11. When they reached the top of the steps, Julia met them. "I just heard," Julia said. "Come on. Follow me."

Brandi introduced Felicia and Mia to Julia.

"I know a place," Julia announced. She led them to a popular sports bar located beyond left field, which featured twenty flat-screen televisions and an outdoor patio and bar with a perfect view of the game. They sat down, drank coffee, and talked while three more innings went by without a score.

Julia knew the story already, but the other two did not. Brandi spoke of her feelings for Cody and his invitation to Detroit.

Mia and Felicia sat mystified and tearful listening to Brandi's romantic story of rescue and love at first sight. Brandi was not accustomed to finding such love among other women her age. Most others had seemed jealous and competitive.

In the top of the eighteenth inning, Cody came to the plate with a runner on base. The four women turned toward the field to watch. On the first pitch, Cody lifted a high fly ball toward the left-field seats.

Brandi immediately realized it was headed their direction. She held her breath as the ball appeared larger and larger descending out of the sky. It struck the patio rail thirty feet in front of them and bounced high as it continued toward their table.

Her three friends scattered, but Brandi reached up and snagged the ball out of the air with her bare hand. The other three laughed and screamed as they reunited around Brandi with hugs and high fives.

"Girl, you made the play of the game!" Felicia was beaming.

The women glanced at one of the television monitors. The broadcast crew was showing replays of Brandi's catch. It was time to go. In only minutes, the patio would be overrun with media.

It was Cody's second home run of the game, and he had also hit for the cycle — single, double, triple and home run — a rare feat in baseball. The two-run homer had made the score 8 to 6 in favor of Houston.

Brandi and her three friends headed back to their stadium seats. It was the bottom of the eighteenth inning, the Pirates' last chance to either tie or win the game.

All the relief pitchers in the Astros bullpen had been used. Aging pitcher Sam McDonough had pitched the previous five innings for Houston and was tired. After two outs, the bases were loaded. The Astros just needed one more out, but McDonough was spent, and everybody knew it.

Astros manager Joe Moran walked to the mound, knowing he had no one left in the pen. Cody had done some pitching in college. Moran had asked him to pitch in another extra-inning game previously, and he had retired all three batters he had faced against the Los Angeles Angels. His fastball was clocked as high as 93 mph, and he had demonstrated a pretty good curve.

McDonough, the veteran, wanted to stay in the game, but Moran had seen enough. "Good job, Mac." He spat on the ground. "But we all know you got nothin' left."

Moran handed the ball to Cody. "It's all yours, Musket. Just one more out."

This was the last thing Cody wanted. He had been baffled when Brandi had reappeared at her seat with a baseball in her hand. Where had she been for the past three innings? Additional police had suddenly appeared on the field but would not tell him why. They looked nervous.

He knew who the next scheduled hitter was. Tanner stood in the on-deck circle swinging a bat, flexing his muscles and flashing his best Cap'n Sly grin.

Cody looked at Moran. "Why me, Skipper?"

Moran spit on the ground again. "Might as well show that lady in Section 11 what you got. I figure you're on a roll. She must be treatin' you right cuz you never swung the bat as good as you have the last two days. Fan this guy!"

The manager walked away, never looked back, but had one parting shot. "Don't let me see you wearing no pink dress after da game."

Veteran Astros catcher Mike Cannon sensed Cody's distraction and recognized the nearly impossible task thrust upon the rookie. He got in Cody's face to make him refocus.

"We're gonna stick with the heater, and don't under any circumstances shake me off, you feel me? Do I have your attention, rookie?"

"Got it!"

Cody took his allotted complement of warm-up pitches. He managed to get only one of them over the plate.

As Tanner stepped into the batter's box, he motioned for the next hitter, Kip Caldwell, who was now standing in the on-deck circle, to move back to the *safety* of the dugout. Caldwell played along. Tanner had briefed him about the on-deck story.

This ploy did not go unnoticed by Cody or Brandi. It made her smile, but she would not return Cody's glance. Cody looked toward the plate again. Glaring at him was Captain Sly, with the tight mustache, bulging shoulders, and that wicked grin, wielding his imposing Tanner McNair model thirty-four-inch bat with the dense head and custom tapered handle.

Cody's first pitch blazed over the inside corner of the plate just under the letters. Tanner's expression was one of shock. He remembered Cody could barely break 80 mph in high school. This pitch was a blur. He never even got the bat off his shoulder. The umpire yelled. "Strieeek one!"

Tanner and Cody both glanced at the radar screen — 92 mph. Cody refused to look back toward the plate, nor would he look at Brandi. He walked toward first base a few steps, removed his cap and wiped his eyes. The crowd was so quiet he could hear Sly's menacing chuckle.

Pirates' first-base coach Willie Moton had fun with it. "Trow dat agin! Trow dat pitch agin! Tanny gonna eat you lunch rookie! He-he! G'bye baseball! U gone be lookin' downtown, rookie! *Downtown!*"

Catcher Mike Cannon flashed the sign for another fastball, this time over the outside corner, but this 93 mph pitch cruised in over the heart of the plate. Tanner was ready. His swing was a thing of beauty, grace, and unbridled rage. The ball took off like a moonshot. Cody couldn't bear to look, but it passed inches outside the left field foul pole — strike two.

*"Time out!"* Cannon trudged back to the mound, his lip snarled, his mask resting on top of his head, and a dirty, sweaty smudge where the mask had pressed against the sides of his face for eighteen innings.

"Look, Musket, I know this guy is your childhood sweetheart, but you throw another one down the middle to him, and you and me gonna have problems. You think you can snap off the Charlie as good as you did in LA?"

"I can throw it," Cody assured, summoning all the gusto left in his tank.

Mike held his catcher's mitt over his mouth and scowled into Cody's face. "Okay. I need the curve in the dirt. In the dirt! You got that?"

"I got it!" Cody pounded his glove. "As good as done. Take it to the bank!"

Cannon turned to walk back toward the plate. He was grinning when the umpire met him halfway. "What the heck's so funny?"

The tired, smiling catcher shook his head and muttered. "No tellin' where this next friggin' pitch is goin'."

"You gonna warn Tanny?"

They walked back to the plate. "Watch yourself," Cannon said as he crouched behind Tanner for the next pitch.

The catcher called for the curve and swiped the dirt with his mitt as a reminder. The strategy was to throw it toward the middle of the plate and make it curve away and down into the dirt. This pitch, if thrown well, could fool a hitter into swinging over the ball.

Things did not go as planned. The ball started toward Tanner's shoulder. Expecting a fastball, he flinched away. As his knees buckled, the ball curved down over the center of the plate.

"Strieeeke three!"

Sly stood there in disbelief watching Cody high-five with his teammates. Finally, with his lethal bat still resting on his shoulder, he left his swagger at the plate, turned around, and lumbered back toward the Pirates dugout. Just before leaving the field, he splintered the bat over his knee. It took him three tries, but on the third, it snapped like a toothpick.

# BUSTED!

As the game ended, Brandi's close acquaintance, Vic Cantouri of the *Gazette*, pulled her aside. "Reporters are waiting at the top of the stairs to ask you to confirm that the guy in the video is Cody Musket."

"What? What video?"

"You haven't seen it? It's gone viral just in the last hour."

"I have been tied up for eighteen innings. What video?"

"Take a look." Vic pulled out his cell. A witness in the theater on Friday night had recorded the entire event on a smartphone.

"That's what the buzz was all about? It's hard to recognize Cody in that video," she insisted. "I know one thing. I can't watch it again."

Vic told her some other bad news, "Detective Dupree's wife has reported him missing."

"Missing? Are there any clues? Do they suspect foul play?"

"I don't know. So far no leads. His car was abandoned, so it doesn't look good. And by the way, do you know a twenty-two-year-old woman named Sasha Williams?"

"Don't know her, but I knew her sister, a former teammate at Stanford."

Vic showed her a brief text — *Sasha Williams, African American female, found dead in her apartment. Throat cut. Hands tied. Tortured.*

"What! Tortured?" Brandi looked around nervously. The crowd was pressing on her. "Um, any motive? Any suspects?" She clutched Knoxi to her chest with both hands.

"They have three suspects in custody. That's all I know."

Brandi's stomach was aflutter. *Detective Dupree missing? Sasha dead?*

*"Vic, I gotta find Cody. We must get out of this town."*

"Okay, okay. Just breathe slow. I'll help you. You think the murder of the Williams woman is related to your attack?"

"I dunno. I don't see how. But I must get my daughter away from here."

"Come down to field level. I can get you through with my pass, and we can avoid the press."

She followed and tried to call Cody. Her hands were shaking, so Vic punched the numbers for her.

"Come on, man of steel, please pick up! Come on Cody." She left voicemail. "Sweetie, we have big trouble. Call me back as soon as you get this, and whatever you do, avoid the pressroom. A video is making waves. *We're busted!"*

*   *   *

Cody already knew about the video. Players were watching it in the clubhouse. He called Brandi. "I think we're in deep trouble here."

"I know. I just voice mailed you."

"I'm expecting a call back from my agent. I wanna see how to handle this."

"Who's your agent?"

"Derek Tyler."

"You're kidding. The former Justice Department guy?"

"Same guy. Former Marine. Smart negotiator. Look, call Tanner and tell him what's up. We gotta figure a way out of town without facing the press. Wait, my agent's calling me back."

"Cody, Dupree is missing." Her voice trembled.

"When did you hear that?"

"Just now. Reliable source. Word is that his wife reported it today." Brandi was now light-headed.

"Slow down, you sound out of breath."

"Cody! You don't know what I've been through during the last five hours since you started playing your silly game. I also found out the sister of a former teammate at Stanford was murdered this morning."

"Okay, okay. Sorry. I guess we know why Dupree never called back. Listen to me, Brandi; breathe slower, otherwise you'll hyperventilate. Everything's gonna — I mean we're gonna get control of everything. You hear me?"

"Control of everything? How can you be so sure?" She exhaled slowly, regaining some poise. "Okay." She breathed a deep sigh. "Talk to your agent."

Just hearing Cody's concern calmed her. Vic ushered her into a private room and stayed with her to wait for Cody's call back.

Fifteen minutes later, her cell rang. "I talked to my agent."

"Well?"

"He said some lady at the outdoor pub caught my second home run. He was watchin' on TV. You got any idea who the lady was?"

"Did he give a description?"

"Yeah. He said she was hot."

"Well, it was pretty warm up there. We were sitting outside."

"I don't think that's what he meant."

"*Cody!* What about strategy? Get serious."

"He saw the video. Thinks we need to get out of town incognito. We can make a statement in Detroit tomorrow after we analyze the situation."

"So you still want me to go with you?"

"What? Of course. I…I mean, it's the best way to keep you safe."

"Okay. Security reasons. I get that. How are we going to sneak out of town without facing the press?"

"Cap'n Sly can think of somethin'."

"I see what you meant about adventures turning into nightmares."

Thirty-five minutes later, they drove away clean. The press was not aware of their plan to drive to Detroit, and had canvassed the airport instead. The McNairs had brought their three-year-old son Jeremy along.

As soon as Cody got into the Escalade, Tanner had words for him. "You struck me out!"

"Well, since I'm so humble I wasn't gonna say —"

"*You struck me out!* Your boyfriend with the mitt told me to watch myself, so I saw it comin' toward my chin and figured it was the high queso! Ain't gonna fool me next time!"

Cody scooted forward and leaned his head over the front seat. "Prolly won't be a next time. Just call it even."

"*Even? Call that even?* I hear you have a pink raincoat and pink rubber booties for your little feeties!"

When Cody glanced at Brandi, she hid her face. "You told these people? Do you know what they can do to me? How many other people have you told?"

"Nobody. I swear it. Well, 'cept Mama and Daddy." She giggled.

"*Your dad? You told Ray?*"

Sly was clearly out for revenge. "Someday, I gonna tell your grandkids how great you look in a pink raincoat and boots," he cackled as he turned onto the freeway. "*Ha-ha!* I gonna tell 'em you *turned pink* when you wore dem boots."

"Fine. So I'll tell *your* grandkids you *turned white* when I struck you out with my Uncle Charlie."

"Turn white? Me? I should stop this car right now!"

Cody leaned back in the seat and folded his arms. "Some other time, Sly. I'm too tired to get beat up. Just drive."

Julia looked back at Brandi with an "I told you so" expression. Brandi felt secure for the first time all day — something about being with Cody and his unhinged friends.

"Julia told me you boys could get quite colorful," Brandi snickered.

Julia slapped Tanner on the shoulder. "Now if you two adolescents can just stop fighting for a minute, these kids are hungry, and so are us girls. Let's hit a drive-thru."

Soon, after a fast meal, the toddlers fell asleep, and the grown-ups engaged in quiet conversation. Julia drove because fatigue had overtaken Tanner, and he could not keep his eyes open.

"Before you go to sleep, Tanner, there is something else Cody and I need to tell you both." Brandi finally spilled the story about the missing detective.

"Also," Brandi continued, "I got some other bad news. Sasha Williams, the younger sister of a former teammate at Stanford, was murdered in Pittsburgh this morning."

Cody widened his eyes and sat straight up. "Sasha? Her name was Sasha? Real pretty, about twenty?"

"She was twenty-two. Vic said she was tortured. You knew her?"

His eyes glassed over, face contorted.

"Cody, what's wrong?"

"It's my fault," he gritted. "She approached me Friday after you left." His dark eyes stared through the tinted window, his fists clenched, the back of his neck ablaze.

"Cody? What did she say? Was someone after her?"

He turned back toward her. "I may have gotten her killed. They must have seen her talking to me. I was just with her for a minute!" He put his hands over his ears. "*Nooo!*"

Cody erupted into a blind rage, flexing every muscle in his upper body like the Hulk. He pulled back his right fist as if to drive it through the glass window, but Brandi grabbed his forearm with both hands and held on with all her 130 pounds.

Julia swerved onto the shoulder and slammed the brakes. Cody got out and ran about fifty feet forward of the car and stopped beside the road.

A second later, he was bent over, his hands on his knees, vomiting. Brandi could only watch in shock, but now things started to add up.

"I get the feeling he was ready to do that all weekend, but he held back for my sake." Brandi was trembling and hoarse.

Tanner got out of the car and followed Cody cautiously. The two women watched as Tanner approached slowly and then put his arm around Cody's shoulders. In the headlights of the passing cars, they could see Tanner speaking, but had no idea what he was saying.

"I have never seen Cody blow up like that," Julia said. "But I do know about his nightmares. Counselors haven't been able to help. The problem is that he's alone even when he's with the team — no family, few real friends, little support, and he doesn't trust anyone." Julia wiped a tear from her eye.

"Now I understand why he's afraid," Brandi said, as she brushed hair out of her face that had been rustled when she had caught Cody's arm.

"Cody's afraid?" Julia was focused on her husband escorting Cody back toward the car.

"Something he said last night outside my room," Brandi answered. "Now I understand."

Julia looked back. "He's afraid he'll hurt you?"

Brandi nodded.

"It was a brave thing you did, grabbing his arm like that. You may have saved his baseball career. What if he had put his hand through that window?"

"I didn't think about it. I just grabbed his arm."

"You may not realize it, girl, but he could easily have thrown you through that glass. If you ask me, it wasn't your strength that stopped him. It was his own."

"You mean —"

"I mean he stopped himself because you were the one holding on to him."

The two somber men arrived back at the car and got in. As Julia pulled onto the highway, Cody was apologetic.

"I'm sorry. The people I touch. Bad things happen. She was so . . . so sweet, so pure. She was crying. I wish I had at least hugged her. I started to but —"

Cody turned his head toward the window, held his hand over his eyes, and shed tears he could no longer restrain. It was awkward for him to show emotion, so Brandi nestled next to him, leaned her head on the back of his shoulder and held him.

"You are with people who love you, Cody. We feel your pain, but it wasn't your fault."

A sanguine smile eased across Julia's lips as she beheld the scene in the rearview mirror. Brandi's heart was on full display. It was breaking. Breaking in a good way. Julia tried not to watch, but couldn't help herself. She reached over and took Tanner's hand.

Cody and Brandi finally leaned against the back cushion. The two children in the utility seat behind them had slept through it all. Cody was exhausted and fell asleep. Brandi never closed her eyes.

# CAMELOT

The travelers arrived at the Great West Casino Hotel in Detroit at 1:00 a.m. The eighteen-inning game had so depleted the guys that they had to be awakened. The two children had never even moved a muscle.

By Monday morning, the media worldwide had identified the "hero" in the video as Cody Musket. Cody received a call from his agent at 8:30 a.m. Derek's take was that the video might not be a bad thing.

Derek Tyler, brilliant, fast-talking, had been one of the 400 officers serving in the Judge Advocate Division of the US Marine Corps. After his military career, he had become a civilian advisor to the Justice Department. Six years later, he became a sports agent and worked his way to the top of the food chain.

Derek told Cody his strategy. "I spoke to a former associate in the DOJ. He said human traffickers like to operate under the radar, to stay out of the news. Anonymity and public apathy are their two greatest allies.

"Look. What you and Brandi have going now is what traffickers hate. The last thing the bad guys want is to harm you and get grassroots America angry enough to pressure authorities into doing something. So, the more popular you get, the better. How serious are you about this chick, anyway? I mean where are you going with this?"

"You never know. But I mean I really like her."

"Okay, the media's gonna love this." Derek's words rolled off his tongue at warp speed. "You meet this peach by chance at the movie. She's being abducted by some creeps in masks. You show up outta nowhere and save her, and then disappear like the humble guy you are! This is Chuck Norris in a baseball cap. This…this is Batman, the Cape, uh, uh, you know, rough justice American style. What movie did you go to see anyway?"

"Superman."

"Are you kiddin' me? Superman?" He tuned up the pitch. "This is over the top — like mild-mannered girl reporter meets real man of steel at the Superman movie. Are you feelin' this? Those traffickers aren't gonna touch this! I assume this girl is pretty?"

"Like right out of *Song of Solomon*," Cody answered. "You remember the lady that caught the ball that —"

"What song?"

"*Song of Solomon*. It's from the Bible."

"The Bible?! Are you tellin' me she looks like a nun?"

"Com'on Derek. You're brilliant, and you're telling me you never read *Song of Solomon*? You know the lady who caught my home run ball? That was Brandi. It was all over ESPN last night."

"No way! This is going stratospheric! Does she already have an agent?"

"Come on, Derek."

"She must be good for you, hitting for the cycle yesterday and picking up a save to boot. I bet your good buddy Tanner wasn't happy about striking out. And she caught your home run? I can see this Solomon lady's gonna be *gooood* for business!"

As soon as the call ended, Cody checked the time. He didn't know if Brandi would be awake. He tapped on her door.

She swung it open. "Take a look at this." The seventy-two-inch flat screen was beaming the story that was spreading across the nation. "We're cooked."

"Not necessarily." Cody gave her his agent's opinion about traffickers wanting to remain under the radar. "Derek thinks we should schedule a news conference for today. The more publicity we generate with this, the better."

"Well, those guys that attacked me didn't mind spitting out who they were, warning everybody in the theater about going against them. That's not what I call operating in the shadows."

"Yeah, good point, but —"

"Makes you wonder whether your agent is right." She turned back to the screen again. "But the news conference can't hurt," she said. "The public already knows who we are, so we don't gain anything by remaining silent."

"Let's do it." Cody banged his fist into his palm. "Two o'clock this afternoon. I'll make it happen."

"Cody, I — Nothing, never mind."

She ambled over to the window and opened the curtains. He joined her. The view was magnificent. The morning sun was brilliant in a cloudless sky. From the twentieth floor, they could see Comerica Park a few blocks away, the site where the All-Star Game would unfold.

A huge Ferris wheel with baseball-shaped gondolas stood out like a giant punctuation mark for the massive stadium. Thousands of summer vacationers covered the amusement area like tiny sugar ants.

Cody leaned his back against the wall, dropped his head, and put his hands in his front pockets — his standard body language prior to revealing deep thought. She waited.

"About what happened in the hallway Saturday night —"

"No need to apologize, Cody. I must learn when to keep my mouth shut." She walked toward the bathroom.

"No, no. Sometimes I just—" He wavered.

She stopped and looked back. "Sometimes you just —?  Just what?"

"Uh. I mean I'm glad you're here."

"I know. I know. Security reasons, of course." She shrugged.

"Uh, yeah. Right. Better to keep you safe."

She continued to the bathroom and closed the door.

\*　　\*　　\*

After lunch, Cody and Brandi continued edgy. Twenty minutes before the conference, sitting in the suite discussing strategy with Brandi, Cody became extremely agitated and began to pace back and forth.

"Cody, what's wrong?"

"Are you kidding? Everything! Are you sure you wanna go through with this? I mean once this news conference is over, things will never be the same. What if it backfires?"

"So what are you saying? You brought me all the way to Detroit to tell me you're getting cold feet? This morning, you were all cranked up about it. The news conference was *your* idea, your agent's brilliant plan!"

"I need a minute." He started toward the door.

"Where are you going?"

"I'll meet you downstairs in the conference room." He opened the door and left.

She plopped down on the end of the bed and hurled her flip-flops at the door behind him. *I'm going to the news conference if it kills me. Don't care if he shows up or not.*

Minutes later, the press gathered in the Rose Calley Room on the ground floor. Brandi was escorted to the head table. Microphones were set up for the couple, but Cody was a no-show. She fidgeted nervously. Finally, seven minutes late, Cody slipped into the room and took his place next to her.

She covered her mic. "Nice of you to join us. Where have you been?"

"Tell you later," he said under his breath. "Let's just get this over with." He leaned toward his microphone, apologized to everyone, and welcomed them.

They had prepared a statement about the attempted abduction. The major points of it were these:

(1) The two had never met prior to the incident.

(2) Neither of them was significantly injured.

(3) The attack against Brandi was an act of terrorism and cowardice.

Cody read the statement. Brandi added her perspective. "The first thing I did was call out loudly for help. That is what anyone should do when attacked. I also prayed. And I do not believe it was an accident that Cody showed up." She looked at Cody. He looked straight ahead.

The floor was opened for questions.

Jon Tsipras of *Global Press* had the first. "I have a question for each of you. First of all, Brandi, did you bring your Cody Musket souvenir baseball with you?"

Chuckles circulated through the room.

"I guard it with my life. Trying to get the nerve to ask him for his autograph. It's exciting to finally make it to *Baseball Tonight.*" Replays of her catch had been shown among the baseball highlights on sports networks ever since the game Sunday.

It was her first exposure to these reporters. She was witty and articulate. Writers showed their appreciation with laughter and applause.

Tsipras followed up. "Cody, were you and you alone the only person standing between Ms. Barnes and her attackers? And, oh yes, are you going to sign Brandi's baseball?"

Cody decided to play along. "Baseball? What baseball?" He turned toward Brandi. "Is that the ball I saw you with yesterday?" Loud chuckles turned the gathering into lighthearted fun.

She reached into her purse underneath the table, pulled out the ball, and presented it to him with a pen. He snatched it and signed it. This brought more laughter and applause. Cody then became uneasy. Serious questions would follow, and he hoped that everyone could change gears to grasp the severity.

"In answer to your other question, Jon —"

"What was my other question? Does anyone remember?" More laughter followed.

Mary Ann Baker of ESPN asked about Cody's self-defense training.

Cody told of his years of training but pointed out that he had tried to scare off the attackers by telling them police were on the way. He also said that Navy SEALs had taught him to never enter a dangerous situation unless he believed he could finish it.

Martin Hardy of ABC News asked. "When you entered the situation, did you, in fact, believe you could finish it?"

"I couldn't allow myself to believe otherwise. Most men I've encountered who cover their faces are not the bravest guys around. They usually run in packs, and they're uncomfortable unless numbers are heavily in their favor."

This brought loud applause and smiles. It was a great live sound bite. Cody had set the stage by playing along with the baseball joke, and now he had dug a deeper hole. If only he could retract what he had just said — not a great start.

Another reporter spoke up. "Melvin Bonner, *Aurora Media Group.* Since the scare tactic didn't work, would you say, Cody, that the three attackers misjudged you?"

"I think the three-to-one odds gave them confidence, so I guess the answer would be *yes.* Of course, they could've been smoking something."

Now the guffaws and cackles ruled the room. Things were out of hand. Maybe he should've asked Derek to fly to Detroit and sit with him on the podium. These were serious matters, but he had not stuck to the script. *Why do I make people laugh when I don't intend to, and bore them when I try to say something funny?*

Brandi placed her hand on his forearm. Cody read her eyes and nodded — "Go ahead."

Brandi nearly swallowed her mic. "I'd like to weigh in, if I may." She briefly covered her mouth and flinched as she cleared her throat. A sudden quietness embraced the gathering. She adjusted her distance from the microphone, and her words became crystal clear.

"Some have claimed that the video looks like a television violence scene, but TV doesn't have the impact of reality. I was just inches from being dragged away, never to be seen again in one piece. My feet, legs, arms, neck, and other places I cannot mention are bruised, lacerated, and painful as I speak.

"They ripped my clothing, verbally assaulted me, tried to take away my humanity, my femininity. I was an object, slammed and tossed around with less respect than a sack of horse manure." She winced, cleared her throat again, and took a sip of water.

Correspondents were motionless. As America watched, Brandi composed herself, looked straight into the camera, and took another deep breath.

"I am troubled in my sleep. I am frightened of shadows. A loud noise makes me jump. I barely hold it together at a ballgame because crowds terrify me. All day long, I have the urge to get into the shower and try again to wash those men off me. I cannot imagine the things I would have endured if — And I…I have a little girl who needs me. She's not quite two years old."

When she had finished, the air was too heavy to breathe. Network crews refocused their cameras to isolate her face. Poise, charm, brutal honesty — Brandi owned the room.

Cody's blue eyes were larger than poker chips. When he delicately took her hand and gazed into Brandi's face, the sudden flush upon her cheeks went unnoticed by no one. It drove the oxygen right out of the building. Forget about traffickers and hit men. The best story was sitting right before them.

Daisy Baird of *Women's Family Culture Magazine* inquired as to Brandi's opinion on waiting until marriage for sex. She cited statements Brandi had made in one of her earlier published editorials.

"Sure. Okay." Brandi told about the abusive relationship that had nearly cost her life and about her decision to return to the Christian values her parents had bestowed.

"I realized that I had been searching for the wrong things in a relationship. For men, love can sometimes be a recreation or an episode. But for me, love is not something I can turn on and off. I need more than just physical intimacy to be whole. I need the security of lifetime commitment, and I can feel safe only with a man who shares my values and who loves me enough to make me his wife before we occupy the same bed."

A soft applause slowly made its way through the room.

"I can speak for Cody and myself when I say that we do not wish to judge anyone else, but at the same time, we would ask that others simply respect our values."

Now the applause was robust. Brandi was not the sort to tap-dance around the issues. Cody stood up and asked for quiet. The room hushed when he turned to face her again.

"So you're speakin' for me now?" Cody folded his arms. "Thank God. Somebody needs to."

Rousing acclamation burst forth and continued as the two worked their way to the exit, shaking hands and thanking everyone.

Cody's cell rang. "You guys were electric! Hey, slugger! What was the name of that Solomon song you told me about?" Derek was certain his strategy would work.

The couple was escorted back to their suite. The next few hours would reveal initial reactions to their first public appearance. Brandi dozed with Knoxi while Cody napped in the next room.

They were awake when it was time for the six o'clock news and were surprised to learn that the televised news conference had already created national headlines. Brandi's stunning transparency, having exposed her personal struggle, trusting millions of viewers with her story, and Cody's reaction, esteeming her to the world, had stirred thousands of grassroots Americans.

Ronald Kingsley of *Deep in The Heart* magazine told it best —

> *"After Brandi had revealed all, killing us softly with a near-fatal dose of bare reality, Cody took her hand and looked into her eyes. We, along with the rest of America, held our collective breath. Would he kiss her? Not one of us would have blamed him for loving her with all his soul. It felt like Camelot reborn."*

# WHAT PLANET ARE YOU FROM?

Sitting in their suite, Cody and Brandi watched the news story unfold in living color while nibbling at room service. Cody got up and paced. Brandi sat on the couch with arms folded.

"I don't wanna see any more," she said. "Just turn it off. They make us out to be two perfect people living in some sort of la-la land. Is this the way it's gonna always be? Is this your agent's brilliant plan? Armed bodyguards following us and standing outside our door? I feel shut in."

Cody made no comment. Instead, he switched channels and sat back down. The televised Home Run Derby was in progress — baseball — his standard escape from troubling realities. The Derby is a popular event the night before the All-Star Game. Players with hefty home run totals are invited to participate. Cody had been asked, but had opted out because of exhaustion, and because the cut on his left arm, which Brandi had stitched, was now red and puffy.

He had seen a doctor after the news conference. Antibiotics and at least 24 hours of rest were the physician's orders.

During breaks in the action, the network showed segments from the press conference along with highlights from Brandi's basketball career and Cody's baseball exploits.

The coverage of Brandi's eighteenth-inning catch in Pittsburgh had spawned a life of its own. The spin was that Brandi had gone to the left-field pavilion to inspire Cody to hit a home run to her and win the game. Brandi's one-handed catch above the bleachers completely overshadowed

Cody's improbable game-ending strikeout of Tanner McNair, one of the premiere hitters in baseball.

The media had now branded them the latest *hot couple* — two faultless people living the ultimate fantasy. Creating a fairy tale was the last thing they had wanted, and tonight they could think of nothing to say to each other.

Brandi now understood Cody's last-minute reluctance to host a media conference, but she was troubled by his alternating explosive-reclusive behavior, and was uncomfortable with someone whose intentions she couldn't read. He was charming, warm, and articulate, but at times stiff and unknowable, with a personality about as engaging as a chunk of Pennsylvania bituminous coal.

Soon, sitting on the sofa across from him, Brandi reached her limit. Stress, physical injuries, fatigue — she ached all over and wanted to excuse herself.

"You wanna keep Knoxi company while I bathe?" She winced after she had spoken. How would Cody fare alone with her toddler for the first time?

He nodded to her while he was glued to the screen watching the Derby. Tanner was taking his turn at the plate.

"Cody, did you understand what I just asked? Hello? Are you listening?"

"Yeah, yeah. I got this."

"*You got this?* Is that *all* you can say? I'd really like to have a few minutes alone to relax. Are you okay being *totally* responsible for her?"

"I mean I got this. Go ahead." He looked at the screen. "Attaboy, Sly!" He turned to Brandi. "Did you see that?"

"*Never mind!* I'll just put her in the bath with me." She attempted to pick up Knoxi, but the little scrambler ran toward Cody and clutched his pants leg.

The tiny girl flashed her huge eyes at Cody, who finally reached down and lifted her up. "See, I told you. We got this." He looked at the toddler. "Isn't that right, baby girl?"

"Her name is Knoxi." She put hands on hips and tapped her foot. "Now listen to me. If she cries or if she even —"

"What is it about '*I got this*' that you don't get?"

Brandi was quiet. Indecision was written on every centimeter of her face. He toned it down. "I can handle it, okay? We'll do fine." He offered her a confident smile.

"All right. But you come get me if anything . . . I mean, just knock on the door, okay?"

Brandi hesitated, then disappeared into the bathroom. Knoxi was crazy about Cody, but he seemed disinterested. Would her daughter eventually get her heart broken? Would Knoxi cry as soon as she realized her mother had departed the room? She left the bathroom door open about an inch — a tiny space through which any sound of travail could make its way to her attentive ears.

Something was certain to go wrong. Cody could handle himself with bad guys and ballplayers, but little girls didn't seem to be his specialty. *I have a bad feeling about this.*

But when she slipped into the whirlpool, she lost herself in the soothing bubbles and soft currents. Time spent alone was rare for a caring single mom. She would wash her hair, do her nails, and thank God for a few moments during which she could be caressed by the water and pamper herself.

In the next room, Knoxi yawned. Cody quietly took her into the adjoining bed chamber, sat down on the bed, and placed her on his lap. He put her head on his shoulder in an awkward attempt to get her to sleep, but she was more fascinated by his nose and wanted to squeeze it with her fingers.

Finally, he reached into his back pocket and pulled out a folded sheet of paper. "I wrote this for you after the news conference today. This will be *our* secret, okay?"

The feisty girl displayed the peaches-and-cream dimples that she had inherited from her mother. Her wide eyes fixated upon his hands as he unfolded the paper and began to read.

His raspy voice made her smile. She placed her hand on his mouth and wrapped her fingers inside his lower lip as if to absorb through her touch the words he had written.

> "Hey there, beautiful,
> Steal my breath away.
> Joy by surprise
> Looking straight into my eyes
> And you're so beautiful.
> Surely goodness and mercy will follow you
> All the days of your life.
> There'll be no mountain so high
> That you cannot one day climb
> For you are the apple of the Father's eye.
> Hey there, beautiful,
> Here's to you, my little princess.
> May the echoes of today
> Love's promise softly lite your way.
> Hey there, beautiful, hey, hey."

When he had finished, she was asleep, her head on his shoulder.

He placed her on the bed and covered her. "You never know," he said quietly. "One of these days, you're gonna talk so much you won't know when to shut up, just like your mom."

Then he turned and saw Brandi standing in the doorway. Dripping wet hair, glassy eyes, and wearing a full-length kimono, her delicately-drawn smile left no doubt — she had heard every word. He folded the poem and stuffed it into his shirt pocket.

Like a pawn in the presence of a queen he stepped timidly toward her. "I . . . didn't mean that like it —" He paused. "Uh, did you know that Albert Einstein's mom thought he was retarded cuz it took him several years to learn how to talk?"

Brandi stared at him like a calf looks at a new gate. Her lips spoke not a word. She fashioned a dry towel around her head to cover her just-washed hair and never took her eyes off him.

Cody hung his thumbs on his front pockets. "Uh, how long have you been standing there?" He waited. Would she at least make a sound?

Sheepishly he dropped his eyes toward the floor. The ends of her wet hair had dripped onto the carpet, leaving a trail behind her all the way to the bathroom. Her slender pink toes, with newly polished Tangerette-Pearl nails, peeked out from below the hem of her robe. A scab that reminded him of a saddle rode atop her left big toe, courtesy of her Friday-night tormentors.

At last, she focused on the folded paper in his breast pocket, held out her palm, and snapped her fingers. He handed it over.

Brandi opened it and silently stared at the crumpled page. Her ocean-blue eyes became moist, her nose blush red.

Finally, she looked up. "What planet are you from, Cody Musket? You may be a son of the thunder where you came from, but not in my world. You don't fool me for a second, but I still can't figure you out." She tilted her head. "That doesn't make sense, does it?"

"No sense at all," he said. "But I prefer *your* world."

"Good night, man of steel." She stepped aside to let him through the door and then caught his arm as he passed. Her wistful eyes blinked twice like a puppy dog pleading to be held. "Cody, I —" She never finished.

"I know." He nodded. "Good night, Brandi Barnes."

\*    \*    \*

Cody awoke before dawn. The digital clock beside his bed told him it was 0530. He turned over. Just then, he was startled to hear a child screaming. The sound was bloodcurdling. At first it was far away, and then close — in the hallway outside his room.

He tried to kick the covers off and run to the door, but he couldn't move. Suddenly, he heard a crash. Three men wearing turbans had burst into the room. They smelled like burning flesh.

They pulled him from the bed and dragged him to the door. He looked out and saw at least five hundred people standing in the hallway of the Marriott with raised arms, shouting, "Death to America! Death to Americans!"

He was on fire. His body felt the sting of ten thousand whips, though no one had touched him. His lower right leg was burned beyond recognition. He could see cuts and burns all over his body. His thirst was unbearable.

Then he looked down to discover that the hallway had morphed into a dusty gravel road — the only passage through a small village — the same street in which the goats and fowl defecated.

The crowd moved back as his abductors threw him into the dirt. Hundreds of voices screamed in a dialect he had never heard. The howling mob was feeding off the collective rage. He would surely be torn apart within moments.

They dragged him through the filth and gravel toward a structure on the other side of the street. He heard the sorrowful sobs of children but couldn't see them.

Just then, a terrified teenage girl was dragged before him. She was screaming, crying, naked, staring through gray eyes nearly swollen shut, abandoned to evil with none to deliver her. He reached his hand toward her. She should at least know someone felt her pain. They threw her upon him.

Suddenly, hatred and rage overtook him. He was the target of a thousand curses, but he lifted his voice and wailed.

*"Oh, God, don't let me die this way! Help me save the kids! Send in the SEALs!"*

His words rang through the village and echoed off the walls of his twentieth-floor suite. Brandi sat straight up. She flew out of the bed and ran into his room. He lay underneath the coffee table in a fetal position, his hands covering his ears.

"Cody! Cody, can you hear me? You're having a bad dream. *Wake up!"*

*"You heard me, Sergeant! Get those kids outta there!"*

Then he screamed like a scalded beast and clutched his left knee. He tried to rise but banged his head on the underside of the table. He fell back to the floor and then crawled away, dragging his left leg as the table fell in the opposite direction. He collapsed temporarily, writhing and coughing.

Brandi wanted to run to the other room and get her phone to call Tanner, but she dare not leave Cody alone. She couldn't control the shaking of her hands and thus doubted she could even manage a call.

Cody began to sob. He moaned out chilling words. "Pleeeese, God. No. Pleeeese, God. I gotta end their misery. *Noooooo!"*

She despaired. *Oh, God, what can I do?* She remembered what Julia had said to her — *"He stopped himself because you were the one holding on to him."*

Something evil was in the air. It smelled like a burning, rotting carcass. Brandi fought the panic as she knelt and spoke tenderly. "Cody? It's Brandi. Cody? I'm here." She wrapped her tremoring arms around his midsection as he crawled again. His shirt was soaked. He stopped when his head bumped into the kitchenette wall, then sat up and looked at her.

His eyes were tearful, wild, distant. *"Brandi?"*

He reached out and clung to her like a drowning man clutching a float. In a few seconds, he leaned back against the wall and rubbed his eyes.

"How long have you been here? Is Knoxi okay?" His breathing was labored, his speech slurred.

"Cody, how often does this happen?"

"How bad was it?" he asked, holding his hand over his forehead.

"How bad? Your head is bleeding if that's any indication. Have you sought help for this?"

"Doesn't seem like it." He lowered his hand, now bloody from touching his forehead. "I recognize your shirt — 'I Love the Son.'"

"Let me help you back to bed and clean up your head. I'm gonna stay with you, okay?"

The stench was gone. In a few moments, Cody was asleep again. She went to her room, checked on Knoxi, got dressed, and returned. She dozed in the recliner beside his bed until he awoke at 9:00 a.m.

When he finally opened his eyelids, Knoxi had wandered into the room and had climbed into her mother's lap.

He rubbed sleep from his eyes. "Good to see — Uh, what're y'all doin here?"

"How much do you remember?" she asked.

He lay on his back and stared at the ceiling. "Too much. Not enough." He rose to one elbow. "But you didn't have to stay in here. I would've been okay."

"Cody, I'm not a therapist, but I know that something is locked away inside your conscience that needs to escape. It tries to come out in your sleep while your defenses are down. Maybe if you could just tell someone everything you can remember, the night sweats and bad dreams would leave you alone."

Cody lay back down and stared upward again. "You never know, but we'll talk about it later."

\*    \*    \*

By daybreak, segments from the media conference had been beamed across the free world. Networks and social media could not get enough of the couple. Candy Mack of *Valley Fervor* wrote, "*There are two things you can't hide — sneezing and romance.*"

Fox Sports analyst Jesse Franklin referred to the couple as "Brandi and the Babe," inserting Cody's military call sign. It caught on.

Individually, Brandi's face had appeared on every news outlet in America. The *San Diego Pacific News* declared Brandi Barnes to be "an overnight international celebrity, whose beauty, transparency and savvy have given a major news story legs — literally."

The *Pittsburgh Post-Gazette* compared her to Jacqueline Kennedy. "*The story of Brandi and the Babe is a match made in heaven, certain to become immortalized.*"

In the Tuesday edition of *The New York Times,* one writer declared, "*She is a Pennsylvania girl who refuses to be a victim, destined to become the most admired woman in America.*"

And Cody was the man of the hour, the guy with the powerful, compact swing both on the baseball diamond and when knocking out bad guys. *Crack! Bam! Oof!* The media hailed him as the union of two superheroes — Batman and Ted Williams.

Reporters researched the details of his short Medal-of-Honor career. Questions arose as to how one could be discharged from the military, having been declared physically disabled, and then just four years later, play in a major league all-star game.

But instead of questioning his integrity, they called it a modern-day miracle.

Even some backwater tabloids abandoned their usual practice of manufacturing sordid details. The real story was better. The media saw dollars. No one wanted to discredit him. It was money in the bank for Cody Musket to be a good man — the American hero everyone wanted to believe in, a distinction Cody feared the most.

The Major League All-Star Game was a destination he could never have imagined at the start of the season while playing third base at Corpus Christi. And how could he have stumbled into ones so priceless as Brandi and Knoxi?

Good things were not supposed to happen to him. Surely it would end in disaster. After the miraculous healing of his leg, why couldn't he have the faith Brandi has?

He told her he trusted God. But did he? If he couldn't trust God with his past, how could he trust God for a future?

He had promised to tell Brandi everything, but he was terrified, afraid of remembering the missing details, but afraid of *not* remembering. He was afraid of committing to her, and afraid of *not* committing.

Would she be disappointed if she knew what he knew? The last few days had been as close to heaven as he could imagine. Could he bear to lose it now?

Three hours before game time, Cody's cell rang. He was in the American League clubhouse, preparing for pregame activities. Brandi's voice was hoarse and uneasy.

"Cody, Dupree is dead. He was found face-down in the Monongahela."

# JUNGLE DAWG NIGHT

T
he annual Major League All-Star Game allows elite players who compete against each other all season to be teammates for one evening that celebrates their accomplishments. Dugout joviality rules the pregame.

Most players did not know Cody because he had not been around long enough, but they had seen the theater video. Some would not come near him at first, but Sly had covertly spread the word that Cody was not looking to smash any mouths or break any necks, and needed as many new friends as he could get.

Players began to reach out, and Cody's friendly response brought on the trash talking — mostly about his hot woman friend. He returned the barbs and began to engage. He was not in the starting lineup for the game but was invigorated by friendship and camaraderie with these great athletes.

Sitting in the dugout, he pondered the dangers ahead. Had the men in black paid the detective a visit? Would they dare attack at a ballpark? Who were they working for? What would Sasha's killers reveal when questioned?

He scanned the stadium. Would another shoe fall during this game like it had Sunday in Pittsburgh?

In the eighth inning, with the score tied, Angels Manager, Bo Phelps, the American League skipper, called out to Cody.

"Musket, grab your bat. You're hittin' for Castillo this inning."

Cody headed to the on-deck circle. Moments later, with his team trailing by a run, he stepped to the plate with a runner at third base and two outs. Pitcher Adrian Lotus of the Saint Louis Cardinals struck him out on a slider low and away, and Cody was through for the night.

*   *   *

After the game, Detroit police escorted Cody off the field and into the home team clubhouse. After he had showered, he dressed in his street clothes and then learned that at least fifty reporters were waiting for him outside the dressing room.

He called Brandi. "Where are you?"

"Julia and I are still in VIP parking, fighting traffic."

"I'm hiding in the clubhouse. Must be a million reporters on the other side of the door. Dunno how I'm gonna get outta here."

"We're listening to CNN in the car. The FBI has taken over the investigation of Dupree's death. They think it may be related to my attack. That's what has the press stirred up tonight."

Just then, Cody heard a loud, booming exclamation behind him. "*Snap ding, yo!*" He turned around.

"*Dawg?* What're you doing here?" Cody yelled. "I thought you were in Mexico." Then he put his phone back to his ear. "Brandi, I'll call you back. An old college buddy just walked in. Tanner is right behind him showin' his Cap'n Sly face. Must be cookin' somethin' up."

JD Blue, former Baylor All-American basketball player, had returned three days early from a trip south of the border. Tanner had walked behind him into the clubhouse but was hidden at first behind JD's imposing six-foot-ten, 290-pound frame. After six years in the NBA, JD was now a megastar with the Detroit Pistons.

"Hello, my brotha Cody! How long's it been?"

"Too long!" Cody answered. "And speakin' of *too long,* I see you haven't gotten any shorter since the last time we saw each other."

"And I see you still ain't tall enough to reach da toppa you own head! Tanny cawled me and said you might need some help gettin' outta here. I was already here, man. I was sittin' right behind da dugout for da game. You didn't see me? Man, dis here my playground now. I'm tight wid evabody here."

JD was a great athlete and wannabe entertainer. Despite his upbringing in the hard streets of New Orleans, he spoke as articulately as any head of state and was fluent in Spanish and French. He could speak like a New England-born Harvard professor, but liked to talk in his "native language"— a well-oiled New Orleans drawl — which he preferred in public. His favorite act was to unexpectedly switch back and forth with his speech styles to the delight of friends and fans.

"Put dese on, man. You know what a hawd time I had findin' gear shawt enough fo you?" He handed Cody a pair of Detroit Pistons warm-up pants, matching jersey, and a motorcycle helmet with a hand-painted pink heart on the side. The paint was still wet.

Cody pitched his eyes toward Tanner. The pink paint was a dead giveaway. Whatever these two were planning had Sly's signature all over it.

"Change into this Pistons gear," Sly swagged. "You gonna be Dawg's bodyguard. You got that?"

"What? You kidding? *I'm* the one who needs a bodyguard!"

"Come on, will you just listen for a minute? You gonna escort JD to his bike, and then y'all gonna meet me and the girls at the hotel. Smoooth as cake, man!"

Cody shook his head. Cap'n Sly was living the dream — anything deceptive or underhanded, especially for a good cause.

Then Dawg switched gears. "You had better be a good actor, Cody, because this is one of Sly's most ingenious flashes of romantic deception ever to be perpetrated upon Homo sapiens since women got the right of suffrage in the state of Texas! And, in case you didn't understand all that,

Homo sapiens is the binomial nomenclature for the human species, and suffrage means —"

"Yeah, yeah. I know all that." Cody waved him off. "You haven't changed much." He had forgotten how wide Dawg's face could get when he grinned that way. "You better not let that wife of yours hear you talk about women's voting like that."

Cody called Brandi back and told her what was happening.

"How would you like to meet Jungle Dawg?"

"JD Blue? Detroit Pistons? You know him?"

"Yep! I'll introduce you. You won't have to get very close to him though cuz his arms are long enough for you to shake hands with him across the room."

Cody donned the gear, including the helmet, and then he and JD went out the door.

"Make way, make way for Mr. Blue," Cody said. "Excuse us. No, Mr. Blue will not be taking questions right now. Make way. Excuse us. No interviews, no autographs." The disguise worked.

Finally, they mounted JD's fourteen-foot-long custom-built Harley, navigated out of the stadium lot, and rumbled toward the hotel. It was the biggest bike Cody had ever seen. They cruised into the casino parking area and loaded the bike into JD's trailer, which Silverbelle, his wife, had just brought to the hotel. Cody invited them up to his suite.

JD's real name was John David, but the Baylor fans called him "Jungle Dawg" because of his dogged tenacity on the basketball court. The nickname, which matched his initials and his physical assets, had also caught on in Detroit and with the national media.

One ESPN columnist, pointing out that JD had founded nonprofit organizations to feed the homeless, house orphans, and provide literacy programs, had declared that his heart was as big as his hands.

Silverbelle was two years older than her husband. She was a master of finance and was the creator and spokesperson for the couple's three charitable foundations. At five foot ten with a photogenic smile, she had become a front-page favorite, having appeared on several women's magazine covers.

They entered the hotel through a back entrance and then took the service elevator to the twentieth floor where they joined the others in Cody's suite.

"*Ha-ha!* How you doin' my man? I see you survived the ride." Tanner slapped Cody on the back and then flashed his sly grin around the room.

"That was quite an act you boys pulled off." Julia sported a grin of her own, making eye contact with JD and Cody but *not* with her husband.

"Yep, Cap'n Sly strikes again." Cody bumped knuckles with Sly. "That was definitely one of your better ones."

Sly looked at Julia. "Man, that ain't nothin' compared to what I got planned for later on when —"

"A'right, a'right. Before you go completely funky on us, we all appreciate your unique skills, sugarplum. And we all love you for it, especially me." Julia kissed her husband on the cheek.

Brandi opened the drapes, unveiling a magnificent cityscape. The large room and death-defying view were perfect for hosting friends at midnight. They munched from a massive fruit basket, courtesy of management.

After thirty minutes, the ladies became weary of hearing the men swap sports stories, so the conversation turned to more serious matters.

"Cody, when Silver called me and said you were shot down, I was at Charlotte in the playoffs. It was halftime, and we were gettin' ready to go back on da court. I gathered my teammates around, and we said a prayer for you, man. Right there in the locker room, man. *Sweeeet!*"

"I knew you'd be there for me, Dawg. I felt it."

Brandi's emotions were getting away from her again. Silverbelle noticed. "So, Brandi, you're goin' back to Pittsburgh tomorrow?"

Brandi glanced at Cody, who hastily took her hand. "I've asked her to go with me to Houston," Cody said, "but we need to go through Pittsburgh tomorrow and get some of her stuff out of the apartment first."

Dawg's face came alive. "*Snap ding!* We gonna hear 'bout weddin' bells purdy soon?"

Brandi's face flushed, but Cody masterfully resorted to his standard response, "You never know."

They decided to break it up just after 1:30 a.m. Silver hugged Brandi and then Cody. "Don't stay away so long, Cody. Come see us, and bring Brandi with you. We used to be really tight. We're still your friends, you know."

"Roger that," Cody said. After handshakes and hugs all around, the two guest couples left the room.

Sly and Julia had decided to leave their son in the room since both toddlers were snug asleep on the foldout bed. Cody followed them down the hall a few feet to ask if they would keep Knoxi the next morning after breakfast so that he and Brandi could talk. They agreed.

When Cody reappeared, Brandi had his phone. "Sweetie, you must have ten text messages here. They are from two different people — Chavez and Sabre."

"Don't worry about reading my text messages." He grumbled as he took the phone back from her. "Let's just get some rest. I'm wrecked."

"I'm a big girl, Cody. I'm guessing these are people you served with, right? And they want to help?"

"They want to get involved if I say the word." Cody took a deep breath. "When I disappeared before the news conference yesterday, I went to call them. That's why I was AWOL."

"Involved? How involved? You mean like bodyguards?"

"Maybe."

Brandi glanced at the two toddlers asleep on the foldout. "Do you sometimes wish you could go back to their age and start over? Don't you wish we could've met under other circumstances?"

"We don't get to choose the circumstances." He sat down on the sofa. "We can only choose where we go from here." Cody stared at the floor.

She waited a moment, then sat next to him and changed the subject.

"I enjoyed meeting Dawg and Silver. They love you. What's their story? What's your history with them?" She rubbed his right shoulder and hoped he would raise his head.

"Our freshman year in college, Dawg and I were thrown together as roommates. He had been one of the top three high school basketball stars in America, so there was lots of pressure. I was just an unknown scholarship athlete. We ran in different circles and played different sports — not much in common."

Brandi got up, walked to the entry, and turned the knob to soften the lights. "I'm listening, Babe. Keep talking."

It was the first time she had addressed him with his military call sign. He lifted his head.

"Midway through the first semester his mom died. She had raised him by herself and worked three jobs to support her family. It hit him hard. Then he tore an ACL in his first game. Several months later, the knee hadn't healed as fast as expected and he got depressed. His grades dropped. I helped him study. We became friends."

Brandi seated herself on the recliner across the table from him. She placed her white tennis shoes next to the chair and removed her knee socks, which she had worn to hide the still painful burns and abrasions.

Cody continued, "When summer came, he called me from New Orleans so depressed that he wanted to end his life. He was drunk. His girlfriend had left him. His knee still hurt. Somehow, he believed he would never play basketball again."

"Wow. Hard to believe it's the same guy I met tonight." She reclined and raised the footrest. Her left foot, both ankles, knees, and shins were inflamed.

Cody stood, moved to the front of her recliner and sat on the edge of the coffee table.

"How do you walk without limping? That's gotta hurt. Your skin looks gross. You gotta stop wearin' the tennis shoes. You got any more of that Blue stuff."

She creaked out a hoarse response. "Blue Tech? In my purse. Didn't want to wear the flip-flops to the game cuz my feet looked so bad."

He reached for her purse and dumped the contents onto the table.

"Cody, don't you know you should ask a girl to open her own purse and let her get what you need?"

"Been awhile since I spent much time with a girl. Guess I'm outta practice."

He retrieved a wet towel from the kitchen, soothed her injuries, and began applying the balm to the inflamed area.

"Oh, Cody." Her eyes were so heavy she couldn't hold them open.

"This is gettin' to be a habit." He grinned.

"And this is for my security, of course, right?" She yawned. "You're gonna put me to sleep."

"That's okay. It's late."

"But I wanna hear the rest of the story about Dawg and Silver first."

"Well, Dawg read me his suicide note. It was nothin' more than a list of failures — stuff he figured he'd never achieve cuz he wasn't smart enough. First item on the list was to marry a woman as great as his mom. He thought he had found her, but she had just dumped him."

Brandi's eyes were shut. Should he go on? Was she still listening?

He dropped his volume. "I reminded him that he was gifted, smart, but several former high school teachers had told him he was dumb and would never amount to a thing if he couldn't play basketball. The only dumb thing he did was to believe 'em."

She opened her eyes. "What did *you* tell him?"

"I asked him what his mother would say. He said his mom would tell him he could be as smart as he wanted to be. So I suggested we keep his list, but change it from a suicide note to a list of goals to accomplish."

"How did he respond?"

"I wasn't very good at praying in those days, but I prayed a short prayer for him over the phone."

"Long-distance prayer?"

"Right. Next semester, he was back in school and he met Silver. After she came his way, the rest of the goals on the list were a piece o' cake."

"What an answer to prayer. Cody, if you —"

"The next year, I met Hanna Kyle. We were sophomores. We fell in love, and I asked her to marry me. But one night, a month before the wedding, she went to sleep in her dorm room and never woke up — some sort of congenital heart thing."

Brandi lowered the footrest and leaned toward him on the arm of the chair.

"I had no parents by then. After I lost Hanna, I didn't have anybody. I hit a low. I planned to drop out o' school. I shut myself off and wouldn't let anyone in the dorm room. But Dawg removed..." He paused, chuckled and took a long breath.

"Cody? What did Dawg remove?"

"Dawg removed the hinges from my door and carried me outside. I didn't have the heart to resist. When he got me to his car, Silver was waiting. I hardly knew her then, but she talked to me like an older sister, scolding and loving me at the same time."

"Oh, Cody. *Sweet.*"

"They lived off campus. Invited me to move in with 'em. With Silver pushing us both, Dawg became an Academic All-American, and I graduated early and became a US Marine."

"I've seen Silver's face on some magazine covers," Brandi said. "She is quite an accomplished woman in her own right."

"Silver is a scrapper, a fighter, grew up in the projects of West Dallas, lost a brother to a gunfight. She earned a basketball scholarship to Baylor, went to grad school, became a financial genius. She's turned Dawg's capital investments into hundreds of millions."

"I didn't know about Hanna. She must have been amazing."

Cody picked Brandi up, cradled her, and carried her back toward the sofa, his forearms so gentle she scarcely felt them. Eyes closed, she was a princess carried on a cloud.

He eased her onto the sofa and knelt beside her, placed a pillow at one end of the couch and motioned for her to lay her head down. She melted into the perfect cushion, soft and light, luxuriously deep.

Cody placed his hand on her forehead and said a prayer. In ten seconds, she was motionless again. He walked to the entry and further dimmed the lights.

As he tiptoed toward the door to the adjacent room, Brandi's shallow voice called, "Good night, man of steel."

When he turned around and their eyes met, she rolled onto her side and faced him. A sudden adrenaline rush had her pulse racing. After a momentary pause, Cody nodded, backed away, and left the room. She breathed a deep sigh of relief — and disappointment.

She lay on her back again, closed her eyes, and scolded herself. *Don't complain. He's exactly what you prayed for.*

She stood up and stepped over to the closet. Exhausted, she changed into her blue "I Love The Son" pullover shirt and dropped the rest of her clothes into the closet floor. Two bloodshot eyes stared back at her in the mirror.

She grinned at her reflection and whispered. "Yes, Cody, I will marry you." Brandi cocked her head. "Uh, of course, I'll marry you, man of steel." Next, she turned up the volume. "Just say the word, Babe, and I'm yours." She placed her hands on her hips and rotated them. "Well, it's about time, Cody Musket. Marry me when? Tonight?"

"What did you say?" Cody had reappeared.

Brandi jumped. She clutched her heart to keep it inside her chest, then scooted over to the refrigerator and opened the door.

"Oh! Cody, you scared me. I, uh, was just getting some water." She pulled a cold bottle from the fridge and shut the door.

"Didn't mean to walk in on you. Thought I heard my name."

Her face, pale when he had set her on the couch earlier, now blushed like a favored rose.

"Don't worry," he said. "I've seen you in that pullover before."

He left again and closed the door. She scurried back to the mirror, pressed the back of her hand to her mouth, and watched herself giggle until she hiccupped.

After drowning her hiccups with the contents of the bottle, she gathered up the extra pillows in the room, threw them onto the king bed, and burrowed into them.

In the other room, Cody collapsed into the middle of his bed.

Brandi's tenderness and the prayer he had prayed over her stayed with him. His sleep was sound. This time, the nightmares stayed away.

# THE LONG TUNNEL

On Wednesday morning, it was checkout day for coaches, players and fans. In two days, the baseball regular season would continue. A security team escorted Cody and Brandi to breakfast at a second-floor coffee shop. Tanner and Julia met them there and took Knoxi with them, as planned, when breakfast was finished.

After they returned to their suite, Brandi went to change in the bathroom but stayed for thirty minutes. Cody decided to lie down on the couch and shut his eyes.

When Brandi finally returned wearing cutoffs and a Pirates game jersey, she was tight and nervy.

Cody sat up. "What's wrong?" Butterflies whiffled inside his gut.

Brandi sat down next to him. "I just got off the phone with Vic at the *Gazette.* Dupree's wrists had been tied."

"So it *was* murder," Cody said. "But I guess we already knew that."

"He also said the Houston mayor is trying to make trouble for you."

"Trouble? What kind?"

"He texted to me a *USA Today* headline which quotes Mayor Leonard Beeker, saying that he questions your medals and says you aren't coming clean. Do you know him?"

"I've met him," he muttered. "He's a Nam vet, seventy something, a popular ol' guy, but he always looks at me sideways."

"Do people take him seriously?"

He walked to the sink and ran the water to splash his face. "I dunno where Beeker gets his information, but I'm not ready for anything to come out in the press. I just want it to go away."

"So now what?"

"We get your stuff out of your apartment in Pittsburgh tonight like we planned and then fly to Houston tomorrow. Derek's arrangin' a charter."

"Is it too dangerous to go to Pittsburgh? I mean if Dupree was —"

"I don't know if Pittsburgh is more dangerous than anywhere else. How large is the trafficking syndicate? Does the location make any difference?" He snatched a towel, dried his hands and face. "All that evidence you've collected. Just need to get in and out quick — hit-n-run."

"Why don't we alert police or the Sheriff? They could provide protection again."

"I got a better idea. Derek can leak a story that we're headed to Houston tonight. What if there's a mole in Pittsburgh? Can't take a chance. No one but your parents should know we're coming."

"Now you sound like Sly."

Cody tossed the paper towel into the trash and then stood motionless, staring at the floor. Brandi stiffened her back.

"I've never been so scared," she said. "I'm used to being in control. Right now, everything is spinning apart."

He took two steps toward her and stopped. "Before I say anything else, you should know that I didn't bring you here just for your security. There were...there were other reasons."

Brandi managed a chuckle. "*Ha!* Did you honestly think I didn't know that?" She wanted to pursue the subject, but other things were pressing.

They sat in quiet reflection for a few moments, and then Brandi broke the silence.

"Cody, what could Beeker say that would be damaging? Why would he want to hurt you?"

He came and sat with her on the sofa. "I didn't want to tell you, but it's time." He pulled in another deep breath. "What you're gonna hear isn't the account written by generals and historians." He leaned forward, hands on knees, staring at the carpet in front of him.

Brandi's thumping heart made her bruised neck throb.

"I told you the story before, but I left some things out. When the seven Taliban showed up at the crash, they had five young boys with 'em."

She caught her breath. Cody stood up and moved to the window and gazed at a passing cloud. "They singled out one little kid. They made him —" He turned around to face her and threw his hands into the air but did not finish his sentence.

"Made him do what, Cody? What did they make him do?"

"They made him shoot Harry."

Brandi didn't make a sound as Cody told her of the decision to leave the other four boys tied up. "We planned to go back and get them in a few hours."

He turned back toward the window and gazed at the rooftops across the street. "Those kids begged me to take them along." He shook his head. "If only I had."

He looked straight down at the street twenty floors below and placed both hands on the windowsill. "For four years, I've —"

He dropped his shoulders and shook with emotion but recovered quickly. Brandi walked up behind him, wrapped her arms as far as she could reach around his broad shoulders, and pressed her cheek against the back of his neck.

"Cody, if you want to stop, it's okay."

Primitive curiosity made her want to know what happened to the four children, but now, touching him with her arms and face, she could feel the tremors that ran through him beneath the surface. He brushed her aside and returned to the couch. She followed.

"The helo never came. We never went back for the kids."

"I was taken to a village near a ravine. They locked me in a truck trailer, a torture chamber — hooks, electric batteries, wires everywhere. Bloodstains and the smell of vomit, urine and feces made me wanna puke. I was left there for what seemed like forever. No water. No food."

Brandi had the crawly feeling again, like during his nightmare. She must hold herself together.

"I heard children crying. It seemed far away, but hard to tell because my only connection to the outside was a small vent on each side of the trailer. Some abducted kids are treated relatively well. I had no way of knowing their condition at that time, but later —"

"Later what? What did you find out about their condition?"

He shut his eyes. "I saw no sign of the POWs. The bloodstains were at least a week old. The helicopter survivors had not been in the trailer."

Why had he evaded her question about the condition of the kids? Brandi walked to the refrigerator to retrieve two bottles of cold water and compose herself. Three swallows, then she sat back down.

Cody just placed his bottle on the coffee table and continued. "Intel had told us that people in this region were more brutal than most because they were secularists and hardliners. They don't torture people just for information. They do it for hate and cold-blooded pleasure."

No matter how well Brandi had prepared herself, it could never have been enough. Something evil and foreboding had invaded their room but she was too old to hide under the bed. She sat on her hands and braced for the worst.

"Finally, this big Taliban officer came in with three subordinates. One carried a small cup of water for me but no food. I learned later that this guy in charge was a wanted terrorist.

"They tried to make me tell 'em where the SEAL team was hiding, but I didn't know. I lost track of time, didn't think they'd ever stop." He shuddered. "I woulda made up any story to get 'em to stop. I told 'em the SEALs had left the area, but they knew it wasn't true."

He reached for the water bottle and downed half the contents. Brandi kept silent.

"Finally, I could hear activity outside the trailer. I assumed it was morning again. Then I heard these indescribable screams. I didn't know if it was even real at first. Sounded like some small animal, but then I realized — Men's voices chanting, shouting, the smell of gasoline and flesh burning. It took a maximum effort to keep my sanity. You can't imagine. Sometimes I still hear it."

He put his hands over his ears, flinched his eyelids shut, and rocked back and forth.

Brandi's eyes burned and she became lightheaded. The rocking scared her.

"Cody, I think —"

"They made sure I heard every sound." He stopped rocking and leaned forward. "Right after that, the soldiers — totaling about three-hundred — decided to move on. They hooked the trailer to a tractor. That's when they threw me on the street.

"At first, the townspeople moved back and became quiet — so quiet I could hear a gasping sound. I looked up and saw the smoking body of a child hanging about six feet off the ground."

Brandi lost all the air in her lungs. *"Oh, Lord Jesus. No. No."* She battled the urge to run into the bathroom and cry her eyes out.

"He was one of the four we had left behind. Didn't make any sense. Did they think he was a traitor? Nothing makes sense over there. His tiny face was beyond recognition, but I knew who he was because two of the older men standing there were holding those little scuffed boots and the pants and shirt he was wearing when I...when I had left him tied up."

*"Ohhh, Cody.* I'm so, so sorry."

He covered his contorted face and sobbed briefly, but no tears.

Brandi's arms and shoulders ached from wanting to hold him, but she resisted. Now she knew why Cody never laughed. Finally, she knelt in front of him, placed her hands into his palms and prayed the worst was over.

He gathered himself. "The mob started chanting again — prolly the only English words they knew — 'Death to America. Death to Americans.' They dragged me across the street. That's when I saw the other children in a holding cell — about thirty of 'em — mostly boys, a few girls."

Brandi's chest throbbed. She wanted him to stop but couldn't say a word.

"Other children stood nearby, 'bout ten of 'em. They were clean, trying to look pious, dressed in turbans and robes. Adult 'mentors' stood with 'em. The rest had been crammed into that cage. Some were naked, like…like cattle." He tightened his lip. "I thought I knew the meaning of evil before, but…"

Brandi sensed a cold shift in the air — the stalking, circling presence of the monster he had told her about — the same deep sorrow and chilling stench as during his nightmare. Her runaway pulse pounded through her neck like a hammer. Her legs — burning, restless — sprung her to her feet and carried her to the window.

She held up both hands. "*Cody, stop!*" Her stomach wanted to erupt.

Cody wiped his face with his sleeve. He glanced at Brandi's mournful face. If he finished the story, she would know everything he knew. He couldn't let that happen. He had already told her too much.

Brandi gazed through the window toward Comerica Park, site of such exhilaration during the game the night before — children on the giant Ferris wheel, baseball-shaped gondolas, moms and dads on summer vacations with their kids. She imagined their laughter.

She looked toward the door. For a brief moment, she wanted to run, but couldn't move. He had warned of things she would not want to know about him. Had he done something in those moments so horrible that it would change everything? Would the events of his past destroy his future? Their future?

She was quiet and still for a moment, eyes closed. She listened. Even the refrigerator motor was now silent. In the quietness, it came to her. It was so simple, so profound. Ray's ninth principle — *Never let who you were in the past define who you become in the future.*

She would no longer let him attempt to hide his vulnerability by shutting her out. Nor would she afford him the illusion that cutting her off would protect her. His open wounds would never heal until someone bore them with him.

The stalking monster could not have her man. Not today. *Not ever.* Cody had called her "armed and dangerous," and that's exactly what she would be.

She left her flip-flops sitting on the windowsill, walked over to the red sink in the kitchenette and retrieved a clean, wet cloth. The red-and-gray wool Berber carpet felt good beneath her feet. She returned and sat on the coffee table again and wiped his sweaty brow and ruddy face with the cool towel.

"I'm all in, Babe. Would you tell me what happened to the rest of the children?"

His eyes were shut. When he tried to open them, he squinted as though he were looking into a blinding light.

"Cody? Did you hear? Can you tell me about the kids in the cage?"

Brandi was not prepared for what happened next. His eyes flew open wide — stricken, wild, like during his bad dream two nights before.

*"God, don't let me die this way! Help me save the kids! Send in the SEALs!"*

"Cody. Cody! Can you hear me?"

He covered his ears again, his nightmare on full instant replay.

"Cody? Answer me!"

But she could only listen and attempt to piece together the events as he relived them. She was in uncharted territory. *Is he hypnotic? In a trance?*

Was he entering a long dark tunnel from which his mind might never return? She had heard of such things. She held on to him with all her strength as if to prevent him from being pulled away into that tunnel. It was all she could think to do.

Cody's memory began to fill in the blanks.

The people in the street had started to run, driven by sudden gunfire. The SEAL team had arrived. They had already rescued the eight helicopter survivors. Now they had come for him.

"Lieutenant, we have to vacate the area now! Our ride is waiting three hundred meters south."

*"Sergeant, get those kids out of that holding cell! What? Not our mission? Of course it's our mission. I'll do it myself. Lemme go! Lemme go! Uggggh!"*

Cody fell to the floor, pulling Brandi with him. They landed hard but unhurt. Cody screamed in pain, like during the dream before. Then he partially returned to his senses, as if he were in two places at once.

One of the SEALs had tackled him after yelling *"incoming!"* When the airborne device had exploded, he had lost consciousness. He recovered quickly and discovered that the SEAL had sacrificed his life, having absorbed most of the blast.

Cody then pushed away the body of the dead SEAL, jumped to his feet, but collapsed immediately. His left leg had been split apart from knee to ankle.

He could see the cage with the children now engulfed in flames, smoke and a pink mist.

A CH-53 transport helicopter flew overhead, spawning a tornado of dirt and debris. But the CH-53, their intended ride home, exploded seventy-five yards away after it passed them by.

Intense gunfire then rang out from the east side of the village. The three hundred Taliban soldiers who had vacated earlier were returning.

The rescue team carried him to the edge of the ravine near the bridge, along with six badly burned children — the only survivors from the cage. In a few minutes, the enemy would be on top of them.

With blowing sand and reigning confusion, Chavez sewed double-time to close jagged wounds on Cody's left leg and foot — the only way to prevent his bleeding to death. No time to clean the injury — dirt, feces and debris.

Brandi sat on the floor with Cody, holding on to him. He finally stopped and snatched up the water bottle that was rolling around beside him. He was no longer choking or screaming, but his wild and distant eyes stared right through her. She picked up the wash towel again and bathed his face and neck. His skin was red and burning to the touch.

Cody slowly came back to himself. Brandi tried to help him up, but he wouldn't move, his eyes still staring straight ahead.

"We were outnumbered, fifteen of us against three hundred. No one was coming to get us. No way to escape."

Brandi moved directly into his line of sight and waved her hands. "Are you back with me?"

He was still distant, but his eyes softer. The redness in his face diminished. His entire shirt and upper portions of his jeans were soaked with perspiration and the runoff from the wash towel. She finally helped him back to the couch.

"Cody, maybe you should stop. You need a break. Give yourself —"

"We knew the Taliban would take the kids alive. We couldn't bear to think about it. The six children were screaming, tryin' to breathe." He took several deep breaths, then finally became calm. "We grieved over them. I mean we wanted to relieve their suffering somehow."

Brandi held her breath.

"I slapped a new magazine in my sidearm and cocked it, I knew what I had to do." He spoke so quietly it was as if he were talking only to himself.

"But all of a sudden, five Marine Super Cobras from Camp Leatherneck appeared from over the hill. We didn't even know they were coming."

"Oh, dear God," Brandi whispered.

"The gunships fired away. Practically leveled the village. I never forget the sound — children screaming, soldiers yelling, gunfire, hot ammo buzzin' past our ears and bouncin' off solid objects, tearin' up flesh and bone. The Cobras sounded like a million horses stampeding. You can't imagine. Deafening. Sickening." He covered his ears once more and began to fade.

"Cody! Please don't leave me. Look at me. Open your eyes!"

Cody dropped his hands. He was quiet, unfeeling, eyes staring at nothing. "I don't know what hell looks like, but I know what it sounds like. I still hear it when things are quiet. Sometimes at night in my bed I tune my earphones to static, just to drown out the sound.

"When the battle was over, the children…the children were dead — all of 'em. The official count was thirty-two dead kids, two dead SEALs, and two Army pilots."

Brandi's throat had tightened up. She held a cool water bottle to her face.

Cody continued, barely above a whisper. "Afterward, all was quiet. I couldn't even hear the voices saying to get me on the helo. Those kids in the cage and Sergeant Jimmy Mason, US Navy SEAL, took an RPG meant for me. That's all."

His eyes were dull, fists no longer clenched, face void. She waved her hands back and forth in front of his eyes, but his expression never changed.

"If only I had gone with the SEALs when they first arrived, those kids might be alive. I went against the mission plan. I can't describe what happens inside your head when so much sorrow and hate flood your mind at the same time. I hate the Taliban. I hate myself."

"Babe, I'm right here." He was still unresponsive. "Babe, here, feel my skin."

She placed Cody's hands on each side of her face. He warmed to her touch and then began moving his hands slowly down her neck and into the top of her jersey.

She tried to remove his hands, but he was too strong and tore the buttons off the front.

"Cody, please. You aren't yourself. Remember what you promised my dad? About my honor? *Babe, stop!*"

He suddenly focused. He panicked as remorse wound fast around his neck like a clothesline. He stumbled toward the door gasping for breath.

"Cody, wait. You didn't hurt me." She ran to him. "Please don't walk out. You can't go in public like this."

"But how can you ever —" He fell to his knees like a prisoner awaiting execution.

"Nothing to forgive." She shivered like a lamb in a blizzard. "You left me again, Cody. That's what scares me more than anything." She knelt and reached for his hands but he pulled away.

"So how much did I tell you?"

# AMALGA OSHIRISH

T he morning sun broke through the lazy, cloudy Detroit sky. Brandi opened the drapes to let the healing light shine in, and then she went into the other room to exchange the damaged jersey for a yellow blouse.

Cody rose from his knees but stood by the door. She tried to pull him toward the kitchen table, but he wouldn't budge.

"Please don't tell Ray what I did."

"We won't speak of it. I'm okay. The Cody I know wouldn't harm me."

"The Cody you know? I don't even know myself."

He finally found a seat at the table. "So how much did I tell you"

"You don't remember? I figured out you didn't shoot any kids. Who was the SEAL? The one who protected you from the explosion?"

"Sergeant Jimmy Mason, Springfield, Indiana. He had a wife and son. I go up there each year to see them. Myra has remarried, but I want her son to know who his father was."

"Cody, how did your scar end up in the shape of a cross?"

"The anesthesiologist, Nikki Corbett, told me that when Captain Jefferson cut across my leg to amputate, he was totally torqued."

"Torqued?"

"That's right. The flesh he encountered was healthy, and the swelling had diminished, so he thought that either I was the wrong patient or someone on his team had screwed up. In a matter of minutes, the infection had disappeared. At first, he couldn't accept the facts. It had to be a mistake.

"He reconstructed the bottom portion of my leg as best he could, considering pieces of bone were missing, and just sewed me back up. Then two days later, the blood flow to my left ankle restored itself, which had been a virtual impossibility — only about an eight-percent chance.

"Then I remembered the silent prayer I had prayed just before going under — exchanging my life for whatever God wanted me to do. I told Nikki about it."

Brandi softened her face with a smile.

"I have the long vertical scar from my toes to my mid thigh, and a horizontal scar just above the knee, where the orthopedic surgeon had intended to amputate."

"Hence, the cross." She folded her hands.

"Roger that. Nikki said the bad news was that I would never be able to walk normally or run again, but a funny thing happened."

"Yay! Let's hear it."

"Okay." He hesitated and issued a disclaimer. "This is the part nobody knows, not even Nikki, cuz I still don't know exactly what to make of it." He paused again. "Whew! I could use a tall cup o' battery acid."

"Okay." She walked to the corner to prepare the coffee. "Keep talking. Tell me what happened."

"Okay, but promise me that . . . I mean —"

"Cody, just tell me. Afterward, you need to take a shower. You're soaked, and you smell like the wrong end of a hippo."

He stared.

"Just learning your flair for words." She shrugged. "Hmm, you nearly smiled."

"Yeah. I'm gonna work on that."

She stood with her back to him and began filling the coffee pot.

"I coded twice on the MEDEVAC to Kandahar, but something happened that . . ." He paused, exhaled heavily. "I mean I didn't remember it until I was in recovery after surgery." He moved his chair closer to the table and leaned on one elbow.

"I, uh — I saw the thirty-two kids when I was on that flight. I saw them sitting in Heaven with Jesus. I swear. It was so real. They were dressed in the finest . . . I mean they — they weren't all burned like we last saw them. They were perfect."

He looked toward Brandi for her response. She stood as motionless as marble.

"I mean they were so happy. They looked at me and smiled. Then, I heard them say, 'Amalga oshirish.' Their lips never moved, but I heard them speak in unison. I swear it."

He glanced up again. Brandi hadn't moved a muscle.

"It happened twice, same voices. 'Amalga oshirish, amalga oshirish.'"

"At first, I figured the words prolly meant nothing, like it wasn't even a real language. I asked Nikki if she knew, but I didn't tell her why I wanted to know. She promised to ask around and find out the meaning. She figured I'd met some local girl and wanted to know if it meant, 'I love you' in her own dialect.

"Later, she came back and told me the words mean 'implement it' or, the loose translation, 'make it happen' in a dialect called Uzbek, one of the languages spoken in northern Afghanistan."

Brandi released the deep breath she had been holding and wheeled around. "Oh, Cody. That's wonderful! God let you see the children in heaven. Do you realize how many people have longed to see what you saw?"

"So you believe me? You don't think I'm crazy?"

"Oh," she breathed out. "Of course not. So what did you make of the words? The translation — *make it happen* — did it have some special meaning for you?"

"I thought about it for a few hours, and then it hit me."

She brought two cups of coffee and sat down. "So what did it mean?"

"When I was drafted by the Astros in the twenty-seventh round after my junior year, I called Tanner. He said, 'Make it happen. Make it happen.'"

"Is that an expression he uses all the time?"

"No. He never says that. But that day, when I told him I'd been drafted, he said it twice, just like the Afghan kids."

"So that's why you decided to make it happen with your baseball career finally?"

"I told Captain Jefferson the whole story — the prayer — everything except the part about the children. I said I wanted to rehab and resurrect my athletic career. He told me I would never enter a major league stadium without the aid of a wheelchair or crutches. I played in a major league all-star game last night because of *amalga oshirish.*"

"God has dealt so bountifully with you, Cody. You should be at peace."

But Cody answered, "Like I said before, I trust God, but I don't trust myself. People lost their lives because of me. And the hate, it still haunts me. I used to have all the answers, but now I'm a stranger to myself. I don't know who I'm supposed to be. That doesn't make sense, but —"

"Cody, if you know who God says you are, no one else can tell you who to be."

Cody drained his coffee cup. Then he walked over to the sink and splashed his face again. "You're right. About the rhino smell."

"It was hippo, and did you understand what I just said?"

"I heard. From Ray's top five or seven or —?"

"Nope. I think it popped into my head just for you, man of steel. If God loves you, how can you hate yourself?" She walked toward him and held out her arms. "I don't care how you smell."

He evaded her embrace and walked to the window. "What if I hurt you, Brandi? Or hurt Knoxi? You said it yourself, I left you again earlier. What if next time —"

"Go clean up. We are exhausted. We'll figure it out later — *together.*"

# MEDAL OF HONOR

"Lieutenant Musket. I congratulate you on your amazing recovery. Are they treating you well here?"

"Yes, sir, General. Hopefully in a few more days I'll be out of this bed and into rehab."

"Lieutenant Musket, I am on official business. This is not a social call. However, I am here for a purpose that gives me great pleasure and a matter I insisted on handling myself."

"Official business, General?"

"Lieutenant, as we have agreed, you are soon to be honorably discharged from your service in the United States Marine Corps. I happen to know a few people, and I'm going to make this as painless as possible."

"Sir?"

The General pulled a communiqué from his pocket and read it. "Second Lieutenant Cody Musket, not only did your actions under fire result in the rescue of eight US fighting men and the salvation of a US Navy SEAL team under the command of Major Simon Hendrix, it also led to the apprehension of Abdul Al-Adami, a wanted terrorist who had eluded US intelligence for over five years. All these acts of bravery were performed in enemy territory under fire of combat and after you, Lieutenant Musket, had been injured in action. Your country and the entire free world owe you a debt of gratitude that can never adequately be repaid."

"Sir, I don't really —"

"I have come to deliver in person the announcement that you are to receive a citation for conspicuous gallantry and intrepidity at the risk of your life, above and beyond the call of duty. For uncommon courage under fire that upholds the highest traditions and honor of the United States Marine Corps, in light of the events above, you are recommended for the Medal of Honor, the highest award for valor in action against an enemy force bestowed upon an individual serving in the armed services of the United States."

"Sir, there is —"

"I'm not finished, Lieutenant! There is another matter, now that I am completely out of breath. Captain Jefferson and Sergeant Corbett told me of this so-called *miraculous* nature of your recovery here. Lieutenant, until you crashed on my battlefield, I had decided that there was no God in heaven. Now I'm not so friggin' sure of myself.

"And as for the shooting of Al Adami, it was an *accident* — that's final. Do I make myself clear? Now listen up! You've been handed a gift. Make the best of it, and that's an order. You go make me proud of my decisions in this matter, son."

The General stood up, squared off, and straightened his uniform. "Are we on the same page here, Lieutenant?"

"Cody, wake up! We're coming into Pittsburgh. Are you awake?"

"I'm not sure about being on the same page. Uh, Nikki?"

"Cody, wake up. You're dreaming."

He sat up. "Uh. Ummm. Guess I fell asleep."

"Oh, you think?"

"What time is it?" he asked.

"Nearly time to meet Mama and Daddy at the Tenth Inning Grill. We all listened to you talk in your sleep."

Sly, sitting behind the wheel, found Cody in the rearview mirror. "Hey, flyboy. We didn't hear nothin'. By the way, who the heck is Nikki?"

"I wuz dreamin' about General Plasket comin' to my recovery room at Kandahar."

"General Abraham Plasket?" Brandi asked. "You mean the Supreme ISAF Commander? He came to see you?"

"So who is Nikki?" Sly was persistent.

"Sounds like a girl to me," Julia ribbed.

"His anesthesiologist." Brandi was quick to answer.

"She was a sergeant. General Plasket came to let me know I was gonna receive a medal. But it was undeserved. I didn't really earn it. I sort o' blundered into circumstances that led to the capture of a wanted terrorist."

"But you also saved eight crash survivors," Brandi reminded.

"Brandi told us that the two of you talked about Afghanistan," Julia said. "She didn't tell any details. You've both been through so much."

Cody stared silently at the Pittsburgh skyline, suddenly detached as though held prisoner to the disquieting reflections in his mind.

Julia and Brandi exchanged glances. Brandi shook her head. Was he retreating again? Would she ever learn to read his thoughts?

Despite her frustration, a strange new peace had embraced Brandi while Cody had slept on the seat next to her in the Escalade. She finally was free of Billy. Today, she had laid herself down like a bridge over Cody's troubled water. Afterward, the hurt and shame from the stabbing had simply left her. Was it gone forever?

Even more miraculous was the sudden feeling of pity, *not hatred*, for her Friday-night attackers. She could no longer feel their collective breath upon her, despite sore bruises that still persisted.

The tears she had cried with Cody in center field had broken some heart fetters, but now, something even more powerful was in progress. A miracle?

An involuntary smile crossed her lips as they traversed the Clemente Bridge. Was her tranquility of heart only the temporary eye of a hurricane, or was it a light at the end of the tunnel? Hope was alive. What would tonight bring? What would await them in Houston? Surely, it would be good.

# GUN SMOKE

The time was 6:00 p.m. when they arrived at PNC Park to pick up Brandi's Mustang. They had stored the car in a secure lot. Cody eyeballed the security personnel on duty for signs of authenticity, but it was still a guessing game. His senses were on alert. He began to second-guess himself. Should he have contacted authorities after all? Had his agent's bogus news leak worked? Did their enemies know where they were?

Tanner stopped the Escalade as close as he could to Brandi's Mustang. Brandi slipped her keys to Cody.

"Do you want to drive? Knoxi and I will be right here." Soft smile.

Cody went to retrieve the car, carrying their bags.

After he walked away, Brandi stood next to the curb to wait for him. Tanner wrapped his big arms around her. "You'll do," he said. "He loves you more than you know, and he needs you more than you know."

"Thank you," Brandi whispered. She looked at Julia who nodded. Brandi felt a warm and pleasant premonition. Sly and Julia could read Cody better than anyone.

Cody put the bags in the trunk. He looked around the parking lot nervously before he dropped into the driver's seat and started the engine. He dug into the glove compartment, pulled out Brandi's handgun and hid it in the front pocket of his jeans. Hopefully, he wouldn't need it. Brandi wouldn't even know he had taken it.

He slipped the Mustang into reverse and backed the car around to pick up Brandi and Knoxi. They said their goodbyes to the McNairs and were on their way.

Knoxi was hungry and fussy, but the couple was silent while the Mustang made its way through the lot and toward the exit. Cody breathed a sigh of relief as they eased past the guarded gate and turned onto the road.

"I know you have it in your pocket." Brandi looked straight ahead. "Thank you for not telling me. Tenth Inning Grill is on the next street. Turn right at the intersection."

Cody offered no response. She put her hand on his knee. "Are you trying to choke my steering wheel to death?"

He eased his grip. "Sorry."

She exhaled a long breath. "Are we gonna be okay?"

"I dunno what to say. There is something else I didn't tell you. I couldn't bring myself — I figured I'd said enough, figured you'd heard enough. The head guy, the one in charge in that village, the terrorist I was credited with apprehending — *I shot him.*"

 Brandi's mouth flew open. She held her breath.

"I couldn't hear anything after the battle. I don't even remember pickin' up my Beretta and wanderin' off. No one even noticed. Mass confusion. They say I used a piece of debris for a crutch and slipped past everybody to the place where five Marines were holding Al Adami. The only part I remember is pointing the gun and shooting him point-blank. After that, I collapsed."

"So he's dead?"

"He's at Guantanamo. I only nicked him in the arm. If I had been in my right mind, I'd have killed him."

"Cody, if you had been in your right mind, you would not have shot him. Did you think of that?"

"If I'd been in my right mind, I wouldn't have attacked you. Did you think of that?" He brought the vehicle to a halt at the intersection. "What scares me is what I might do if my mind keeps playin' tricks." He had a vise grip on the wheel again.

Brandi looked away. "You can go right on red here, you know."

He turned the corner. "Just like the kids I saw in heaven. All this time, I figured it was just another hallucination or dream."

"*No!* That's the most *real* thing that's happened. Without that, you would not have played baseball, and we would never have met. I would have suffered a horrible death last weekend, Knoxi wouldn't have a mother, and you'd be living in a VA hospital with a wheelchair and nightmares."

"You have a way with words. I'll say that much."

"Listen to me, Cody. If God healed your leg, and He let you see those kids in heaven, don't you think He can heal your mind?"

"Is that the place? Half a block up on the right?"

She nodded.

"They ruled it was accidental — the shooting. The general made sure. The official report claims that Al Adami was nicked in the arm by a stray bullet from some place. My Beretta was supposedly never found. General Plasket died last year."

"I believe he's proud of the decision he made, Cody. Did you hear what I said about God healing your mind?"

"Did you hear what I said?" Cody asked. "I shot an unarmed man. I went through psych counseling for a year while I rehabbed my leg — was told I was okay. I mean, aren't you scared I'll do something crazy?"

Cody parked the Mustang in front of Tenth Inning Grill and turned off the engine. Brandi looked behind into the back seat. Knoxi's head was drooped, her eyes nearly closed.

Brandi turned toward Cody and softened her voice. "You were God's gift to me at the theater, you know. And the way Knoxi looks at you —"

"*Stop.* I don't need that kind of pressure right now."

\*　　\*　　\*

Tenth-Inning Grill was nearly empty because the Pirates were not playing that night. Just as they finished their meal, reporters began gathering in the parking lot. The headwaiter gave Ray a heads-up, so the party decided to escape through the back exit and head to Mayfield Tower.

The apartment was stifling hot. Air-conditioning had been off for three days, and July heat had returned to Pittsburgh. Brandi lowered the thermostat. The air unit kicked on, but it would take a few minutes for the apartment to cool down.

Meanwhile, they took refuge on the secluded outdoor patio, which afforded a dazzling view. The convergence of the Allegheny, Monongahela, and Ohio Rivers at dusk, coupled with a lighted Pittsburgh skyline, created a stunning metroscape.

Brandi retrieved five bottles of cold water from the refrigerator, and they all sat at the patio table for small talk while they waited.

Cody got up and slowly ambled over to the railing and stared down at the traffic three stories below. His face was tight, his thoughts distant.

"Expecting someone to climb this wall, son?" Ray had followed.

"You never know." He continued to look at the street.

"Something on your mind?" Ray asked.

"Among other things, I think we should conclude our business here and move on as soon as possible, sir."

"Agreed. But it's the 'among other things' I was referring to."

"Does it show?" Cody's eyes were unfocused, his elbows resting on the railing. "My life's changed in the past five days. I'm more scared now than ever before. I'm afraid I'm gonna unravel. I didn't have much to lose a week ago, but now I do."

"Is that why you haven't picked up Knoxi? She's reached for you several times since we've joined you this afternoon, but you've looked the other way. Is that why you and Brandi barely spoke at dinner?"

"You noticed."

"I haven't talked to my daughter since you came back from Detroit, so I don't know what transpired between the two of you. But let me guess. All of a sudden there are people in your life that you care about, and you're afraid you won't have enough man in you when they need you."

Cody raised his head and looked Ray in the eye.

"Oh, you think you're the only one?" Ray crossed his arms and leaned back against the railing. "After I got home from the Gulf, my habit was to get up in the middle of the night and go outside to sleep on the concrete driveway. Some nights, I couldn't sleep in a bed. No one understood. Whitney hurt for me but had no idea what I was going through. I've been where you are, Cody."

"Do the scars ever go away?"

"No, they don't. But you have to eventually face whatever is stalking you." He banged his large fist into his palm for emphasis.

"Your daughter is the strongest woman I've ever met."

"And you want to protect her from shadows that lurk?"

"Yes, sir. I hope I haven't said too much. And the hardest thing is…I don't trust myself."

"She doesn't want you to protect her. She wants you to let her in. You don't trust yourself because the demon stalking you has convinced you that you're just like he is. *Listen to me!* Don't you ever let an enemy tell you who you are. What do you think your father would tell you if he were here?"

Cody nodded pensively.

"After Operation Desert Storm, Whitney loved me back into reality. I rescued her when she was sixteen. She rescued me when I was twenty-five. Don't think for a minute that we're meant to face it alone, son. And don't think there's a quick fix. Problem is, you've had no family to lean on."

Whitney and Brandi had gone into the apartment with Knoxi to check the comfort level. Soon they reappeared and stood in the patio doorway. "Hey, guys, the apartment's cooler now and —"

They were silenced by the sight of a gigantic orange moon that now hovered on the horizon and filled up their view. In front of the huge fiery ball stood two stoic silhouettes in an uncharacteristic embrace. Even the toddler seemed mesmerized. To make a sound would have seemed a sacrilege.

"Mama, they don't know we're watching."

The women disappeared. Ray and Cody would come when ready.

In a few minutes, the men walked in. They pulled out empty boxes and began to pack essentials, including Brandi's valuable research and editorials.

Ray and Whitney worked in the bedroom. Brandi was in the kitchen. Cody gathered items from the hall closet while Knoxi played on the living room floor a few feet away from him.

"I'm done." Cody yelled to the others. "Let's get outta —"

*Boom!* He never finished his sentence.

Cody recognized the sound. The front door had been blasted off its hinges. The repetitive rattle of automatic gunfire followed. Knoxi's piercing screams were drowned out by the clamor of shots fired from three assault rifles. Bullets ripped through drywall and stucco while Cody instinctively threw himself to the floor.

Then he looked up. Three armed, hooded gunmen stood in the entryway. Muzzle flashes, smoke, bullets ricocheting — Cody's nightmare lived once again.

Knoxi stood frozen only a few feet away, trying to catch her breath. She was in the line of fire with bullets passing just inches from her head. There was no decision to be made. Cody vaulted toward her, gathered her up with his hands and leaped back into the closet with a single bound.

He frantically yanked Brandi's gun from his pocket and cocked the weapon. One of the hired guns appeared at the closet door. Cody pointed and pulled the trigger. The gun misfired. He shielded Knoxi with his body while he desperately attempted to clear the chamber, but it was too late. From point-blank range, Cody and Knoxi would be easy money.

At that moment, a single booming shot rang from the other side of the room. It had a familiar, friendly sound, much different from the sterile *rat-tat-tat* of the intruders' weapons of choice. Ray's Colt .45 had reported loud and clear from the bedroom doorway. His bullet ripped into the back of the shocked gunman who had stood ready to murder Cody and their little princess.

With shattered ribs and a pierced lung, the wounded man staggered forward. His rifle discharged several times as Cody wrestled it away from him. The close-range muzzle fire set Cody's jeans ablaze just above the right knee, but none of the stray bullets found flesh.

With the killer's assault weapon in hand, Cody sent the injured intruder to the floor with a fierce blow to the head, but two armed assailants were still loose in the living room. The cold-blooded *rat-tat-tat* continued. Brandi hugged the wall in a corner of the kitchen — shocked, frozen, vulnerable.

Cody caught sight of Ray tumbling backward into the bedroom. Ray's contorted face and cry of pain told him what he did not want to know — Ray was hit.

The shooting stopped momentarily. Cody peeked around the corner into the living room. Gray gun smoke and a white powdery dust from the bullet-battered stucco filled the air, creating a perfect smoke screen. *The time is now.*

He needed to move into the open to get clean shots, so he checked his weapon, took a deep breath and bolted toward the coffee table across the room. After two strides, he dropped into a perfect slide — the kind he would execute with a daring attempt to steal third base.

He skimmed along on his back across the smooth wooden floor while firing at his two living targets with lethal results. He had drawn their fire, but with the low visibility, the assailants' bullets had flown over him as he had ducked and slid. Now all three intruders were down.

*   *   *

Brandi's world was pitch-black. The last thing she had seen before squeezing her eyes shut was Cody running into hell's fury to snatch Knoxi off the floor. *Everyone I love in this world is dead. Why else would the guns have fallen silent?*

*   *   *

Cody was wide-eyed and focused after the gunfire ceased. The smoke and dust cloud hung motionless and filled his lungs. He coughed. Both his ears rang. The sound of every shot still echoed around inside his skull.

He squeezed his eyes shut. When he opened them, he was at the bridge on the outskirts of the Afghan village — cries of death, the stench of hell.

*"Phillips? Chavez? Secure the children! That's an order!"*

His ungainly commands were but hollow echoes against the battered walls of the smoke-filled apartment — none present or accounted for.

He coughed again as he clung to the edge of the coffee table and pulled himself to his feet. He stumbled toward the entryway until he saw an overturned sofa that had been obliterated by scalding bullets. Somehow it looked familiar. *How did it get here?*

Then the clamor in his head ceased. It was replaced by a coughing, gurgling sound that made him shudder. He moved forward slowly with weapon raised. Two men wearing black ski masks were lying on the floor. One was not moving. The other was thrashing back and forth, covered with blood, his hands wrapped around his own neck. Cody bent over and moved the bloody hands of the wounded man away from his throat to take a look. Blood spurted forth from a gaping bullet hole.

The thrashing and gurgling stopped. Cody unmasked them. Who were they? Why were they in this room? Why did everything here look familiar? This was just another of his nightmares. Wasn't it?

In the distance, he heard a single child crying and coughing. It sounded at least fifty meters away at first, and then just a few feet. The ringing in his ears was like a fire alarm, but he recognized the cough, didn't he?

Cody tracked in the direction of the child. He stumbled upon another masked individual lying face down in a pool of blood. Something then latched onto his left knee.

"*Knoxi!*" The toddler was trying to crawl up his leg. "Knoxi, what are you doing way out here? This is no place for you!"

Then someone else coughed at his six. He wheeled around and spotted Brandi on the floor in the kitchen. His senses returned.

He lifted Knoxi and tried to look her over for injuries, but examining her was impossible because she clung to him so tightly. He did not know the fate of the others as he raced into the kitchen to check on Brandi. She was still crouched against the wall, motionless. Hadn't she just coughed? Was she dead?

"Brandi? Brandi, it's me."

She looked up in disbelief. "Oh, Cody!" She scooted forward and latched onto his knees. Dazed, she pushed her fingers through the burn hole in his jeans above his right knee and then gazed upward for an explanation.

"Here. Take Knoxi. She has blood on her, but I don't think it's hers. I'm gonna check on your mom and dad. Brandi? Can you get up? Are you hurt?" He lifted her up with his free hand and hurriedly scanned her from head to toe. *No blood. Thank God!*

From the end of the hallway, Whitney screamed, *"Somebody help! Call 911. My husband is shot!"*

# THE ABYSS

Strobes and beacons reflected upward into a low-hanging haze. An eerie, flashing, flickering glow hovered over the steel city. Emergency lights, sirens, crackly radio sounds, but it wasn't the president who had been attacked. It was Brandi and the Babe.

In the wee hours, Pitt-Sinai Medical Center was lit up like daytime, swarming with federal and local law enforcement officers. News teams with cameras lined the streets.

Whitney was sitting with Ray in a recovery room under heavy police protection. The surgical team had removed a bullet from Ray's shoulder. The prognosis was good. Neither his shoulder joint nor internal organs had been injured seriously.

Brandi and her toddler had been escorted to a grand hospital suite while Cody remained at the apartment giving a detailed report to police and FBI agents.

This suite was the best hospital facility Brandi had ever seen, with two rooms — one for a patient and the other for family. The family room had two double beds and two foldout couches. The bathroom was L-shaped, with two showers and a whirlpool. The other bath, situated on the patient side, was the typical hospital type — utilitarian.

Brandi's throat felt like she had swallowed sandpaper. It was ragged from inhaling the gritty cloud in the apartment. She battled nausea and tried to calm Knoxi. The toddler had not ceased crying since the attack.

The sudden pandemonium of guns and smoke, discharges of more than a hundred rounds, and the sight of blood and human remains spotting the walls were more than Brandi's system could handle in one evening.

Her bruises from the theater attack were still painful, and her head was splitting. Ringing in their ears would not go away. Knoxi was cold and shaking. Mother and daughter coughed intermittently.

After a warm shower with Knoxi, Brandi dressed in scrubs provided by the hospital and then collapsed on one of the double beds. She wrapped her daughter in a blanket and cuddled with her. They finally dozed.

Whitney had insisted that Cody be allowed to stay with the Barnes family. When he at last dragged himself through the door, Knoxi awoke and reached for him.

Brandi sat up and stared. His eyes resembled those of a relic statue, his face deathly, ashen. Bloodstained head to foot, he labored just to put one leg in front of the other while making his way toward the bathroom door.

Brandi's life was a train wreck — attacked twice in one week? When would she wake up from this nightmare? The words of Dupree haunted her — *These guys are part of something much bigger.*

Cody and Ray had made them pay this time, but what about next time? Her crusade against the traffickers had come at a steep price.

She struggled to her feet, moved over to the window, and raised the wooden shades. Outside, the light of a full moon was washed out amidst the glow of searchlights and flashing beacons. From the twelfth floor at 2:00 a.m., the flickering haze above reminded her of muzzle flashes and gun smoke. She closed the shade.

She headed back to bed. It was then that she noticed a trail of bright red blood on the floor — a trail that led directly to the bathroom where Cody had retreated.

Whitney arrived. "They're bringing your father up in a few minutes."

"Oh, thank God." Then Brandi calmed herself. Cody needed her.

"Mama, could you take Knoxi for a minute? I can't get her calmed down, and I am about to go crazy. Beside that, I need to check on Cody." She pointed to the blood trail.

Whitney's face flashed alarm. "Does he know he's bleeding?" She took the toddler.

"No. He's like a sleepwalker. Need to get his attention and convince him to come out. I might even have to — Um, we'll ring a nurses' station if…" She looked toward the bathroom door.

"All right, baby, but he may just need some space if he isn't hurt bad."

Brandi nodded and then cautiously approached the bathroom entry. He had not latched the door. *Hmmm, not like him. He always locks it.*

She gently tapped. "Cody? Are you okay, sweetie?" No response. She nudged the door open slightly and peered through the small space.

His blood-spattered clothes were on the floor — jeans, tennis shoes, socks, and shirt all lying together. Then she saw a pair of orange sports boxers lying at the far end of the room with two holes in one of the legs. The boxers were soaked with fresh blood. The words on the large waistband were still visible — Under Armour American League All-Star.

Her heart galloped, sending adrenaline to every cell. No more nausea. No more fatigue. The water was running, but no one was in the shower. She tentatively walked in, turned off the water, then quietly listened. She could hear him moaning and sobbing around the corner at the dark end of the room.

She tiptoed carefully toward him, trying to avoid bloody smudges on the floor. Brandi wanted to peek around the corner where he had taken refuge, but she was afraid. She remembered being eight years old and approaching an injured German Shepherd while Ray warned her to not approach the scared, hurting animal. She had ignored her father and the dog had attacked her, drawing blood from her arm and leaving teeth marks that lasted several months. Ray's .45 may have saved her life that day.

Now, standing in Cody's blood, emotion overtook her and she tossed her fear. "Cody?" No answer.

Slowly she walked the last two steps and glanced around the corner. There he stood in the shadowy recess, his back to her, head hanging low, elbows resting on the shelf. He had knocked most of the towels into the floor. Had he even noticed?

The light in the corner was off, but when her eyes adjusted, she could see that a wound on his left hip was bleeding, not gushing. It was about four inches long, two inches below his waistline. A bullet had entered and exited, leaving a dark purple tunnel underneath the skin, his hip and leg covered with blood that dripped down to the floor.

Her mind raced. Her heart pounded. Cody had taken refuge in the one place he did not expect to be disturbed and had not invited her along.

He had not locked the door. Had he subconsciously hoped to be rescued? The guns and violence had sent him back. How many more times would this happen? Would Cody have been better off had they never met?

She would back away. He would never know she had intruded. But when she turned around, her mother was standing firm in the bathroom doorway.

Brandi read Whitney's face. *Get in there and save your man.*

She cherished the mother and daughter moment with a thankful nod, and then turned back toward the corner. Again, questions came — What if this time he would not let her in? Had he finally given up?

She had come too far to let him go now. If only she knew where his mind had taken him. The Taliban torturers again? Another night trap in a thunder squall? Into what abyss had he fallen? *Will he see me as an intruder?*

She paused and calmed herself. For two days, a story had rolled around inside her head. Why had she not been able to put it out of her mind?

It was the story of Esther, the young Hebrew woman chosen from among commoners to become the Queen. To save her nation, she had summoned all her courage and risked death to intrude uninvited before the King in his court. Her godly cousin, Mordecai, suggested to her that she had been born for that moment.

Now the story came to life, resonating in her heart. *Oh, God, was I born for this moment?*

With nervous fingers, she dialed up the lighting a quarter turn. Suddenly, she gasped. She had betrayed him. Brandi wanted to dim the lights again, but now that she knew, she could not unknow it — the reason he would not change his shirt in her presence.

The shock of cold discovery could not be silenced by covering her lips. Her cry echoed off the tile walls, muffled only by the steamy air. The hideous scars that extended from his shoulders to his knees were four years old, but she had only now felt their sting.

She cried softly as she pulled a towel off the rack and fastened it securely around his waist. Her fingers gently traced over the wounds on his shoulders and back as if to erase the pain the injuries had once caused, and to absorb from him the agony in his soul.

"Cody, sweetie, can you hear me? Babe, it's me. I want to be there with you. Is there lightning where you are? Angels two zero? Let me lead you back to the deck. Cody?"

He made no response.

"Babe, *please* come back to me."

At last, she squeezed her arms around him with all her might and screamed desperately, *"Oh, God, please save my man of steel!"*

Brandi's unbridled prayer pierced every corner of the bathroom and resounded like the battle shout of an angel warrior.

Slowly he turned around. He clutched her and drew her close. He still reeked of gunpowder, but his arms were cotton-soft around her.

Finally, he spoke. "I'm sorry you had to come in here and see me like this. Every dark corner where I set my feet reminds me of who I am. That will never change." He lowered his head. "I prayed you'd never see what

I'm capable of. I don't want the people I care about to be afraid of me. I don't want my grief from things I've seen and done to wreck the lives of people I love. You don't deserve that. Your parents don't deserve that."

She was blindsided, wanted to reassure him somehow, but her father's eleventh leadership principle reminded her — "In a life-altering crisis, choose carefully your first words, for they will be remembered forever."

She waited and listened. If ever she needed something profound — a wise saying, a Bible story or verse, a courtside pep talk — it was now. But this time, she had only one thought: *Just tell him what is in your heart.*

*Really?* It seemed random, insignificant, and way too simple, but she was losing him, and it was now or never. She gave her heart permission to hold nothing back, and then slowly began. Her breathy words — candid, unrehearsed, unashamed — floated from her lips and gently swirled around him like a sweet fragrance from the purest summer spring.

"I've seen all your scars now, Cody, and I am not afraid, because each mark shows me what you are capable of. These wounds brought soldiers home to their families.

"I know exactly what you are capable of. Tonight I saw you charge into a cloud of gun smoke to save my baby. I froze, but you never hesitated."

She gripped his shoulders. "In Detroit, when you read your poem to Knoxi, I knew you were the man I had prayed for every lonely night for two years when I asked God to send me a *real* man who would love my baby girl as much as he loves me."

She placed her hand on his heart. "Cody, you grieve for the Afghan children because you couldn't save them. The only heart that cannot be broken is one that has no love in it." She lifted up his chin. "You're the man who brings hope to kids by the hundreds in every stadium and dark corner where you set your feet. That's who you are.

"Tonight was killing, but it wasn't murder, and when the sun rises in a few hours, America will know that three killers no longer steal children from their parents or abuse women for sport, because you and my father were capable of stopping them."

He straightened his back and squared his shoulders.

"Cody, you asked God to forgive you. You're clean, so stop calling unclean what God has cleansed."

"I guess I'm the one who doesn't deserve you," he finally drawled out.

"You mean, I'm not bad for a girl?"

He shook his head. "You're not a girl. I went into that theater to see Superman, but I walked out with Wonder Woman."

"Now listen to me. You are wounded. You are bleeding."

"No, I wasn't hurt. I'm fine."

She could barely manage a whisper. "Cody, you have a *bloodeus' maximus*. I'm gonna have them send a doctor. Wash the blood off. Pull the shower curtain, but don't lock the door. I don't want you passing out in here alone. Do you copy?"

"Copy that, ma'am. Did you say *bloodeus maximus?*"

She giggled and turned to go. "Affirmative. *You look shot!*"

# YOU NEVER KNOW

A moment later, Brandi came bounding from the bathroom sporting a huge grin. Whitney sat on the edge of the bed with Knoxi in her arms. "That evidently went well. Is he hurt? And what was that laughing I heard? Was that Cody?"

"I told him he looked shot."

"Shot? Well, you both look shot if you ask me."

"Roger that, but Cody has a bullet wound on his *retrosphere.*"

"*Retrosphere*? Is that a language I don't know?"

"On his butt, Mama. He has a wound on his butt!"

"Ohhh." She put her hands on her hips. "Wait. You mean like *shot*? How bad?"

"Just a flesh wound." Brandi shrugged it off as she scooted over to the window and opened the shades again. "It's the first time I've heard him laugh. Gives me hope that — Oh, how's Daddy?"

"Resting. So how bad is Cody hurt? Does he need —"

"A doctor? Affirmative. We need to initiate communications with the nurses' station."

"Now you're even startin' to talk like him. Baby, is he okay? I mean *really* okay?"

"Oh, Mama, he's beautiful. He's the most gorgeous man I've ever seen." Then she composed her feverish smile and straightened her face. "What I mean is, if he hadn't been there tonight —"

"Baby, none of us should've been there tonight, but as your man says, '*you never know.*'"

"Roger that. He still hasn't said he loves me. I pray he'll be able to express himself enough someday to tell me."

Whitney hugged her. "Your father's in the other room, still groggy. And tell that man in the bathroom he needs to get out here, *shot or no shot*, and pick up the baby. She really needs her new daddy."

Brandi's eyes brightened up. She set some scrubs inside the bathroom door. "Babe, I'm puttin' some clothes here for you. Everything okay?"

He extended his hand through the curtain and signaled thumbs-up.

In a few minutes, Cody emerged and then collapsed face down on one of the beds. The legs of the scrubs were too short, lacking about four inches.

"Cody, I'm gonna see if I can find some socks for you to cover the scars."

"Don't worry about it. Doesn't matter anymore."

"Any itching this time?"

"Nope." He exhaled a long sigh of relief. "And your *shot* joke?" he groaned. "That was pretty sick."

*"Ha!* You laughed didn't you?"

His eyes were shut.

Moments later, two doctors and an intern nurse arrived to take care of the "emergency" surrounding Cody's wound. Brandi retreated to her father's bedside in the other room.

When the medical team had finished, the doctors agreed he should not play baseball for at least two weeks. He protested. "I can just slide on my other side."

They chuckled and gave him a bottle of antibiotics. "Two weeks, Mr. Musket. Doctor's orders."

"Okay, okay. Two weeks," Cody grumbled.

Brandi was amused as she overheard a conversation between the intern — a baby-faced young woman named Lilly — and the doctors as they departed.

"Wow! I never saw a famous person's butt before," the starry-eyed intern declared. "He's lucky he didn't lose his hip."

One of the doctors, a tiny woman with dark hair and thick glasses, spoke up. "His hip? Lucky he didn't lose his life. They said one of the walls in that apartment was almost destroyed by bullets."

The other doctor, a tall man with a booming voice, answered back. "I heard Wyatt Earp was involved in numerous gunfights and never even got a scratch."

"Guess he'll get pretty antsy not playing baseball for two weeks."

"Are you kidding me, Lilly?" the tall doctor spouted. "He'll just get a couple of buddies to slap some pine tar on it, and he'll be back in the lineup again tomorrow night."

Brandi chuckled as she came to check on Cody. He was motionless with his eyes shut, still lying on his stomach. No! He would *not* be playing ball any time soon. She would make certain of that!

In the other room, Knoxi whimpered again. Brandi went to her, but the distraught child would not be comforted. Moments later, Cody appeared in the doorway. When Knoxi saw him, she reached out. Brandi handed her off.

Ray asked the ladies to give him a few moments with Cody. The two women went into the other room.

Knoxi finally caught her breath. She was now quiet and content. It was 4:15 a.m.

"That baby girl really loves you, son. I guess you know that."

"I know. Feeling's mutual." He wrapped his arms even tighter around the child. "How's the shoulder?"

"I've been hit worse." Ray's voice was crackly but unwavering.

"Roger that. You saved my life. Your hunch was right. Good thing you brought the .45."

"You saved my girls," Ray answered back. "But I think we should give God the credit."

"Is that one of your Top Five?"

"Oh. Brandi told you about that?" He chuckled.

"How many are there now?" Cody inquired.

"Fourteen."

"If I may ask, what principle is number *one* on your list?"

"You will learn that on your own, Cody. When you do, I'll tell you and we'll compare notes."

"Fair enough." Cody took a deep breath. "I've invited Brandi to come to Houston with me. I want to pull a surprise and propose to her Saturday night during the seventh-inning stretch at Minute Maid Park. If you aren't able to travel by then, I'll wait, but I want to marry your daughter, and I am asking your blessing."

"That's my girl, Lieutenant. It would take at least ten divisions to keep me away." He chuckled, and then his voice deepened.

"I want to ask you a question, Cody. Do you believe in the devil?"

"The devil?"

"Affirmative. Do you believe in the devil?"

Cody thought for a moment, then answered, "Any man who's been to hell believes in the devil, sir."

"We are warriors, Cody. We've taken lives. That'll never change. What we've been through will always be part of who we are. That's why you gotta remember you were created in God's image, *not* the devil's image. If you're gonna marry my daughter and be a father to my granddaughter, you *will* remember that."

"Loud and clear, Captain. I read you loud and clear."

"Son, until five days ago, I didn't believe there was a man on earth good enough for my girl. I know your old man would be proud of who you've become." Then Ray shut his eyes. "Prove me wrong, Marine, and I'll fan your butt…" He drifted off.

Cody looked at Knoxi staring him in the face. "Aren't you sleepy, little girl?"

He held her on his right arm and waltzed her gently, floating around the room hoping she would fall asleep, but her pearlescent blue eyes would not give up. He gruffed out a familiar tune, humming at first, and then trying to sing. Knoxi curled her fingers inside his bottom lip again, like when he had read his poem to her.

Brandi and Whitney appeared in the doorway when they heard Cody's attempt to carry a tune. Despite his gritty monotone, something about it was heavenly at that hour. Brandi decided to video record the event with her smartphone, but the reluctant hero and the willing princess never noticed. Locked in a visual bond, they were oblivious to all else.

In a few minutes, Cody paused. "Baby girl, I got a secret. You're not the only blue-eyed lady I've fallen hard for in this town lately, so what do you think of that?"

Ray awakened just in time to see the corners of Knoxi's lips turn upward. *"You never know,"* she said, her blue eyes twinkling like the little star.

Whitney gasped. Brandi tossed her phone onto Ray's bed, scooted to Cody's side, and squeezed him with both arms. The toddler's first spoken words — Cody's favorite catch-phrase — had arrived with a perfect Texas drawl.

Brandi's squeaky voice hoarsened her response. "Something I've wanted to tell you, Mr. Texas; I would be so honored if you would take me to the beach with you sometime."

"Hmmm. With me? Well, I been told there are no beaches around here."

"Well, I been told there are plenty of beaches near Houston." She moved her lips next to his and closed her eyes. "Oh, I'm so totally going to cry all over you. I'm so sorry."

Despite her meltdown, he clutched her with his free arm and kissed her with an ardor that dispelled any notion of subtlety. Afterward, Knoxi, who still occupied his other arm, clapped her hands and let it fly, *"Yaaaaaay!"*

Cody tossed Ray a glance. The wounded old warrior shut his eyes and nodded as if he had just seen heaven. "Principle number one," he said with weak vocal cords. *"The ability to bring healing to others is granted in deepest measure to those who carry scars."*

He drifted into a dreamy, restful sleep.

\*   \*   \*

At dawn, news of the attack at Mayfield Tower sent repercussions around the world. War had been declared on America's darling duo.

Brandi and the Babe had captured the imagination of a country weary of violence. The valiant couple had made bad guys pay a dear price, and it was to the delight of a nation desperately in need of heroes.

Cody wanted to get them all out of Pittsburgh as quickly as possible. He would take his Tyler Rose and his little princess home to familiar surroundings. They would be more secure in Houston, wouldn't they? Would his agent's strategy finally pay off? Could they ever just get back to baseball? And love?

# HATE IN THE WIND

E veryone slept all day Thursday. The shootings of Wednesday night had left them depleted.

Cody woke up Thursday evening when Lilly, the intern, returned. She had been assigned to change Cody's bandage and check for infection. She was alone this time — no doctors. Her hands were shaking, and she kept apologizing for interrupting his evening.

"I will try to not hurt you. If anything doesn't look right, I'll call a doctor. I promise."

Lilly was a nervous wreck. Brandi didn't like it. "If it's okay with you and Cody, I can stay here and assist you. I've had some experience with wounds and changing bandages."

"Thank you, ma'am. I'm nearly through with nursing school, but I'm always afraid I'm gonna hurt someone. This is the first time I've seen a real bullet wound since I was ten years old. Guns make me nervous. My little brother shot himself."

"Well, I am so sorry to hear that, Lilly. So, what happened?"

"He died, ma'am. He was seven. I didn't know what to do. We were in the woods behind our house and found the gun. When it went off, there was blood everywhere. My back porch was just fifty yards away, but I couldn't find my way home. The next day — Never mind, I can't talk about it. I want to be a doctor someday, but sometimes when I look at my hands, I still see my brother's blood on them. Even a simple task like changing a bloody bandage…"

"I had to change my own bandages when I was stabbed several years ago," Brandi offered. "It's a piece of cake." Then she looked at Cody. "Uh, you're gonna have to turn over, sweetie."

Lilly removed the bandage. "The doctor said these older scars were from the war. I read that you were a hero, Mr. Musket."

Brandi bit her lip. "Uh, Lilly, Cody is sensitive and doesn't like to talk about his —"

Cody cleared his throat. "What kinda hands do you have, Lilly?"

"What kind of hands? I guess just regular hands. I don't quite get your meaning."

"May I see 'em?"

She stepped forward and showed him her hands. He reached out with his left palm and asked her to take hold. Her hands were cold and shaky.

"Hmmm. Just as I thought, young lady. These aren't regular hands. These are *healing* hands."

"They are?" she asked, studying her hands. "Well, how can you tell?"

"A good friend patched me up in Afghanistan. He blew up things and he was a sniper, but he was also a medic. When he dealt with wounds, he had to remind himself his hands were meant to heal, not hurt. He said it's all about where you set your mind. He saved my life."

"Right now, I can't stop my healing hands from shaking."

"Oh, well. I'd have never noticed," Brandi teased. "I have an idea. You just change the bandage, and I'll shake my hands so you won't have to shake yours."

*"Ha-ha!* That's funny. Nobody ever offered to do that."

Lilly managed to calm down, clean the wound and re-bandage it — no complications. After she had left, Brandi handed Cody the latest edition of the *Gazette*.

"Here, read this." She had circled a news article about the torture and murder of Sasha Williams.

"I must say," Brandi observed, "Lilly seemed relaxed when she left. Maybe she'll —"

"*Did you actually read this?*" he interrupted, slamming the paper down.

Startled, Brandi wheeled around. "*Shhh!* You're gonna wake everybody up."

He softened his voice but not his intensity. "Did you read about the things they did to her?" He clenched his fists.

"*Cody!* Get hold of yourself. Yes, I read it." She picked up the page. "I shouldn't have handed it to you right now. What was I thinking?"

"We should go." He reached for the paper again.

"Go? Where?"

"The memorial service. It's tomorrow, 'bout two hours east of here."

"What about security?"

"I have a team coming in tonight. They can take us. The police and press won't even know we're gone. These guys are that good."

\* \* \*

The memorial service for Sasha Williams was scheduled for 10 a.m. Friday morning at Central City AME Church in Herronburg, Pennsylvania, a two-hundred-year-old community east of Pittsburgh.

Cody and Brandi rode in the back seat of a dark green Hummer with bullet proof, tinted windows. Stan Knight, a former FBI agent, now ran his own security company. He was driving. Hunter Page, former Army Ranger, rode shotgun.

They had used a clever ruse to fool the press into believing they were still holed up in the hospital. They managed to sneak out of town without alerting anyone, and they were not followed.

Soon, Pittsburgh was in the rear view mirror. Cody gazed out at the grassy Pennsylvania countryside. The rolling hills, an occasional barn, and intermittent forests along the highway made it a welcome change from the industrial complexity.

Cody picked up a folded tabloid that Brandi had brought along. "What's this?"

"Oh, you'll love that." She sounded like her mother when she wanted to be sarcastic. "That's called the *Renegade Brigade.*"

"Never heard of it."

"You haven't missed anything. One of the nurses gave it to me. Makes a big issue of the fact that the three guys who attacked me at the theater were black. Says it was racially motivated."

"No way," Cody said. "Don't they know about your parents?"

"Probably, but it doesn't matter to them. The piece quotes some militant group saying they want to kill all white people. *Scary. "*

"Hate. It's nothin' but hate. Just when I think I'm gettin' past it, I read about Sasha. I wanna kill 'em — the three guys in custody. Sasha was so...so innocent." He pounded his knee with his fist.

"You have gotten past it, Cody. Don't allow yourself to believe otherwise." She put her hand on top of his.

He relaxed his fist and gently clasped her fingers. "The pain of Afghanistan is gone. Since the other night in the shower, it has just disappeared — *after four years.* How do you figure it?" He leaned his head back.

"Don't try to figure it out. I reminded you of who you are and that God had forgiven you. Somehow, in those moments, He took away your pain. That was a miracle. He did that part. It wasn't me."

"Yeah. I was startin' to see that, but now, this funeral, more reminders. Where does it end — the killing, the hate? I can't help it. I wanna kill 'em. It's happening all over again."

He took a long breath, looked out at the hills again, and exhaled slowly. "Stan, how much farther to the church?"

"Just a few more miles, Cody. We're gonna make a drive-by for recon."

"Roger that." Cody was already fatigued, and his sore hip ached from riding in the vehicle.

They crossed a railroad track and saw a large contingent of bikers — about fifty of them, all white — parked near a creek bed. It was not what they had expected to see in a predominantly African American community.

They continued two blocks and saw the church on their left. The parking lot was full. Stan slowed as they approached. It was his job to be suspicious. No one knew they were coming — no security detail waiting to protect them.

Hunter looked at his watch. "You sure the start time's ten o'clock? We're an hour early, but looks like the church is full."

Sasha had been popular. Her uncle, Dr. Jonathan Williams, was the senior pastor. His son, Johnny, a former Army specialist, was his associate pastor.

They had hoped to avoid walking in after others were seated, but most of the seats were already filled with mourners humming the familiar tune of "Amazing Grace."

The couple squeezed into a pew on the back row near the door. Brandi sat next to the aisle, with Cody crunched in beside her. No one had recognized them.

The building was a modern A-frame with sleek wooden beams that began at floor level, extended upward, and then curved gracefully into bold rafters angling overhead. Seating capacity appeared to be about two hundred. The architecture, simple but magnificent, reflected a harmony between man and nature.

Skylights invited healing radiance into the midst. Sweet, natural fragrances of magnolia and northern red oak filled the air, blending the sanctuary seamlessly into the lush Pennsylvania landscape. On such a day as this, it reminded one of realms brilliant and balmy where Sasha now reveled in her glorious eternal future.

Cody was surprised to see smiles on the faces of those who had known Sasha. It was not like military funerals he had attended. This meeting was more like a celebration.

After several lively presentations by the Central City AME Dancing Choir, a local rapper performed a number he had just written in tribute to Sasha. It brought tears to Brandi's eyes.

Next, the pastor introduced his son, Johnny Williams, who stepped up to the pulpit.

"Good morning, ladies and gentlemen. I'm Sasha's cousin. She lived with us for the past eight years since her mother died. She was a sister to me and like a daughter to my mom and dad.

"Four years ago in Afghanistan, I was one of eight survivors of a helicopter crash. I was captured by the enemy. Sasha prayed for my freedom for several days without eating or sleeping. My release seemed impossible at the time, but —" He stopped suddenly.

Brandi whispered to Cody. "Was he one of the guys on that Chinook?"

But Cody ignored her question. Something was wrong. Johnny was frozen at the pulpit. His eyes were focused on an individual who had just entered the building from the back.

Next, a chilling voice called out. "*We will cleanse the earth!*"

The shrill interruption stunned everyone. Cody turned to his left. What he saw sent tremors down his spine and brought his protective instincts to full alert. Standing in the aisle next to Brandi was a white male, about five feet six inches tall, brandishing a semiautomatic handgun. *How did they find us?*

The individual with the gun fixed his gaze upon Brandi and pointed the weapon toward her head at point-blank range. *"Traitor!"* He pulled the trigger.

But Cody had already become airborne, flying horizontally across Brandi and stretching his right hand toward the weapon. He managed to get two fingers around the muzzle, deflecting the gun the instant it fired.

Hunter Page, who had ridden shotgun, fired his weapon and struck the shooter in the chest, but Page took a shot in the leg during the process.

Screams and panic — everything was chaos. Then, more shots rang out. Cody looked toward the opposite side of the church. A second individual standing over six feet tall was discharging another handgun, firing blindly into the crowd. Bullets found targets.

"Everybody down! Everybody get down!" But Cody's voice could not be heard over the crying and screaming. He pulled the handgun away from the wounded first shooter in hopes of stopping the second one, but too many people were in his line of sight.

"*Everybody down!*" This time, people heard and jumped out of his way.

Stan Knight then fired a kill shot through the heart of the second gunman. The shooting stopped.

At first, Cody was disoriented and could not remember where he had left Brandi. When he turned around, he saw her lying on the bench, her face and dress covered with blood.

"*Brandi!*" He screamed above the noise and knelt beside her. "Brandi?"

Brandi covered her face. "Oh, Cody!" She coughed. Blood came from her nose and mouth. "My nose!" She was panting. "*My face! Uggggh. It hurts.*"

"What? How?"

"When you jumped over me your elbow caught me in the nose." She struggled to catch her breath.

"Oh, thank God! I thought you'd been shot!"

"*Well, it feels like it!*" She coughed. "Ohhh! My head is exploding." She tried to sit up but collapsed. Now, writhing on the bench, the sounds of the wounded filled her head — moaning, sobbing, vomiting, crying out. Cody had told her what hell sounded like. Now she had a small dose.

Why had this happened? Most people go through life only *hearing* about violence, but in one week, she and Cody had been in three life-threatening violent encounters. This time, countless others were suffering. *Is this our fault?*

Cody fumbled through Brandi's purse and pulled out a handful of tissue which he gently held over her nose. She was still coughing, gasping.

"Brandi, can you sit up? Breathe through your mouth." He helped her rise to a sitting position and supported her head with his left hand. He looked around the room hoping to spot someone who could help Brandi, but he saw only chaos.

What had been the scene of tribute to Sasha's life was now a disaster zone. The shuffling feet of emergency responders made a rustling sound along with sirens, the loud clopping of rotor blades echoing through the sky, and the rumbling of motorcycles on the church grounds. *Motorcycles?*

Cody checked two weapons he had taken from the first shooter. How much ammo was left? Would there be more shooting? More death? *If only we had stayed in Pittsburgh.*

A quick count revealed only four fatalities so far, not including both assailants. Fourteen additional worshippers had been wounded. Responders had their hands full with the seriously injured, so Brandi and Cody were on their own.

After several minutes, Johnny Williams, whose presentation had been interrupted, came and knelt next to Brandi. He had recognized Cody. "Ma'am, can you stand up? Please come to my office. My wife is a nurse. I'll ask her to attend your injury." They tried to help her up, but her knees were shaking, so Cody lifted and cradled her.

"Thanks for your help. Brandi's really shook up. Just lead the way. I have two weapons in my belt. We may need 'em."

"No need for that. Just follow me."

Johnny wove between the wounded and the emergency responders, working his way to his office. Cody followed and then carefully placed Brandi on a sofa next to the window. He winced. The flesh wound on his hip had reopened when he had leapt over Brandi. It felt like a wasp sting.

Johnny's wife, Charlie, an ER nurse, introduced herself. Brandi's nose and mouth were swollen and still bloody. Charlie cleaned her up and gave her a soft ice pack for the swelling. Cody held the ice to her face.

"Thank you for your kindness, Charlie. My head is spinning." Brandi rubbed her temples.

"Lean back against this cushion, ma'am. My mother is a resident ER doctor at Hopper Memorial. She's on her way. You could have a head injury. We should leave nothing to chance. Meanwhile, here are some clothes you can change into."

They heard a soft knock. A uniformed police officer nudged the door open a few inches. "May I come in for a minute?" He quietly swung the door open. "Mr. Musket, I am Clarence Danforth of the Herronburg Police Department. Mind if I talk to you?"

Danforth had several questions but kept it brief. Afterward, Cody had several questions of his own.

"Officer Danforth, can you tell me who the shooters were and why they attacked? Did it have anything to do with Sasha? Were they after Brandi? Were they after me? Also, sir, would it be possible not to mention that I had any part in stopping these men? Give the credit to the others. I know it's asking a lot, but I still have a hard time with —"

"Mr. Musket, I won't even remember who you are after this meeting. As for motive, these guys were from a white supremacist clan that operates in the southeast part of the state. It had nothing to do with you or Sasha Williams. It was about hatred for all people with black skin. They want us all dead."

"I guess you'll be glad when I leave your state," Cody muttered. "Since I showed up, I've been involved in an abduction attempt, a shootout, and a hate killing. I seem to attract violence." He gave the two weapons to the officer.

"I take issue with that, Cody. If your security team hadn't been here, the victims would have numbered more than — well, I hate to think about it. They attack a church because it's a soft target. They weren't expecting any resistance."

The tall officer nodded to Brandi. "Ma'am, I'm sorry for your injury. I'll leave so they can finish taking care of you and help you get changed. Hated to barge in, but it's my job."

As Danforth left, Charlie's mother arrived. "Hello, Ms. Barnes, I'm Dr. Brown. Just call me Sam. Hello, Mr. Musket. Are you injured?"

Cody subconsciously placed his hand over his injured hindquarter. "Uh, no, ma'am, but Brandi took an elbow in the nose — an elbow from me."

"He was too busy saving my life to watch out for my nose." Brandi was wobbly, but she hadn't lost all sense of humor.

The doctor examined Brandi's face. "Hmmm, eyes look fine, the nose does not show signs of a break, but when you get back to Pitt-Sinai Hospital this afternoon, have them run these tests. I'm writing them down for you." Sam handed the list to Cody.

Charlie looked closely at one of Brandi's arms. "What about these abrasions on your forearms ma'am? Do you have serious injuries elsewhere?"

"Oh, here and there, yes. And please, both of you, call me Brandi." She reached down and pulled off her shoes. "These heels are hurting my feet."

That prompted Sam. "Brandi, have you had a medical exam since your attack last Friday in that theater? Your feet and ankles are swollen and inflamed. If you have other injuries, you should be checked. The hematoma and skin abrasions do not look good."

"Well," Brandi said, glancing at Cody, "I have been treating them myself, doctor." She blotted her eyes. "And we've been through so much this week."

"Perhaps while Charlie and I help you change we could take a look at you if you don't mind."

"I'm not leaving you alone." Cody placed his hands on her shoulders. "How secure is this office? It was my idea to come today. All my fault."

Brandi's voice was unsteady. "Um, is it okay if Cody stays? I mean I don't mind." Her face was puffy, her nose and right eye turning purple.

"I'll just sit in the corner and look the other way," Cody suggested. "You won't even know I'm here."

"Mr. Musket, Cody, your girlfriend will be in good hands. I promise we will not harm her, and this office is secure from outside entry. I would prefer you wait in the next room, please."

Cody's glowering eyes looked to Brandi. She nodded her approval.

"Okay, doctor," he grumbled. "I suppose the last thing I wanna see right now is more blood and bruises."

Cody looked back once more to make sure Brandi had not changed her mind and then limped out and closed the door behind him.

"He didn't mean that like it sounded," Brandi offered. "He just has a way with words now and then."

Sam displayed a guarded smile. "Apologies not necessary. You didn't see the tears in his eyes, child. He doesn't want to let you out of his sight right now."

A buoyant smile softened Brandi's distended face. "Yes. I know. And he feels responsible for the bad that has happened, even though it wasn't his fault."

"Not unusual when one has lived through his experiences," Sam said.

"*Traitor.* He called me a *traitor*."

"Who did, ma'am?"

"The shooter. I remember now. He called me a traitor. I guess I looked like a white girl in a black church." She shook her head.

With glistening eyes, Charlie and Sam somberly examined Brandi's bruised ribs and other injuries.

"There are seriously injured people in the next room," Brandi said. "Don't they need you worse than I do? You both seem to be taking this in stride."

"The injured have been evacuated to hospitals in the area, dear." The doctor's tone was calm. "And you mention taking it in stride? I know you have some African blood in you, Brandi, but you don't live in the neighborhood I'm in. Here, in a black community, we live with the threat of this violence all the time. We fight a constant battle with hate."

"How does this ever end?" Brandi picked up the ice pack again. "Cody and I have been hunted by organized traffickers. It is so hard to believe that we have been involved in another incident here, and it had nothing to do with trafficking. It was just pure hate for no reason."

"Jesus said to love your enemies," Sam pointed out. "Dr. King declared that hate does not defeat hate, and that only love can conquer hate. This church is called to lift up the light. When folks see the peace that Jesus gives, they run to Him. We see it every day."

# LOVE IN THE DARK

Cody stood in the sanctuary looking over the crime scene and waiting for Brandi. Two police officers searched the floor for shell casings. A teenage girl worked hard to clean Brandi's blood off the back pew. As Cody watched, his anger escalated again.

Would they reschedule a memorial service? No one had yet spoken of Sasha's sweet, easy-riding demeanor. She had put him at ease, had honored him, and had transparently revealed her affection for Brandi, a woman she did not even know. He had known Sasha for only a moment, but that was long enough to realize she was a rare soul. Someone should have said so. The service had been interrupted way too early.

He wanted to take up arms and kill three men. Though they were in custody, he had already killed them in his mind a hundred times in a hundred different ways. Sasha must be avenged. He thought he was rid of the hatred, but with a new enemy came new challenges. Was it a test?

"Mister Musket?"

Cody turned around. It was the pastor, Dr. Jonathan Williams.

"Hello, Cody. I'm Jon Williams, Sasha's uncle."

The senior pastor, despite sad eyes and trouble, managed a keen and distinguished smile. He had removed his coat and tie.

"Hello, sir." Cody paused. "I...I don't know what to say to you right now."

"Johnny, my own son, would have loved to visit with you, Cody, but he has left to be with the shooting victims in the hospital. I will be going there in a few minutes. When I found out you were here, I wanted to stay behind and take a minute to talk."

The pastor paused and placed his left hand over his forehead. "I'm sorry. I hoped this wouldn't happen." His deep voice broke. "Sometimes I get so weary, Cody."

During the previous seven days, Cody had seen plenty of tears — something to which he was not accustomed. But he was becoming more comfortable, even entertaining the notion that male tears might not always be a sign of weakness.

The man standing before him was struggling. Who could blame him? Two deranged individuals had attacked his beloved congregation. People were dead. Cody knew all too well what that felt like. He recognized the charisma this man carried along with the onus of command that had brought him to such sorrow.

Other people in the building had now departed. The two men stood alone in the sanctuary. It was an awkward moment.

"Pastor, is that your picture on the bulletin board riding that big Harley?" Cody hoped to kick-start the conversation again.

"Yes, Cody. That was six years ago when several of us took our message of redemption on the road to biker meetings in Pennsylvania, West Virginia, and Ohio. We saw miracle after miracle and — How 'bout you? Do you ride?"

"Well, in Detroit, Tuesday night, I rode with a friend on the biggest bike I had ever seen."

"Fun? Did you enjoy it?"

"*Ha!* Never been so scared in my life."

The two men laughed briefly and then came to another pause.

"Cody, the first thing I want to say is…" He fought for his composure again and then continued with a steady voice. "I wanna thank you for giving me back my son. He is here ministering the Gospel with me. That would never have happened if you hadn't…"

Cody lowered his head, shut his eyes briefly, and then opened them again.

"Johnny told us that when the chopper came to transport you to Kandahar, he and the seven other survivors moved up in front of the Navy guys, picked up the transport gurney themselves and lifted you on board. Nobody thought you would survive. I am so happy to see you here in my church. It's an honor I thought I would never have."

"The honor is mine, sir. Sasha told me Johnny was on that Chinook."

"So you knew her?"

"Only for a few minutes, but it was enough time to know that she was a beautiful person. I...I may have been partly responsible for her death." Cody's eyes began to burn with hot tears that quickly overflowed onto his face. "I know she was like a daughter to you. I seem to be really good at being in the wrong place at the wrong time, getting people killed — like today, for example."

The patriarchal minister looked confused at first, and then his face completely reconfigured as though he knew every thought in Cody's mind.

"Now you listen to me, son. You listen real good. What happened today was gonna happen with or without your being here. Your security men saved countless lives. You may think you've been in the wrong place on occasion, but today wasn't one of those times.

"And about Sasha. Yesterday, Johnny and I went to the jail where the suspects are held. One came out to talk but spit in my face. The second one didn't want to see us at all, but the third one — age seventeen — embraced the person of Jesus and asked Him to forgive his sin. He cried bitter tears. We cried happy tears. I know it's what Sasha would have done and what she wanted. Who knows how much good that young man may do in the future. He might even save the world someday. We only know that the plans God has for us are good — plans for us to prosper and be in peace."

Cody hung his head. His thirst for revenge had brought him to shame in the presence of such greatness.

Brandi emerged from Johnny's office carrying her shoes. She walked gingerly toward the two men and then stopped about twenty feet away next to a grand piano. Her first thought was to turn back and wait, but something stopped her where she stood.

A Presence hovered. It was overwhelming, older than the earth, sweet, irresistible like waves of liquid love. It was infinitely more powerful than the monster that had seemed to invade their suite in Detroit when Cody had fleshed out his tale of child carnage and bloody sorrow. Brandi sat down on the piano bench and bowed her head, listening to the venerated pastor break open his heart and pour out its contents over her man.

"Cody, there is something else I must ask you."

"What's that, sir?"

"Do you know what thin line separates a hero from a murderer?"

*"Thin line?"* Cody asked. "I don't understand."

"A hero doesn't want to hurt anyone but sometimes has to, while a murderer doesn't have to hurt anybody but *wants* to. In every man there is a hero, and in every man there is a murderer. It only requires stepping over that line. Mind your heart, son, that it knows where to stop."

Pastor Williams turned and headed toward the door. He paused to look back. "I have suffering people I must go to, Cody. Several of our church family are dead and many injured, including a pregnant teenager who is fighting for her life. Come back and see us, and bring your family next time."

"Family?" Cody looked to his left and saw Brandi approaching.

She stopped a few steps away, a shoe in each hand, and opened her arms. With no hesitation, he walked right in. It was the first time they had held each other and wept together. It was not for shame, not for sorrow, but for the peace and the undoing of shackles. For the revelation that there is an empty place in the human heart that cries out to be occupied by the Ancient of Days — a union where only love hides in the shadows and where there is no pit so deep that He is not deeper still.

As they prepared to leave the building, Stan met them in the doorway. "Don't go out this front door. We need to move out through the side exit — too many reporters in the front. They've been looking for you. That cop in charge — Danforth — he's standing guard out front. He won't let the press into the building until I get you out. I've arranged for a chopper. It's waiting on the south lawn."

"So, how many people are waiting for us on the south lawn? The helo is bound to attract everybody, and it's a long walk to the landing zone."

Stan had an answer, "It's about thirty yards, but I took care of that too."

Cody pushed the side exit door open a few inches to take a look. Filling up his view was a giant gray-haired man wearing a red bandana and a snaggletooth smile. When Cody swung the door fully open, he was promptly greeted with a salute.

"Hello, Lieutenant! Corporal K. Bob Braddock at your disposal, sir."

The man standing before him looked to be about six four. He wore jeans cut off below the knees that appeared old enough to have been worn by Noah on the Ark. His combat boots looked brand new. With massive sun-freckled arms, a neck and face that resembled aged leather, and a long ponytail that was tangled and weather-beaten, he and his muscle shirt both had enough years to be considered relics.

Cody finished looking him over. "Well, Corporal, how'd you get fresh blood on your shirt?"

"Volunteered my services a few minutes ago to help with the wounded, Cody. Served as a medic with the 5th Cavalry in 'Nam. I'm eighty and still goin' strong."

"Funny. You don't look a day over seventy-nine."

"*Hahaha!* I've never heard that one before, sir. Ma'am. So check this out." He flexed his biceps. "See, the thing about getting old is, you know you still got it, 'cept nobody wants to see it anymore!"

Braddock's untamed humor was a welcome breeze clearing the air and did not seem out of place even after the tragedy. His deep laughter made the porch vibrate. Brandi, still carrying her shoes, could feel it in her toes, even though the pain medication Sam had given her was beginning to take effect.

The two men shook hands, and then Braddock explained. "I was able to organize an honor guard to your ride, Cody. Ma'am." He turned and pointed. "Take a look."

They stepped down and went through the gate. A path led directly to a helicopter thirty yards away, its turbine engines idling and rotors already turning. Bikers, both men and women, had lined up along the sides of the pathway — helmets, snarling faces, muscle shirts. It was the same group they had spotted near the railroad track, but it now appeared to number at least a hundred. The group stood facing outward, daring anyone in the clamoring mob to cross the line.

Brandi leaned on Cody. "My head's spinning again." He picked her up.

As he carried Brandi to the waiting helo, their biker honor guard stood fast. Braddock, with the non-stop voice, was at no loss for words.

"A hellish week for you, Lieutenant? I read about it."

"Roger that, Corporal. I keep ending up in the wrong place — three times in one week. Just wanna play baseball, but —"

"Cody, in November '65 at La Drang, we got sucked into the worst fight I've ever seen. I got almost no shut-eye for six days. The blood on my hands never dried cause o' the wounds I was treating. If ever I was in the wrong place at the wrong friggin' time, that was it, but when it was over, I had saved seventeen lives — seventeen kids who needed me to be in the wrong place at the wrong time."

When they arrived at the helicopter, Cody was still carrying Brandi. He stood by the door, turned around, and nodded to the crowd.

Despite the whirling hum of overhead rotor blades, a booming voice sounded off loud and clear. *"Ten-hut!"* It was Braddock standing at attention. When he saluted, Brandi returned the honor for Cody since his arms were occupied. At least thirty bikers saluted her back.

Cody and Brandi strapped in. "Stan, how's Page?"

"Gonna be okay. The bullet missed his knee joint."

"Thank God," Brandi said. "Did the bikers already know Cody?"

Stan shrugged.

"Understood," Cody said. "Nice work Stan. Very professional."

As they lifted off into the sun-bright afternoon sky, Cody looked down. Police cars, television crew vans, scores of reporters, and bystanders behind the roped-off perimeter created an ominous sight. But the people here — loving souls, kindred spirits, peacemakers — whose ancestors had endured slavery of the worst sort, refused to be put in irons again by walking in hatred. They had found love in the dark.

Like a child gazing through the rear glass of the car when leaving relatives behind after Christmas, Cody put both hands on the cabin window and stared as long as the people were in sight. It had been a long, painful journey from the valley of the shadow of death in Afghanistan to a small gospel church in Herronburg, Pennsylvania, where the bikers and locals now mingled, hugged and chest-bumped on the south lawn.

People here represented all that was right in America. Someday, he must return. Next time, he would bring his family.

After the church had faded from view, he turned to Brandi. "Your face is a mess. You want me to help you fix it?"

"Keep your hands to yourself," she mumbled, her eyes shut, her head bobbing gently with the soft turbulence. Where are we?" Her light was out.

He put his arm around her and let her head rest on his shoulder. She nestled her swollen face onto his chest. Tonight would complete the first week of their lives together — a relationship that had begun when they had met in the *wrong place* because they needed each other. No matter what tomorrow might bring, he and Brandi could face anything. He knew that now. For better, for worse, they would find a future in Houston. Together.

# DESTINATION HOUSTON

I n Pittsburgh the next morning, thick fog and slow drizzle presaged a melancholy Saturday. Brandi sat next to Cody aboard a chartered jet awaiting take off, weary eyes fixated on the concrete runway below her window.

The two turbofan engines rumbled at full throttle, sending tremors through the fuselage as the aircraft began to accelerate. The powerful thrust forced her backward temporarily against the cushy leather seat. The runway rolled by faster and faster, then dropped completely out of sight as the aircraft ascended into heavy clouds that hugged the ground.

They were airborne at 7:10 a.m. Their destination was Houston Intercontinental Airport as per their official FAA flight plan. The trip would take three hours — plenty of time if malefactors chose to prepare a deadly welcome upon their Houston arrival.

Cody and Brandi sat in the front section of the cabin near the cockpit. Ray, Whitney, and Knoxi sat behind them in a club seating arrangement.

"We're off!" Cody's graveltone voice tried to sell optimism, but no one was buying it.

"We're gonna be in the soup most of the trip," Cody rattled off. "Layers of stratus clouds all the way up through thirty thousand feet this morning."

"Hmmm." Brandi's empty response was nearly inaudible. Cody may have been hyped about rocketing across the sky at 400 knots through solid clouds, but she didn't share his exhilaration. The plush Learjet Model 60 failed to find any sunshine in which to bask while climbing toward its assigned cruising altitude of twenty-eight thousand feet. She was a sunny-day person, and today even the sun was in hiding.

Three days earlier, after Knoxi had spoken her first words, a supernatural peace had settled upon the entire group. The media had painted their lives as a picture of intrigue and adventure, but now Brandi's Saturday morning had arrived with a hundred shades of gloom. Was the dismal mist a message? A warning? Was it nature's way of mourning for the carnage they had left behind? Or a trepidation of more to come? Or maybe just innocent clouds?

Could her depression be due to the pain meds Sam had given her yesterday? She needed to look no farther than her own bruised shins to be reminded of dangers that might lie in their pathway. Would things be any better in Texas?

"Cody?" She tapped his knee. "You awake? Cody?" If he had loved her, he would have stayed awake. If he really cared, he would have asked her to marry him already, right? How many more nights to sleep alone? Brandi sighed and stared out the window once more. *Solid clouds. Why did I even bring my sunshades?* She kicked off her shoes, leaned back, closed her eyes, and fell asleep.

Ray had also nodded off. His wounded shoulder was painful, and he was clearly under the influence of his medication. Whitney's self-appointed mission was to make her husband comfortable during the flight. Knoxi slept soundly.

After three hours, the aircraft approached the South Texas Coastal Region and descended to eight thousand feet. Brandi awoke from a deep slumber and looked around through drowsy eyes. With unhealed lacerations and bruises, her pain medication now wearing off, she could not remember boarding the jet. She looked to her left. Cody's eyes were shut and he would not budge.

Bees began to swarm inside her chest. She was trapped, claustrophobic, aboard a vessel from which there was no escape. She gazed out the window and searched for any trace of blue sky above or green earth beneath, but her efforts yielded nothing save endless gray. Was the plane even moving? Were killers lying in wait at the Houston airport? Her nervous fingers fidgeted with her seat belt.

Cody opened his eyes and took hold of her fumbling hands. "Take a deep breath," he assured. "Can you feel it?" He smiled. "We're good."

Warmth traveled up her arms, through her shoulders, and into her racing heart. Was that what Lilly had felt when Cody held her shaking hands and told her they were meant to heal? Brandi exhaled slowly and leaned back against the headrest. If only he would smother her in his arms. But for now, she would relish just holding on to his toasty fingers, knowing that he sensed her feelings.

"I'll be right back," Cody told her, just before he stood and stepped to the cockpit. After a brief conversation with the crew, he returned. All aboard were now awake.

"We're not going to Intercontinental," he announced to everyone. "We're headed instead to Hobby Airport near downtown Houston. ATC just now approved a last-minute change of destination."

Ray and Whitney nodded, but Brandi wasn't as quick to catch on. She spelled an inquiring look toward Cody, but he was busy putting on an aviator headset provided as a courtesy by the crew.

Ray looked at Brandi's face. "You want the short version?" He smiled. "It's known in the field as tradecraft, deception, bogus intel. If the bad guys were planning a welcoming party at Intercontinental, they're gonna be disappointed."

"Never intended to fly to Intercontinental," Cody said. "We filed our FAA flight plan to the wrong destination just to throw everybody off."

Brandi backhanded Cody's shoulder. "Who's idea was that?"

"It was Ray's idea."

"Oh, no it wasn't!" Ray stated emphatically.

"Ha!" Whitney chuckled. "They'll never tell."

"Well, which one of you heroes forgot to tell me?" Brandi scowled at both men.

"Need to know only," Cody told her as he slipped the headset over his ears.

Brandi's mouth flew open, but before she could set him straight, Cody was busy eavesdropping on the pilot's conversation with air traffic controllers.

"*Houston Approach, Learjet seven-six November, eight thousand, with Hobby information tango.*"

"*Good morning, Learjet seven-six November. Radar contact. We just received your new clearance to Hobby. Descend and maintain four thousand, fly heading two-four-zero, expect a visual approach, runway one-seven.*"

As they continued their descent, the aircraft suddenly emancipated itself from the gloomy nebula and burst into clear air. Brilliant solar rays beamed in through the windows of the cozy jet. Lush Texas grazing lands now sweetened their bird's-eye view as they looked down from four thousand feet. Straight ahead, a mere forty miles, stood a splendid sun-splashed Houston skyline. A world was out there after all.

The last-minute change of destination — a clever ruse — combined with the sudden arrival of friendly skies. Everyone brightened. Like the Pilgrims who once landed in the new world, they couldn't wait to see what fortunes might lie ahead. Hope ran high that they had seen the last of the cloak and dagger. Cody removed his headset.

Brandi rubbed her face with both hands to clear the cobwebs. "Daddy, are you okay? Your pain meds are in Mama's purse — those orange pills."

"I'm good, baby girl. Nothing's gonna keep me from . . . I mean, I'm good."

"Cody insisted that we wait to come until you could be with us," Brandi told Ray. "He wanted you and Mama here this weekend for some reason."

Ray knew the reason, but he dared not spoil the surprise awaiting Brandi at the ballpark that night.

"Speaking of pain meds, whatever Dr. Sam gave me yesterday absolutely knocked me out." Brandi stretched. "I slept splendidly."

"Tell me about it," Cody said. "What's the last thing you remember?"

Ray and Whitney snickered. Brandi noticed. "What're you both grinning about?"

Then she turned to Cody. "And why are you so smug?"

"Well," Cody replied, folding his arms, "you fell asleep in the helo yesterday, and when we arrived back at the hospital, I carried you from the landing pad to —"

"I don't remember that," she interrupted. "What was wrong with my legs?"

Whitney spouted off. "What he's trying to tell you is that he carried you from the helipad all the way to your bed and laid you in it. You never even peeped. He collapsed beside you, and I just covered both of you with a blanket."

Brandi grinned as her memory began to return. "So that's why I awoke and found Cody in bed with me this morning? I supposed that with all the confusion, maybe we'd gotten married and I just didn't remember." She pounded Cody's knee.

Cody raised his hands to his head. "Are you kidding? *Us? Married?*"

Brandi's soft smile disappeared. He could have gone all day without trying to be funny.

Whitney decided to come clean. "Baby, we're just messin' with you. Cody wanted to be next to you so he would know if you had problems breathing during the night — that swollen nose of yours and all."

"Really, Cody? Is that why?" Brandi's dimpled smile reappeared and she leaned back against the headrest again. "So did anything else happen that I should know about?"

Cody turned toward the opposite window, rubbed his wounded hip and tried to reposition himself to take the pressure off the injury.

Brandi moved close and lowered her volume. "There was blood on the sheets where you slept. Are you bleeding again? I forgot to give you this." She pulled a small bottle from her purse. "Sam gave it to me because she saw you limping. Wash the wound twice a day and then use this on it." She flashed him a smiley face. "Can you do that by yourself or do you need help?"

"Where's Lilly when you need her?" Cody smirked. "I bumped my *bloodeus maximus*, as she calls it, during the scuffle yesterday," he told everyone.

*"Well!"* Ray boomed. "All we gotta do is find a doctor of *buttology!* They have those in Texas, don't they Musket?"

Cody moved his lips next to Brandi's ear and cupped his hand around his mouth. "I wonder how many of those *ornge* pills the old man took."

*"Ornge?"* she asked. "What's that? Do you mean *orange?"*

"Yeah. That's what I said — *ornge."*

Ray changed the tone. "I have a good feeling about coming here."

Brandi's face lit up. *"Roger that!"* She pulled her Astros cap down to just above her eyebrows and pretended to spit. "I'm *sooo* ready to meet Houston!"

*    *    *

After the wheels had touched down on the runway with a gentle nudge, the shiny Learjet taxied to the Lancelot Aviation Services ramp — their designated parking assignment. When the aircraft came to a stop, Brandi gasped at the scene outside her window — at least a million law-enforcement vehicles, lights flashing, moving toward the plane.

"Cody, how did all these people get here so fast? Didn't you change our destination just a few minutes ago? How did they know to come here?"

"Like I said, need to know. *These* people needed to know earlier."

"Well! What about me?" She crammed her swollen feet into her shoes and threw on her mirror shades. "This isn't over!" She headed for the exit.

Cody glanced at Ray, but he conveniently looked out the window and focused on something outside the aircraft.

They were allowed to deplane, and were escorted to a new state-of-the-art VIP welcoming area with a waiting crowd of press, corporate execs, and Astros front-office honchos.

Most of the swelling had disappeared from Brandi's face, but her right eye had turned dark underneath, so she wore the shades even after entering the building. She wanted to remove her shoes again, but decided to gut it out.

Cody saw a familiar face. Derek Tyler, his agent, had just arrived. "I forgot to tell you Derek was coming," he told Brandi. "I'll introduce you."

"Hey, Slugger! Wow. She was great on TV, but I mean in person, honey, you are —"

"Brandi, meet Derek." She shook his hand.

"Just make a brief statement," Derek said to Cody. "No need for a long speech, and don't take any questions. By the way, here comes the mayor."

"You're kidding. The mayor?" Cody's face tensed.

Brandi impulsively took Cody's arm. "I don't think the Houston mayor likes Cody," she told Derek.

"Haven't you been watching the news?" Derek gushed. "You kids are the biggest story in America. You think he's gonna miss being here with all the media present?"

"I hope he doesn't call Cody out or something like that," Brandi said while she watched the mayor mingling, shaking hands. "That's all we need on a day like this."

"Call me out?" Cody forced a grin. "Which movie did you get that from? Look at the old codger. He ain't even wearin' no cowboy hat or big bubba boots."

"Careful," she snapped. "I'll take off these shades and he'll wonder where I got the shiner."

"Let's don't build up harsh expectations ahead of time," Ray suggested. "Maybe he's changed his mind."

"You never know," Cody agreed. "Here he comes."

Mayor Leonard Beeker was a short, stocky man with a crooked nose and dark hair. A 73-year-old son of Holocaust survivors, he had become very popular during his two years in office. Smart, efficient and jovial, he had made a fortune over four decades with a major chain of automobile dealerships throughout South Texas and was also a Vietnam veteran.

He and Cody had crossed paths. Their brief relationship had been strained. The mayor had suggested on more than one occasion that Cody was covering up secrets about his military service. Some of his comments had been carried earlier that week in *USA Today*.

"Hello, Cody. It's good to have you back in our city. I recognize this lady." He addressed Brandi and offered his hand. "I saw you on TV. Hello, Ms. Barnes."

"Hi, Mr. Mayor. Please call me Brandi."

"Hello, hello. And please call me Mr. Mayor," he snorted. "I'm only kidding, Brandi. At my age, I have to act like a clown sometimes to remind myself I'm alive. Just call me Leo. And you may slap me if I get too brash."

"Howdy, Leo," Cody said. "We like the turnout. Uh, we're sort o' tired and —"

"I'll handle this crowd, Cody. Just follow my lead."

"Ladies and gentlemen, welcome." The mayor flashed his familiar charm. "As you know, security was tight today," he paused and scanned the room, "so I don't know how the heck some of you got in."

Joviality ruled. The Saturday morning crowd was hyped — lots of coffee and the anticipation of hosting the newsiest couple in the country.

"Cody has a limp, but despite being among the walking wounded, he has agreed to make a brief statement." Beeker stepped aside and began to applaud.

As Cody stepped to the podium, the crowd erupted. He held up his hands for quiet, but the psyched attendees would not be denied. Brandi held Knoxi close as the toddler placed her hands over her ears. Ray put his good arm around Whitney. Flashing bulbs, a million smartphones clicking, it didn't take a genius — Cody Musket was no stranger to this city.

Finally, everyone settled down. Cody began. The audience remained hushed as he thanked them for being there, and then introduced Brandi and her family.

They left to a standing ovation. Despite correspondents calling out questions, police quickly ushered them to a bulletproof vehicle. Their small motorcade pulled away and then turned back through a security gate, trapping followers outside the perimeter. A helicopter was waiting to take them to the Astro Merry Yacht Hotel.

The group arrived at the hotel at 11:00 a.m. and were promptly treated to a dining experience in a private room similar to the one Tanner had reserved for their after-game dinner in Pittsburgh the previous Saturday. The meal featured the finest in Gulf Coast cuisine. Afterward, they retired to their rooms across the hall from each other.

\*     \*     \*

Ray collapsed on the bed. Whitney pulled off his shoes. "Now, sugar, you need to rest this afternoon. This is gonna be quite a night," she blurted.

Brandi overheard. "Quite a night, Mama? What do you mean?"

Ray to the rescue. "Tonight will be Knoxi's first ball game. Quite a night, indeed."

"You didn't eat much, child." Whitney breathed a sigh after Ray had bailed her out.

"It was hard to get used to so many security guys," Brandi lamented. "So many eyes on me I wanted to hide behind something. Took away my appetite."

"Uh, you better get accustomed to it," Ray pointed out. "Things have changed."

"Oh, Daddy, I love Cody more than I ever imagined I could love a man. If he doesn't ask me to marry him soon, I know I'll go crazy. I've only known him a week, but —"

"Good thing you didn't accept Speedy's offer to move in with him," Whitney declared. "You would not have been at that theater. You would never have met Cody, and those killers would have caught up with you somewhere else."

"Mama, moving in with another man was never an option. I had already made my decision about that. Now I just wish Cody would ask me…ask me to be his wife. Do you think I should just ask him? I mean sometimes he just needs a little push."

"Like with the 'need to know' episode?" Whitney teased.

"Yes, but maybe if I become his wife, he'll figure I need to know before anybody else. What do you think?"

Whitney glanced at Ray, but he turned his head. "Well," Whitney said to Brandi, "you don't really want to know what these men are thinking, anyway. Of course, you could try beating some sense into him with one of those Louisville Muggers." She picked up Knoxi, held her on one hip and headed toward the bed.

"Louisville Muggers? Mama, what on earth are you talking about?"

"You know. One of those things he bats the ball with."

Ray smacked his forehead. "Gramma, you can't be serious. It's Louisville *Slugger.*"

# HERMOSO DIAMANTE!

T hree hours before game time, Cody stood in front of his locker at Minute Maid Park. He donned an Astros batting practice jersey and warm-up pants.

"Hey, Joey, did you get it?" Cody saw José Bustamante walk into the clubhouse.

"Si, señor. I got it, man."

"Should we do this in English or Spanish?" Cody asked.

"We better do it in English, man, judging by your Spanish. The last time I ask in Spanish how you doin', you thought I was asking if you had a sister named Esther."

Cody chuckled. "Okay, 'ta bueno, amigo. You have the ring?"

"Yeah, man, take a look. She'll love this one. Hermoso diamante! Mia find it in Bolivia. It is just the one you ask for."

"Yeah, I figured since Mia's family owned the largest jewelry business in South America she would be able to find it."

José grinned. "Well…maybe not the biggest, but maybe the best."

He handed Cody a small box that contained a halo engagement ring with a heart-shaped bluish-pink center-mounted diamond.

"Way cool! You're right, amigo. She'll go crazy when she sees this."

"Oh, is you she crazy about, man. Everyone can see. Whatever you get her, she like."

"Well, this is exactly like the photograph. No one in the US could get one in less than three weeks. Is this number the total for everything? I'll ask the bank to wire it. Dawg co-signed a note for me."

"Das it man — signed, sealed and deleted."

"You mean *delivered,* man. Signed, sealed and delivered. I'm gonna take some swings in the cage."

José was from the Dominican Republic, and Mia was from Venezuela. He had never spoken English before coming to the United States as a minor-league player three years earlier. Mia had taught him to speak the language. During the past couple of weeks on the road trip, the two men had become good friends.

Hitting in the batting cage was on the doctor's list of approved activities. After the short workout, Cody lay down near his locker on a bench and went to sleep. He was awakened thirty minutes later when the rest of the team showed up to dress for the game.

*    *    *

The first pitch was delivered at 6:10 p.m.

Minute Maid Park was built on the site of the old Union Station alongside Highway 59 near downtown. The beautiful modern stadium, built to replicate one-hundred-year-old architecture, retains the flavor of the old train hub, complete with grand arches and even a steam locomotive atop the left field bleachers that travels along a track and blows its horn after one of the Houston players hits a home run.

The Astros' home dugout sits along the first base line. Cody had positioned himself at the farthest end away from home plate. He wasn't used to riding the bench, and it made his bullet wound throb. He stood during most of the game.

In less than two weeks, he had become a media magnet. Brandi and the Babe, the iconic pair, had not existed before he had left town. Now the VIP boxes were overflowing, and extra security personnel were posted throughout the stadium. Thousands gazed into the seats behind home plate with binoculars, hoping to see Brandi.

The game crept slowly along. For Cody, tonight was all about the seventh inning, and the longer the game dragged on, the more time he had to think. Would he remember what to say? Was he rushing it too much? What if she said no or hesitated? Would the entire crowd be listening? What if the ring didn't fit? *This was a bad idea!*

Too late. His plan was already in motion. He clutched the small leather case in his palm and never set it down. He checked it repeatedly to make sure the ring was still inside.

As the Astros came off the field before the bottom of the seventh inning, Whitney and Ray could hardly contain themselves while they awaited the arrival of their future son-in-law in the box seats behind home plate.

Security police accompanied Cody as he made his way toward Brandi. All had been arranged. As he approached her, a special welcome came from the public address announcer.

> *"And now, ladies and gentlemen, turn your eyes to the screen in right field. The Houston Astros are proud to welcome Ms. Brandi Barnes, her daughter Knoxi, and her parents, Captain Ray and Whitney Barnes."*

Brandi's cheeks flashed hot when she suddenly saw herself on the huge screen, and she began waving to the crowd which had risen to its feet. She turned and threw kisses in every direction. When Cody neared, fans erupted with deafening screams and applause as both he and Brandi were now in full view.

> *"And you may recognize the gentleman wearing the Astros uniform approaching Ms. Barnes. That's number 12, Astros third baseman, Cooooodyyyy Musket!"*

Brandi was still waving to the crowd when she gazed up once more at the screen to notice Knoxi reaching toward someone wearing an Astros uniform. Brandi had not heard the introduction of Cody because the crowd noise around her had risen, drowning out the public address. Ray and Whitney tried desperately to get her to look to her right so she would notice Cody.

Finally, she turned. "Cody? What are you doing?" She planted her hands on both sides of her face when she saw the box he was holding. Cody's skittish grin would otherwise have made her smile, but now she could only cover her mouth and try to contain herself. Could this be real? When he knelt, it removed all doubt.

The women in the crowd were quick to catch on. *"Awwwww."*

Melanie Spence of the television broadcast team arrived with a microphone, but many, particularly the women, seemed disappointed when Cody's proposal was drowned out by the clapping and whistling of the men.

However, all fans caught a thrill when Brandi responded to Cody. "Oh. Yes! Yes! Yes!" With each *yes*, she leaped higher into the air, stretching her arms outward and upward. Ray reached out with his good arm to steady her so she would not lose her balance. The crowd caught the fever.

Her *yes* had been years in the making, and once she started, she could not stop. Finally, she covered her face again, realizing how many people had just shared the moment she had dreamed of for a lifetime.

Knoxi reached up, pulled Cody's hat off, and placed it on her head. Fans watching the jumbo video screen above the right field bleachers saw the hatless Cody slip the ring onto Brandi's finger and kiss her. Knoxi peered out from beneath the oversized cap and began wildly clapping her hands. The already ecstatic crowd became delirious.

Astros principle owner, Dale Scott presented a bouquet of bright red Tyler Roses to the gushing bride-to-be. Brandi was now officially a Houstonian and the twenty-month-old Knoxi an instant heartthrob. Brandi and the Babe had won the heart and soul of Space City and Minute Maid Park was in liftoff mode.

As Cody headed back to the dugout, country artist Andy Jayne added the seventh-inning tradition — the singing of "God Bless America."

\*   \*   \*

Post-game, Brandi called Cody. "After I get Knoxi to sleep, I need to see you."

The Barnes family had been placed in the Presidential Suite on the ninth floor of the hotel. Cody was across the hall in the Admiral Suite from which one could see much of the southern half of the city. Brandi told Cody she would knock on his door when she was free to talk.

The knock came at ten thirty-five. Brandi could not contain her exhilaration. She launched herself, squeezed him with all her strength and would not let go.

She finally loosened her grip and looked him in the eye. "No other man has ever asked me to marry him and make my home with him forever."

"I'm glad it was a hit. I was purdy nervous."

"Nervous? Why? Did you think I would turn you down?"

"Well, in front of forty thousand people, that wudda been hard to —"

"I will marry you, Cody. But, when?"

"When? I'm leaving that to you. You attend a big church in Altoona and have a lot of friends and family. I assumed you'd wanna get married there. 'Bout the only friends I have are military buddies and ballplayers. You make the call."

"Now."

"Uhh, now? Right now? You mean like tonight?"

"Cody, I have waited for you all my life. I don't wanna wait any longer. We may not have tomorrow. You gave me a huge surprise earlier. I've prepared one for you."

They heard a knock. Brandi giggled while Cody went to the door.

He was shocked to see a crowd standing in the hallway. Leading the way was Rev. Ron Summers, pastor of Church On the Meadow, a small community church in South Houston where Cody was involved on Sundays. Mark and Sandy followed, along with José, Mia, and several others.

Whitney and Ray brought Knoxi. "We figured Knoxi could stay up late tonight."

Ray had a sling on his right arm and was walking as though his shoes weighed fifty pounds each. Brandi motioned for him to sit on the bed. She leaned two pillows against the headboard and made him recline against them. "Don't argue with me, Daddy. This is my party."

Then, she turned to Cody. "I hope this impromptu gathering is okay with you."

"Just one question — how did you get these people here this fast? And who's this guy setting up the camera with all the wires and a screen?"

"That's more than one question." She giggled again and backhanded his shoulder.

"She called me during the eighth inning," Sandy said. "Mark and I got it done with the help of Mia and José. The camera is so you can video the ceremony on a live feed to Los Angeles and Pittsburgh. Your friends want to watch. The Pirates played the Dodgers today in LA, and Julia stayed home in Pittsburgh."

"Unfortunately, Dawg and Silver left for Spain yesterday," Brandi said, "but they can see the replay after we let them know."

The most conspicuous guests were from the umpiring crew. José had managed to recruit them. "I figured you might need groomsmans, amigo!"

"Groomsmen," Brandi said. "Thank you, José. That was thoughtful."

Bellevue Connors, who had called the balls and strikes that night, had somehow managed to obtain a chocolate cake with pink icing. "Hope this'll do," he said, baiting Cody.

"You know I don't ever argue with you, Bell. Not since that call you made in Seattle, that is. I still say that pitch was away."

"Oh, Cody!" Brandi scolded.

The umpire fired back, "That pitch was down the middle, and you know it, Babe. I might just have to toss you outta here!" This brought cackles from the others.

"Guess I'm gonna have to learn how to be a ballplayer's wife, huh?" Brandi looked at Cody.

He took her hand. "Let's do this." He raised his hands for quiet, and then gave her the floor.

"Each of you has made this night even more meaningful than I could have imagined," she said. "I love you all." Then looking at Cody, "*We* love you all."

They managed to clear a spot near the window to say their vows. No rehearsal, so Pastor Summers made it a "repeat after me" affair for simplicity.

After the ceremony and rationing of the cake, Brandi, never at a loss, concluded. "I have known Cody for barely eight days. Marrying him is the scariest and most wonderful thing I've ever done. I now have a new place to live, and it's with my husband. Tonight, that place is in this room. So everybody out!"

More laughter, handshakes and kisses for the Bride as everyone filed out. Before Whitney and Ray left, Cody had some special words for his new in-laws.

He embraced Whitney. "Thank you for my wife," he said. "The courageous decision you made twenty-four years ago has changed my life forever."

"And Ray, without you, none of this — What I mean is…."

The two men nodded.

Just then, Cody's cell rang. "Hey, flyboy! I heard she cornered you at the ballpark. Hahaha! Uh, say, do you got a few minutes to hang out on the phone?" Everyone heard the crowing voice at the other end of the connection.

Brandi wrenched Cody's phone from his hand. "Sly, I'm definitely gonna have a talk with Julia about your adolescent behavior!"

"Whoops! I shudda known the lady of the house would be home!" The line went dead.

Brandi glared at Cody. "You'll get this back when I say you can have it, and not a minute sooner!"

"Aye aye, ma'am." None of them had ever seen his grin so large.

The grandparents slipped out with Knoxi. After Ray had closed the door behind them, he and Whitney heard unbridled laughter drifting into the hallway.

"Good enough," Ray said. "She'll have him tamed before morning."

"Tame that boy? No way."

They entered their room, closed the door, and sat down. The curious girl looked up. "Is Cody my daddy now?"

Ray's eyes fogged. "Yes, but it's a good thing."

"But, will you still be my grampa? Can I still love you?"

"Of course." He pulled her close with his left arm. "You'll always be my granddaughter."

"But Mama told me you should love just one man."

"But…but that's different. What your mother meant was, uh —" He looked to Whitney for help.

Whitney reached for more tissue. "Baby, your mother loves Cody in a different way than she loves Grandpa. And Cody loves you in a different way than he loves anyone else. And don't worry, your heart has plenty of love for everybody."

# The Morning After

"Cody, are you awake? You said to wake you at eight."

"Uh, what time is it?" He rubbed his sleepy eyes.

"Nine!" She declared.

"Nine?" He sat straight up.

"Nine Eastern, that is," she giggled. "It's only eight here. Just making sure you're awake. I have your coffee ready."

He plopped back facedown on the pillow. "I can see we're gonna have problems if you keep messin' with my mind like that." His voice drawling, grinding like a tractor.

"Oooh, are you gonna get rough with me?" She snickered and popped him on the backside opposite from where he was wounded. "Took me a few minutes to figure out where you hid my gown last night."

He turned over onto his back. "What gown? The one you have on? Uh, where did you find it?"

"Right where you hid it." She pinched his big toe through the sheet. "You said Pastor Ron is planning a breakfast meeting in the Galveston Room near the lobby at nine o'clock, and he wants you to speak, so I made the effort to fix your coffee."

"Even though I hid your gown?"

"So you're admitting it?"

"Never!" he growled. "Come here." Cody caught her hand and pulled her to the bed. "Did we really get married last night?"

"I certainly think so." She sat on the edge of the mattress. "You called me Mrs. Brandi Musket just before we jumped into the hot tub."

"Yeah. Splashed water all over the floor."

She pulled the sheet off him, "Babe, why do these pajamas you're wearing have holes in the knees?"

Cody tightened up.

"Oh, sweetie. I'm sorry." She lay beside him and stroked his face. "I pray you won't have those nightmares any more. I'm gonna get you a new pair of PJs."

"Speakin' of the hot tub, you're beautiful," he doted. "I can't even remember what a Tyler Rose is anymore."

"And my bruises? I wasn't kidding when I told the press —"

"Yeah. Made me wanna hurt those guys again. You look like a train ran you down. Are you sure you don't have some busted ribs?"

"Ouch! Don't be poking around on me like that. What's the matter with you? Last night you were so gentle."

"Yeah, but I just wanted to see if you have any broken bones."

She pulled on his chin whiskers. "Ya betta not mess with me, sucka."

"Ohhh, now I got goose bumps." He pressed gently on her ribs. "But seriously, does that hurt?"

*"Yes!"*

"Well, maybe you should see Doc. Have x-rays?"

"Look, if I get checked out, *I'm* choosing the doctor. Don't want some baseball trainer gawking at me."

"But he's a *real* doctor and — No, no, I didn't mean…of course you should choose."

"I'm sorry you had to meet me on the worst day of my life and then marry me eight days later when — I mean I was worried that it would dampen our wedding night when you saw how much damage those guys did when they manhandled me."

His voice deepened. "Well then, like Tommy Lee Jones asked Robert Duvane in *Lonesome Dove*, 'You want me to kill 'em for ya?'"

"It's Robert *Duvall*. And I know it sounds impossible, but I'm not afraid anymore."

He softened his tone and delicately wrapped her in his arms. "I noticed the old stab wounds. That was a bad day too. I nearly lost you two years before I met you. So how do you feel about your former boyfriend?" He propped himself on one elbow.

"I was able to forgive Billy, even though he's dead. I don't feel the pain anymore."

"The black cloud of Afghanistan has left me, for now at least," Cody said. "Do you reckon a miracle has happened to me?"

She smiled, then pulled him close and let him place his ear next to her heart. "Do you feel that? You're listening to a miracle, Babe. My heart never beat with more joy." She looked into his eyes again. "So how do you feel about the men who tortured you?"

"The hate's gone, finally. Dunno if I'd call it forgiveness though."

"Hate was causing your pain. If they asked you to forgive them, could you do it?"

"If they asked me? Hmm…yeah, I guess I could. I asked God before I left Afghanistan to take away the hate, but it never happened."

"Not until now," she declared. "Before now, you weren't willing to forgive *yourself*. You can't stop hating others until you stop hating yourself."

"Still hard to believe Pastor Williams actually went to the jail to pray with the guys who killed Sasha," Cody said. "I always wanted to beat the truth into guys like that with a Louisville Slugger. I figured they didn't deserve forgiveness."

"But now? What do you think now?"

"You are all I can think about right now." He held her tighter and began kissing her face.

"Man of steel, it's after eight." She fought him off. "We need to get ready." She crawled out of the bed. "I'm in this gown and I want to go across the hall to get dressed, but the security guys are standing outside our door. I need to borrow your robe."

"Yeah, roger that."

"Are we gonna always have to live under heavy guard?" She walked toward the closet. "We can't exactly disappear like people in witness protection."

"We could disappear," he said, "but that wouldn't be any fun."

"Get serious." She pulled his robe from the closet and put it on.

Cody sat up and leaned back against the headboard. "The Astros have been trying to sign me to a five-year contract for an average seven million per year."

"Wow. They're taking a big chance with a rookie." Then she crossed her arms. "By the way, Captain America, are you telling me about this because I'm finally on your *need to know list?*"

"Lets just say it's something you need to know. Derek says I could make twice that much if I wait a few years 'til I'm a free agent, but I wanna start a foundation now to reach out to abducted children and prevent...I mean if I —"

"But you would be confronting the same forces who already want us dead. You *know* that, right?"

He lowered his face with a long sigh. "This is difficult. It involves you. That's why you need to know what I'm thinking. I'm tired of us hiding, tired of you being a target. I want to turn the tables and change the odds — to hit 'em where it hurts — in the wallet."

"And what happens if the bad guys get wind of it? What if they find out what we're doing?"

"I know some people who are good at what they do, and one thing they're really good at is keeping secrets. The traffickers will never know who's behind it. Besides —"

"Listen to me, husband." She came back to the side of the bed. "I woke up three hours ago. What you're suggesting has already been on my mind since before dawn. I even have a name for it — Planned Childhood."

"You already thought about it? You already have a name for it?"

"The way I see it," Brandi said, "we're already in a battle because someone has declared war on us. Daddy's eighth principle — *You either cower in fear or you answer the call.*"

Cody's stormy brow eased.

"Babe, this is our time, a fight we can't walk away from. We either win or we die fighting. I don't want Knoxi growing up in a world where evil men can rule by just intimidating innocent people into doing nothing. I'm all in, man of steel. All in."

He stared at her for a moment, eyes wild, playful like when he had swept her up and kissed her the first time. "Babe?" She took a step backward. "What are you thinking?"

"You are a *dangerous* woman!" he rumbled.

He lunged, but she scooted away, screaming, laughing like a playground child. "I'd love to do what newlyweds do," she was out of breath, "but right now I *must* get ready." She ran to the other side of the breakfast table. "Cody! I'm warning you." She giggled. "Stay back!" He stopped.

"Did you think of the name *Planned Childhood* before or after you found your gown?"

"I'll never tell."

"Well," he conceded. "We'll have to continue this later. I guess that's what God made Sunday afternoons for."

"Unless you play baseball." She caught her breath, still giggling.

"Well, there's always the off-season," he growled.

"Roger that." Her happy feet waltzed her toward the door.

"And I plan to make good use of the off-season!" Cody shouted as she left the room.

# MR. MAYOR

The Muskets and Barnes families with security escorts arrived in the Galveston Room at 9:00 a.m. Attendance at the breakfast meeting was expected to be about forty, but word had circulated on short notice that Cody Musket was going to speak. Nearly a hundred people showed up.

Umpire Bellevue Connors, who made his off-season home in the nearby city of Katy, arrived with his wife and twin granddaughters, as did members of the Houston Press, a few players from the visiting Chicago White Sox, and players, wives and girlfriends from the Astros.

A surprise guest was Mayor Leonard Beeker. Cody, who was already nervous about agreeing to speak that morning, felt even more uneasy when Beeker arrived.

After breakfast, Pastor Ron Summers invited Cody to the microphone. "Remember, this is a devotional meeting so watch your language," he snapped.

Everyone laughed since they knew that Cody's teammates often teased him for not employing enough "colorful metaphors" in his speech to adequately represent the Marines.

"I heard him say *damn* once," shouted shortstop Dancer Coleman, "when he made his first error this year. Good thing he don't make too many."

Loud cackles and guffaws circulated through the audience.

But Felicia poked her husband and apologized to the group. "I been tryin' to teach him manners for five years," she said. "Now, honey, you apologize. You know you never heard that boy swear."

Now the laughter resonated out into the hallway and brought curious bystanders into the room to fill empty chairs.

Cody, who had tried to avoid public appearances, felt awkward at first. His handling of the press conference in Detroit had not helped his confidence, and this morning, Brandi would not be able to bail him out. He looked at her, then Ray. They both nodded. Knoxi was sitting on Whitney's lap, her baby blues fixed on Cody's face.

"Thanks for the endorsement, Dancer. As I recall, you cut in front of me and deflected the ball, and they gave me your error. I nearly got into a fistfight with the official scorer over that!"

After the light-hearted fun, everyone settled down.

Cody began, "I have a new family this morning." He introduced Brandi and Knoxi, referring to Knoxi as his daughter. Brandi tried not to cry. He honored Ray and Whitney, saying that he felt like a son to them. Brandi reached for the tissue in her purse.

"Today, you are looking at a new Cody Musket." He waited a few seconds for the room to quiet down. Would anyone even be interested?

"For the past four years, I've lived a secret life of deep agony and personal sorrow."

Cody revealed the emotional torture he had endured since he had been discharged from the Marine Corps. Though he was not specific about the children, he mentioned the wounds left on his body and soul from traumatic events in Afghanistan.

"To this day, a stigma persists toward those who suffer from post traumatic stress, and yet it is an epidemic in our modern world." He took a sip of water.

"I couldn't tell anybody about the pain. My life was unbearable when I was not on a baseball field. A few suspected, but I tried to play it down and even hide it."

Hearing this swashbuckling hero openly reveal his hidden struggle produced an eerie hush. Soon, the word had reached the hotel lobby, resulting in more late arrivals. It was standing room only.

Cody gave them a quick overview of his improbable recovery while at Kandahar — restoration that the trauma team had called a miracle. "I shouldn't be able to walk, or even be alive today."

He paused. The room was silent and still. Even the servers in blue aprons had ceased refilling coffee cups and were standing motionless.

"Psalm 23 says, 'Though I walk through the valley of the shadow of death, I will fear no evil, for You are with me.'

"I know all about that valley — the shadows, death. I know what it is to fear evil. I have seen the lowest of humanity. I saw it abroad. I've seen it here. It changes you. It can make you become just like your enemies.

"Most people choose happiness as a goal, but my expectations did not reach even that high. My goal was to somehow keep my sanity. I had to *man up* cause I had too many people counting on me. Everyone wanted me to be a hero, so I hid my weakness." He took another sip of water.

"Nine days ago in Pittsburgh, my life changed forever. We were rained out. I went to a movie. That night, I met the most beautiful creature God has ever made. She was courageous, understanding, and tough as nails. When I met her family, I found out where she got her mettle."

He paused again and looked around. He had never imagined himself speaking words that would move a crowd to tears.

"I've seen things that no human should see, and done things I did not believe I could be forgiven for. I was in a pit so deep that even God couldn't find me, or so I thought.

"But Brandi? Well, she doesn't believe there is a pit that deep, and she loved me too much to leave me in that hole. After the gun fight in Pittsburgh four nights ago, I completely tweaked out of my mind. I blocked out everything — all reality, light, sound. I finally gave it up. It was a battle I just couldn't win. But then, I felt her arms around me and I could hear her crying, pleading with God for me."

The mayor, seated at the head table, was fixated, staring at the uneaten pastry on his plate. More arrivals had quietly gathered along the back wall.

"All I can tell you," Cody said, "is that somehow the pain I had carried for four years just went away." He paused again.

From the sanctity of the silence arose the tender voice of a woman seated somewhere near the back of the room. "Oh, sweet Jesus."

"I've seen the shadow of death, and I know the fear of evil," Cody continued. "The shadow arrives when all hell is breaking out in your life and you become convinced God doesn't love you. The fear of evil comes when you lose hope.

"I have concluded that if God has one big flaw, it is that He loves us way too much, and you're lookin' at one thankful Marine."

After he had spoken, many came to shake his hand. Some wanted an autograph, but most asked for his prayers. Ballplayers' wives and girlfriends surrounded Brandi.

The last individual to shake Cody's hand was a man in his middle thirties with dark hair and handle-bar mustache. A brunette woman accompanied him. She was thin, her face drawn and pale.

"Could we talk to you sometime tomorrow, Cody? I'm Baker Rafferty, and this is my wife, Elena. We were both police officers, but now we…we are not working. And —"

Brandi overheard. She moved closer. Cody introduced her to the couple. "We could have breakfast here tomorrow," Cody suggested. "Just the four of us."

It was agreed.

"Elena seems distraught, but Baker looks okay," Brandi observed as she watched the couple make their exit. "What do you think?"

"He's the one hurting," Cody said. "He's hiding it. Covering it up. They aren't Texans either. They sound like New Englanders. They've come a long way from home."

*     *     *

After the Sunday morning crowd had left, Cody, Brandi, Knoxi, Ray and Whitney sat down at one of the tables. The meeting hall was deserted but for two young attendants who were cleaning the room and a couple of police officers who stood guard. Ron Summers had left just as Cody had finished speaking because he had duties at his church.

Cody set Knoxi on his knee and told her he was going to legally adopt her. She didn't understand. He explained that it meant he would always be her daddy.

Her face lit up, and she became animated, running out of breath before she could finish her response. "Then I'll adopt you too, so I'll always be your little girl, but it's okay cuz you love me different than you love Mama, and I know I'm supposed to just love one man, but I love Grampa too, and don't worry," she stopped to come up for air, "cuz there's plenty of love in my heart to go around for everybody!"

Cody's eyes were as big as baseballs. Brandi snickered, and Ray totally lost it. Cody had never seen the captain lose control of his internal funny bone. Everyone was still adjusting to the toddler's recent acquisition of speech.

Now Knoxi was feeling it — the exhilaration of discovery — she could make grown-ups laugh.

"I know you understood us before," Cody told his daughter, "but how come you never spoke until just three days ago?"

Knoxi cocked her head to one side and stared back, suddenly speechless.

"You don't know the reason, do you," Cody concluded.

Her lower lip began to pucker, and her face clouded up.

"It's okay, baby girl," Cody assured her. "You haven't done anything wrong. We aren't disappointed in you. It just took a little longer for you than some other kids."

Knoxi lunged forward and threw her arms around his neck. Whitney cried.

When Cody hugged Knoxi back, his affirmation loosed her tongue. She looked him squarely in the eye. "Now I'm talkin' so much I don't know when to shut up — just like my mama."

Ray howled, bent forward and grabbed his hurting shoulder as he tried to control himself. "Where on earth did you hear that?"

Cody covered his mouth, took one glance at Brandi, and instantly read her thoughts. *I hope you're satisfied.*

"Never mind where she heard it!" Brandi vented, as she pulled Cody's hat down over his flushed face. "Like father, like daughter."

The tiny girl lifted Cody's hat above his eyes. She wasn't finished. "What did Grampa mean when he said Mama would tame you before dawn?"

Whitney gasped and thumped Ray on his forehead. Ray was suddenly silent.

Knoxi knew she was on a roll. "Mama said sometimes you need a push, and Grandma told her she should beat some sense into you with a Louisville Slugger."

No one took a breath. Brandi and Whitney looked at each other, trying to decide whether to laugh or hide. Ray hid his face in his hands. The merriment that followed was as much about the girl's perfectly adult-sounding diction as anything else.

Then the toddler decided it was time to go for the home run. "Daddy, there's only one thing I want from you." She placed her hands on both sides of Cody's face like she had seen her mother do. It was the first time Cody had ever been called "Daddy." Brandi moved her lips close and kissed his ear lobe.

Cody removed his cap. "This ought to be good. I hesitate to ask. What one thing do you want from me?"

"I want one of those *ornge* hats like yours, only it needs to be my size."

"I think she let you off easy, Cody."

Cody looked behind him. It was Leonard Beeker who had just entered the room.

"Excuse the interruption. When you get a break, could we talk?"

Cody looked at the others. "Okay, Mr. Mayor. Uh, how's right now?" He had been dreading the inevitable meeting with Mayor Beeker, but it seemed like a good time to get it over with, and an opportune moment to break up the family chat before Knoxi could spill the beans about anything else. Good thing no one had ever mentioned the word *blackmail* around the child.

It was time for the rest of the family to leave Cody and Mayor Beeker alone, so they gathered themselves up and walked toward the exit door. Knoxi's tiny voice punctuated their departure.

"Mama, did you let Daddy have his cell phone back yet?"

Brandi scooped her up. "We need to talk!"

\*　　\*　　\*

Cody and Leo found a private conference room. A two-man security team stood guard outside the door as Cody and the mayor shut themselves off from the world.

"Cody, you aren't the man I thought you were. For the last few months, I have been critical of you because I knew something wasn't right. Now, today, I don't know what to —" He stopped.

Cody wore a stiff face as he sat across from this man who was his senior by nearly a half century, and whose parents had known the death stench of Nazi oppression — the Gestapo, the Schutzstaffel, terrorism of another era.

"You are right about one thing, Cody. You're a new man. The first time we met, I could see...I mean I knew that something didn't add up."

Beeker dropped his eyes. Cody's pulse began to race.

"July, 1969, I volunteered for a secret mission in enemy territory in Laos, near the Ho Chi Minh Trail. There were three of us, all enlisted men, along with six South Vietnamese regulars. Officers rarely led these clandestine missions, and it was strictly volunteer work."

Cody looked Leo in the eye. He had never sensed a bond with this crusty politician. Instead, the wrinkled old man with the crooked nose made him nervous. This morning was no different. Where was he going with this story, and what did it have to do with him?

"It was all jungle and a few rice paddies," Leo continued. "Lots of small villages hidden in the back country. We came to a small settlement — seven, maybe eight huts. It was deserted except for seven children. Their parents were working a rice paddy 'bout 200 meters away. We knew they doubled as enemy soldiers at night and used the Ho Chi Minh to transport supplies."

Leo's eyes began to turn red in the corners. It took Cody by surprise. Something was up. Something had happened.

"We were a half day's march into enemy territory. We knew that as soon as we left, these kids would run to their parents and give away our position. We would be ambushed before the end of the day. We would be coming home in body bags."

Cody knew the look. He dreaded Beeker's next words.

"We drew straws." The mayor's voice dropped to a whisper. "I pulled the short one."

Cody leaned back. "You've carried this all these years?"

"For forty-five years I've kidded myself. Maybe it wasn't me. Maybe I just dreamed it. Maybe all soldiers do it, even some of the medal winners like…even guys like Cody Musket." He glanced up briefly.

"But now, I'm an old man. I found out four days ago that I have about six months — glioblastoma, brain cancer. I can't pretend anymore. My parents survived the Nazis only to give birth to a murderer. What you said about becoming like your enemies…" He covered his face with his hands.

It gave Cody no pleasure to see Leonard Beeker crumble. "We lose a piece of ourselves in war, Leo. It sometimes makes us do horrible things our hearts don't want to do. We feel broken, dirty, like Satan's offspring."

Leo stared into Cody's face. "When I heard you speak this morning…" He folded his hands on the table in front of him. "The shadow of death — you said we see that shadow because we don't believe God loves us. I know God couldn't possibly love someone like me, and I never thought you would forgive the things I said about you in the press."

Cody trusted Leo with the rest of his own story, the parts he had not shared earlier — the children who had died because he departed from the mission plan, the secrecy, and having to live with a medal he did not deserve. He told about shooting the unarmed Al Adami.

"Jews and Christians are brothers, Leo, and I would count it an honor if you would let me say a prayer with you."

"Don't waste your breath. I'm not worth it."

"I believe Jesus suffered to pay for the unthinkable things I've done cuz He believes I'm worth it. But you gotta decide for yourself what you believe about that. What you did is horrible but not beyond God's forgiveness. You may think of yourself as a worthless ol' fossil that nobody could love, but God doesn't see it that way and neither do I."

Cody said a prayer to the God of Abraham, Isaac, and Jacob for an enemy — now a friend.

A Presence hovered.

# BAKER AND ELENA

O n Monday morning, Cody and Brandi met for breakfast with Baker and Elena Rafferty. Brandi had reserved a booth near the back of the coffee shop.

Baker was tall and muscular with a deep timbre in his voice. His handlebar mustache was curled on the ends, a la Rollie Fingers, a Hall of Fame pitcher Cody had once met. He tended jovial, but Cody sensed he was covering for deeper sorrows.

Elena was frail and quiet, but she had a pleasing smile. She sat close to Baker and kept her hand on his knee when he talked.

"I hope you folks don't mind," Cody began. "Brandi and I did some checking on you late last night. Your background story is the subject of several blogs."

"We didn't wanna pry," Brandi assured. "Just wanted to gather public information to help us understand why you are unemployed."

"We noticed you're from Chaserburg, Maine," Cody said. "Are you in Texas to find work?"

"I joined the Chaserburg police force when I was discharged from the Navy," Baker responded. "After that incident with the kid, things totally fell apart. Now, no law enforcement agency will hire either of us. We finally started driving five days ago in search of work. Two years now without a job."

"So you're just wandering across the country?" Brandi asked.

Elena spoke up for the first time. "We left our three-year-old son with my mother and emptied our savings and just took to the road. We had received a response to our inquiry about a job here in Houston at a private security company. They wanted a husband-and-wife team, but by the time we arrived here, the opening had been filled by a local couple."

Cody addressed Baker, "We know about the mission in the Chechen Republic ten years ago that went wrong. You were the leader of that SEAL team."

"Yes. So you know I was the only one to survive. It was a judgment call, my call — a fatal error."

"I understand," Cody said, "but you were promoted and given a medal. You and your men saved everyone in that compound."

"Correct, with the help of three brave locals who picked up weapons my fallen fighting men had left in the street. There isn't a night that passes I don't dream about it. I was getting past it until I shot that kid in Chaserburg. And now…"

"But honey, the kid was with guys who had guns, and they were shooting at us." Elena looked across the table at Brandi. "We weren't married then. We were partners on patrol looking for a gang of five who had just murdered a judge and his wife."

"I know." Brandi leaned forward. "Baker returned fire and hit one of 'em — a fourteen-year-old boy."

"But when the fight was over, we couldn't find a weapon on him," Baker said. "The kid was a bystander caught in the middle of the fight. The incident went viral. All the information about my PTSD counseling and the men I lost in Chechnya became public."

"We both were exonerated for the shooting but eventually fired due to political pressure," Elena added. "But what you said yesterday…" She looked at her husband. "That part about the shadow of death and losing your hope —"

Baker stepped in. "You see, two days ago, we had reached the point of just giving up. Our savings runs out in a month. We have my military retirement, but we have an autistic son, and —"

"Then, yesterday," Elena smiled. "We…" She glanced at Baker and grasped his hand. "We prayed. For the first time in our four-year marriage, we prayed, just the two of us, together."

"Yeah," Baker affirmed. "See, we were supposed to meet a guy for breakfast in this very same coffee shop — another job interview. He never showed. We went back to the car."

"That's when it happened," Elena broke in. "I was crying. Everything was all wrong. There was just no place for us in this world. Then he grabbed my hand and said two magic words — *let's pray.*"

By now, Brandi's eyes were filling up. She pulled a tissue from her purse and offered one to Elena.

"I rather think she was shocked. I prayed, or at least I tried. Wasn't much of a prayer."

"Ohhh. It was a great prayer." Elena leaned her cheek on Baker's shoulder.

"It was a first for us," Baker asserted. "I said *amen* afterward because I once heard a Navy Chaplain say that. Then I turned the ignition, but the friggin' car wouldn't start."

Elena chuckled. She looked across the table at Brandi and Cody as Baker continued.

"Finally, I sat there banging my fist on the steering wheel and this van from Fox News shows up. But instead of asking for a jump-start, I roll down my window and ask him what's happening. This media guy gets out of the van and says, 'Cody Musket is speaking.' I ask him who the heck Cody Musket is."

Elena jumped back in. "So I say to him, 'Honey? Seriously? You don't know who Cody Musket is? Brandi and the Babe?'" She chuckled again. "I couldn't believe he didn't know, after all that news about you guys last week."

"Yeah. She knew who you were, so we followed the Fox News guys into the meeting. Then, when I heard you speak…" He put his hand over his eyes.

With a weighty expression, Elena finished his thought. "He said that when he heard your story at the meeting, he knew for the first time in his life there was a God."

Brandi touched Cody's forearm and leaned close to him. An impulse of the moment took him. He cleared his throat. "So, you see, it's like this. Brandi and I plan to buy a home here in Houston. My apartment is too small for the three of us. We can't live in a hotel forever, and we've got a security problem. We need someone to guard our property twenty-four seven, uh, preferably man and wife." He looked at Brandi. "Right?"

Brandi's lips parted, but she offered not a word. The couple across the table now stared incredulously at each other.

"I mean, we talked about this didn't we, Wonder Woman? About a live-in arrangement? For somebody just like the Rafferty family?"

Brandi's face lit up like the sunrise over Galveston Bay. "You mean we're gonna buy a home here?"

"We talked about it," Cody prodded. "Don't you remember? We have a daughter who is almost two. She needs to be protected."

"*Ohhhhh,* of course, *that* home," she gushed as she looked across the table again. "Um, I'm sure we can find one with a guest house big enough for the three of you in back of the Olympic pool with a —"

Cody held up a stop sign. "Uh, we haven't discussed the details yet, remember?"

She put the brakes on. "Well, man of steel, I hope Elena likes shopping for furniture and picking out interior colors. We're gonna have a lot of decorating with *two* houses!"

"We don't know what to say," Baker answered. "I can't think of a better gig. Only problem is," he smirked, "I'm a Red Sox fan. Must we watch your team play?" His handlebars seemed to vibrate.

"I don't believe in cruel and unusual treatment of employees," Cody assured.

"Well then," Brandi shook her shoulders, "I have an appointment this afternoon at the spa here in the hotel. I think Elena should join me for a facial, mani and pedi. We have a lot to discuss."

"*Oh, how much fun!*" Elena was exuberant. "You guys can argue about sports or something. We girls have important things to worry about."

"Okay, you're both employed," Cody said. "But these women are gonna have to lighten up a little, don't you think, sailor?"

"Roger that, Boss."

# MAKING GOOD USE OF THE OFF-SEASON

C ody resumed baseball activities seven days later. He was voted the league's most valuable player and won American League Rookie of the Year honors while leading the Astros to a playoff berth. They were defeated in the American League Championship Series by the New York Yankees. A New York reporter pointed out that baseball fans in the Big Apple were known for being verbally brutal to visiting players. Referring to those fans, he asked Cody what it felt like to be in enemy territory.

"You gotta love these fans," Cody said. "They paid good money, and they're just havin' fun. I know what it's like to face *real* enemies, and baseball fans do not fall into that category."

Brandi managed her newly found fame well. She became accustomed to the tight security and all the eyes that watched her. Her appellation, First Lady of Camelot, did not stop her from being tough as nails when it came to keeping Cody focused.

Planned Childhood would become more than a dream as Brandi forged a solid foundation with help from Julia and Silverbelle. Future plans called for establishing bases around the world which would serve as safe houses for rescued children. They secured financial commitments from professional athletes and other compassion-minded celebrities. Brandi formed alliances with several organizations that reached out to displaced or abused children and young women.

When Brandi asked Cody how he planned to "hit the bad guys where it hurts the most — in the wallet," he would always say, "You never know."

Was she, or was she not on his *need to know* list? But did it really matter? She had his heart. Did she really want to know everything that was in his head?

Cody's new pajamas, courtesy of Brandi, never became *holey* in the knees again. He began to grow in stature among his peers and took a leadership role in veterans' outreach programs. The Muskets would enjoy a period of relative quiet for the next four years, as traffickers decided to keep a lower profile until a more opportune time.

Knoxi became a straightforward media darling. Always quotable, she was never at a loss. On November 29, her second birthday, she was asked by *Fort Worth Star Telegram* reporter Sam Hummer what Cody did in his spare time now that the baseball season was over. She replied that she wasn't sure, but that something secret went on every Sunday afternoon in her parents' bedroom.

"It must be good," she said, "cuz I heard my daddy tell my mama he was makin' good use of the off-season."

The End – Book 1

---

Turn this page and receive a special gift from the author.
To learn about real events which inspired parts of this story, see page 284.

A Special "Thank You"

As a way of saying "thanks" I want to offer you a special gift. If you will simply email me, James Miller, at the address below, I will gift you a **free Cody and Brandi 28-page short story** entitled "Nikki." This story is a bonus, not part of Book 1 or Book 2. It will be electronically delivered to you via return email. Make your request here: codymusket@gmail.com

Lions Tail Books is dedicating all profits from The Cody Musket Story to Franklin Graham ministries — Samaritan's Purse — which feeds and clothes the poor and supports US wounded war veterans through Heal our Patriots. Profits to include paperbacks, ebooks and audiobooks. On the following page, you will find a brief description of the next installment of No Pit So Deep, The Cody Musket Story.

## A PEEK INTO BOOK 2

The second installment of No Pit So Deep will carry you on an adventure, a journey which will once again include real events woven into the plot.

The story begins four years later. Cody has become an American baseball icon, but plays an even more dangerous game — rescuing children from traffickers through a clandestine arm of Planned Childhood. Brandi is kept in the dark about the shadow operation until traffickers retaliate by snatching six-year-old Knoxi.

Cody assembles a team of commandos for a rescue attempt in South America. He is unable to prevent the headstrong Brandi from going on the mission, but her presence becomes vital as she once again proves her mettle.

Things heat up when they encounter additional abducted children being held for auction. The Muskets and a team of only fourteen avengers must rescue and lead a child brigade on a twenty-seven-mile exodus through the rainforest with an army of assassins in pursuit. Miracles (inspired by real events) leave hardened commandos scratching their heads, and the mission turns on a desperate prayer from a most unlikely source.

If you liked Knoxi in Part I, you will love her in Part II, where she inspires a South American nation to rise up and take back its country. Jungle Dawg shows up just when all appears lost, and Lilly, the timid intern from Pittsburgh, becomes a thorn in the side of a mass murderer.

Finally, the conclusion, which has more twists than Chubby Checker, reveals Cody's fate as he lies in Methodist Hospital lingering between life and death after having been shot by police in a case of mistaken identity. Cody visits Heaven and returns long enough to deliver a message to friends and family.

But no one will be able to predict what happens next, nor will anyone be prepared. The Cody Musket Story, Book 2 now available in paperback and electronic transfer.

## Real Events That Inspired No Pit So Deep

The miracle healing of Cody's left leg at Kandahar, which resulted in the conversion to Christ of the orthopedic surgeon, was inspired by the verified experience of Dale Black, the lone survivor of an aircraft crash, as told in his biography *Flight to Heaven* (Published 2010 by Bethany House Publishers)

Cody's encounter with the Taliban and the child traffickers in Afghanistan was similar to several real incidents, though the story was not based on a *specific* case file.

The symptoms of PTSD as experienced by characters in this novel are realistic and typical, as discussed in widely-circulated publications, congressional hearings and case files available to the public.

The story of hate killing at the AME church in Pennsylvania, and the subsequent forgiveness, was inspired by recent events in American history.

The title *No Pit So Deep* was inspired by the life of Corrie ten Boom, a Dutch Christian whose family hid Jewish citizens during the Nazi occupation of their homeland. She is best known for her quote, *"There is no pit so deep that He is not deeper still"* — a truth she learned while in a Nazi concentration camp. The most widely-read of her 46 books is *The Hiding Place* (Published 1971 by Bantam Books)

Leonard Beeker's dreadful tale about the killing of children near the Laotian border originated from a real event as told to this author by a former soldier who was involved. The location, circumstances, and names were changed to maintain privacy.

Child human trafficking is symptomatic of our modern culture. An Antioch University study indicates that 300,000 children are used on front lines in battle zones today. Also see *Growing Up Naked: The Untold Story of Children at War,* by McAnthony Keah.

Do you hunger to know a God who really sees, really hears and loves you? Message me - www.facebook.com/nopitsodeep

"Jesus, I want to know you. I believe you laid down your life to pay the penalty I owe for my sin. I am willing to lay down my life in exchange for the wonderful destiny you have planned for me. I believe you rose from the dead to demonstrate that you have the power to forgive sin, and that you can work miracles in our lives. Forgive me, and send your Holy Spirit to live in me to change me forever."

Proof

Manufactured by Amazon.com
Columbia, SC
04 April 2017